Glenrannoch

I jerked erect. I could hear the ancient oak floor creaking loudly as the steps approached. An unknown figure was walking with measured tread along the short passage leading from the minstrels' gallery to my door.

I held my breath as I listened and waited, my eyes on the great iron key which I had instinctively turned the first night I slept here.

The footsteps came nearer, the floor creaked louder, and then there was silence. Someone was out there, standing on the other side of the panelled door.

Slowly, the iron latch lifted . . .

D1549809

Available in Fontana by the same author

Dragonmede

RONA RANDALL

Glenrannoch

Collins

FONTANA BOOKS

First published in 1973 by William Collins Sons & Co Ltd
First issued in Fontana Books 1976

© Rona Randall 1973

Made and printed in Great Britain by
William Collins Sons & Co Ltd Glasgow

CONDITIONS OF SALE
This book is sold subject to the condition
that it shall not, by way of trade or otherwise,
be lent, re-sold, hired out or otherwise circulated
without the publisher's prior consent in any form of
binding or cover other than that in which it is
published and without a similar condition
including this condition being imposed
on the subsequent purchaser

CHAPTER ONE

I paid little heed to the footsteps, that first night at Glenrannoch. If someone from this isolated mansion chose to walk abroad at midnight, they were more spartan than I, coming as I did from the milder south. Besides, I was too tired to pay more than passing attention as they approached along the wide stone terrace, paused beneath my window, and then went on at the same measured pace, gradually fading into silence.

It was the same the second night, except that this time I was more wide awake, stimulated by a day spent in meeting my hitherto unknown relatives and seeing, for the first time in my life, my father's background, the place where he and his ancestors had been born and on which he had turned his back when he married my mother, a 'heathen Sassenach' whom my tyrannical grandfather refused ever to meet.

So the second time I heard the footsteps, curiosity drew me to the tall bedroom windows overlooking the grounds of Glenrannoch and the wild stretch of Glencoe curving towards Buchaille Etive Mor, 'The Great Herdsman of Etive', which pierced the night sky like a giant sentinel guarding the eastern entrance to the pass.

I could see no one. The jutting stone balcony hid the terrace from view, but I could still hear the footsteps and at that precise moment they paused beneath my window yet again. By the time I had grappled with the unfamiliar lock and stepped on to the balcony they had moved on, and as I leaned over the balustrade, clouds obscured the face of the moon, leaving only a world of shadows below. The midnight walker had gone, but the echo of his footsteps remained.

Something about this echo caught my attention. The sound came from no ordinary shoes. There was a metallic ring about it, like that from the spiked soles of golf shoes or a climber's boots. Probably the latter, since this was climbing country. But why wear such boots for a midnight stroll? The grounds of Glenrannoch were smooth, well tended, and the walker must have known that pacing the terrace in such footwear could disturb those members of the household who slept on the south side.

The third night was different. The footsteps came again, jerking me from sleep, not by their metallic echo on stone, but by their heavy tread coming to my room.

I was dreaming, and in my dream someone was walking towards me, a person I could not identify, a face I could not see, and when I wakened it seemed as if I still lingered in that dream world although my eyes were open, for the unknown figure was still coming towards me, walking with measured tread along the short passage leading from the minstrels' gallery to my door.

I jerked erect. I could hear the ancient oak floor creaking loudly as the steps approached, and it struck me that there was nothing furtive about them, nothing secret. Their owner knew precisely where they were going and obviously had no objection to being heard.

Unreasonably, my hand shook as I fumbled for a bedside lamp and switched it on. It was foolish to be afraid, and I knew that I trembled only because I had been wakened from sleep so abruptly, and because the echoing boom of midnight sounded in the great hall below, as it had sounded on the previous two nights. It was those twelve solemn strokes, echoing in the silence of the vast house, which added an eerie touch.

The only other door leading into the short passage was from my adjoining bathroom, made *en suite* with the bedroom when my grandfather married again, after which the door leading from the bathroom to the passage remained permanently locked. I had learned all this from Brenda, my grandfather's widow, on arrival at Glenrannoch.

So I knew that those deliberate steps could only be coming to me.

I held my breath as I listened and waited, my eyes on the great iron key which I had instinctively turned the first night I slept here (was it really only three days ago?) and had continued to turn since. Never in my life had I locked my door at night, but there was something about this gaunt, shadowy room which compelled me to. From the first I had felt it to be a room of unrest. It made me uneasy, tense, insecure. Turning the key in the heavy iron lock had been prompted by a compulsive need for security, but now that I was threatened by unknown footsteps the lock appeared flimsy and unreliable.

The footsteps came nearer, the floor creaked louder, and then there was silence. Someone was out there, standing on the other side of the panelled door; a person I could not identify, a face I could not see. I felt menaced, and my throat went dry.

Slowly, the iron latch lifted. I watched, mesmerized, wanting to call out but unable to. I could only clutch the bedclothes and wait, while pressure against the door forced a groan out of the unyielding lock. Ancient iron and oak combined to keep out the intruder, and the latch fell back into place with a sharp, frustrated sound.

The floorboards creaked again as the footsteps retreated. They went straight back to the minstrels' gallery, which told me that their owner knew the outer bathroom door was locked, thus preventing access to the bedroom that way. It also told me that the midnight walker was familiar with every part of the house, aware of which doors could or could not be opened.

Long after the house was silent again I remained as I was, sitting upright in bed, hugging the bedclothes against me, with the lamp burning and the feeling of menace refusing to be stilled.

I was afraid to sleep again, although reason argued that there must be some logical explanation for the visit. Could it have been Brenda MacDonald, wondering if I needed anything, or fussy Aunt Mary with the same idea in mind? (Not that her chilly reception of me on arrival had indicated the least concern for my comfort.) Or perhaps it had been Duncan Campbell, who had met me at Renfrew Airport, but that idea I dismissed immediately. Duncan might be attracted to me, as I was to him, but he would not be so tactless as to force his attentions on me at night. Not after an acquaintanceship of only three days. I had a feeling, a hope, that this acquaintanceship might develop into something stronger and that he shared this hope, but he was more sensible than to act prematurely.

One by one I went over the occupants of Glenrannoch. They were few enough, consisting only of my father's sister Mary, Brenda – my step-grandmother if there was such a term – and Duncan himself, her son by her first marriage. Duncan was not only the family lawyer but in charge of legal affairs at the MacDonald-Matheson Mills outside Fort William, founded by one of my ancestors generations ago, and famed for their fine Scots tartans and tweeds. It was this prosperous business on which my father, Andrew MacDonald, had turned his back when a young man, preferring to marry the girl he loved than one he was expected to.

For years the many branches of the MacDonalds and Mathesons had married whenever possible, because in the early days a Matheson had joined the mills at a time when they threatened to founder, adding the ballast of money and knowledge to steady the boat; not too much money, not enough to wrest the balance of power from the MacDonalds, but enough to earn for the Mathesons a sound place in the establishment.

Ever since then the two families had kept the ever-expanding mills beneath their joint ownership, the Mac-Donalds remaining dominant. Who would replace my grandfather as chairman now, I had no idea. All I knew was that the two families had devoted their lives to the mills, endeavouring to bring in no outsiders even in personal relationships, and as they all had large families, with branches expanding and diversifying throughout the years, partners were carefully chosen to avoid any risk of inter-marriage.

There had been an Isabel Matheson lined up for my own father from an early age, so his break with tradition had never been forgiven, and for this reason I, daughter of his unacceptable marriage, had never expected even to visit Glenrannoch, let alone inherit it.

I could scarcely believe it was true, for I felt a stranger in this sombre place.

Gradually I slid down amongst the pillows, still thinking about the inhabitants of this house. Glenrannoch had been built to accommodate generations of MacDonald families, but now there was only Aunt Mary, pathetic and irritating, with her embittered mouth for ever nibbling the sugared almonds which emerged in an endless supply from her capacious bag of faded *petit point*. The bag hung like a sack from her thin arm and bumped against her bony hip as she walked. On such a constant diet of sugar she should have been fat. Instead, she was a lean rake of a woman, nerve-ridden, agile, giving the impression that a smouldering fire burned up this constant source of energy.

An unlikeable woman, too; totally different from what I expected, for my father had always described her as pretty. It was hard to credit. Increasing gauntness and passing years had sharpened the outlines of her figure and blurred the contours of her face.

And that, apart from myself, was all that remained of my grandfather's particular line of MacDonalds. There was no male heir at Glenrannoch to pass on the name, but old James, cunningly evading any possible claim from other off-shoots of the family, had insured against this in a codicil to his will. On marriage, he decreed that I should retain the name of MacDonald, linking it with my husband's, but taking precedence, so that it became MacDonald-Matheson, not Matheson-MacDonald.

'And what Matheson did he line up for me?' I demanded indignantly when Duncan Campbell revealed the stipulations of the will, but he had merely laughed and said, 'I'm sure James quoted it merely as an example. The same arrangement would apply if you linked your name with, say, a Campbell.'

'In *Glencoe*? I thought the old feud between the Mac-Donalds and Campbells had never been forgotten.'

'It hasn't – but neither has it remained. And it was never the personal enmity which history records, but the result of political rivalry for leadership of the Gaels.'

'Despite the Massacre of Glencoe!'

'Even despite that. In any case, I was only quoting the name as an example.'

His words held no significance, but I was faintly and somehow pleasurably embarrassed because the first name he thought to link with mine was his own.

Now I thrust the recollection of that moment aside,

also the picture it conjured up of Duncan's features etched in profile against the gathering evening light as we drove from Glasgow to Glencoe. I had expected a middle-aged, dry-as-dust lawyer, not this vigorous and attractive man of around thirty.

I turned my mind to the domestic staff, which comprised only Flora Fyfe, housekeeper at Glenrannoch for well over thirty years and who ruled the two girls under her with a rod of iron. Flora was a dour woman; I had not yet seen her smile. She had a son named Luke who did odd jobs about the place, mainly on the estate. I found it hard to imagine Flora Fyfe ever bearing a child because it was even harder to imagine her ever firing a man's passion, much less yielding to it. I was curious to find out what this son was like. Luke was the one remaining member of the household whom I had yet to meet.

There was now a deep silence in the house. This silence had impressed me on my first night. I had never realized before, accustomed as I was to the eternal hum of London's traffic, that silence could seem to have substance, like a wall or a tightly enclosing shell.

Suddenly stifled, I flung aside the bedclothes, crossed to one of the three tall windows and pulled the curtain rope. The floor-to-ceiling curtains of heavy lined brocade swished aside, revealing the outer world bathed in moonlight. I could see the towering strength of Bidean Nam Bian – 'Summit Peak of the Mountains' – thrusting three spears towards the sky.

It was well named, I thought, as I stared at its stark outline and marvelled that I was here at last, in the glen about which I had heard so much. The wild, beautiful, haunted Glen of Weeping.

Occasionally I had contemplated coming as a tourist to see the country which had bred my father, but so long as he and my mother were alive I never put forward the idea; and after the plane crash which had killed them a couple of years ago I lacked the heart, convinced that there was no place for me in Glencoe, just as there was no place for me at Glenrannoch.

But fate, in the person of my unyielding grandfather,

had decided otherwise. Was it a belated desire to atone, or simply the knowledge that there was no other MacDonald left in direct line from himself? No young one, at least. Mary was now too old to produce an heir, even if she married belatedly — which, I thought with pity, was not likely to happen to a woman of her acid personality.

Unlike Brenda, her stepmother, Aunt Mary had spared little greeting for me on arrival, merely surveying me coldly and then commenting, 'You must resemble your mother, girl. I can see no likeness in you to a MacDonald.'

To that I had answered amicably, 'Neverthless, I am one,' and, glancing down at my trouser-suit, added: '*And* entitled to wear the tartan.'

At that her thin lips tightened. 'Only gentlemen's trews were permitted to be made in tartan,' she pointed out.

'That was centuries ago, Aunt Mary. No chieftain campaigning on foot in the Highlands would wear trews, only the leaders on horseback, because the kilt was too cumbersome to ride in. So the trews became a sign of rank. My father told me all this when I was small.'

'I'm glad Andrew remembered *some*thing about his ancestry, and if he still had anything of the MacDonalds in him I'll warrant he wouldn't have approved of your parading the tartan in that fashion.'

Far from annoying me, she amused me, and before Flora could show me to my room, I had pointed out that my tartan trouser-suits had been a great hit everywhere and must have boosted orders at the mills, for I had designed them exclusively in Mactweed, the MacDonald-Matheson weave.

'So the family should be grateful to me,' I told her lightly.

Brenda MacDonald's warm eyes had sparkled with amusement. I wasn't surprised that Duncan had a mother like this, in her late forties but youthful, elegant, and friendly. Nor that she had a son such as he.

I had had no further skirmish with Aunt Mary. Since that first meeting she had been, if not affable, at least reasonably polite, and as I now climbed back into bed I found myself wondering what sort of life she had had with her father, of whom I had grown up with my own mental picture, and not a pleasant one, which was why I had felt little reaction when reading the newspaper reports of his death.

He had died at the age of seventy-six, at his home in Glencoe – the manor of Glenrannoch, built a century after the famous massacre of 1692. He left a wife, his second, twenty-eight years younger than himself. Also a daughter of his first marriage, now aged forty-six.

To learn that his widow was merely two years older than his daugher had sparked inevitable questions in my mind. How had the two women got on together? How had they lived together? Why had his daughter been content to remain in the same house when her father married again at the age of sixty-four, choosing a bride of thirty-six?

I recalled that Mary had been at a finishing school in Paris when my father left home. 'Being polished for the marriage market,' as he put it when relating the story to me years later, 'although the choice of a husband was a foregone conclusion. Some Matheson or other would be lined up for her, and she would do the right thing and marry as she was told. Poor Mary. She was always weak.'

But apparently no Matheson had been lined up for her and she had never married. Had her dominating father decided that he needed her services as mistress of his house and she, in weakness, obeyed? And was it weakness again which had kept her there, even after James remarried so unexpectedly and brought a person like Brenda to be queen of Glenrannoch in her stead? Or had she merely given up hope of marrying, decided that home was the place where her bread was best buttered, and that, family pride being so strong in her father, he would naturally bequeath Glenrannoch in the direct line if Brenda gave him no heir to replace the disowned Andrew?

And that was the way it had happened. Brenda had given him no children, so Mary's expectation had been justified, although the final execution of it was surprising. James MacDonald bequeathed the ancient mansion, with its famous collection of antiques, to the daughter of his disinherited son – myself, Lavinia MacDonald, hitherto not even acknowledged as one of the family.

'There are provisos covered by a codicil to the will,' Duncan Campbell had told me during the drive to Glenrannoch. 'My mother is to remain, unless she marries again. James made generous financial provisions for her, also for Aunt Mary – your aunt really, not mine, although I've called her that ever since Mother married James when I was sixteen. Another proviso is that you make Glenrannoch your permanent home and take your place in the family business. If you turn your back on either and return to live in London you lose all claim to your inheritance and it will be divided equally between my mother and your aunt.'

'In other words, I am to remain here as a good and worthy MacDonald, never following in my father's footsteps.'

When Duncan failed to answer I had smiled and said, 'Don't be embarrassed – I am well aware of my grandfather's dictatorship.'

I had come to Glenrannoch out of curiosity, not because comfort and security were a couple of juicy plums dangled before me. I had other plums already; a rapidly growing career as a dress designer, an adequate life annuity from my parents, and a comfortable flat which had been the foundation stone for Andrew MacDonald's career as an interior decorator. Despite my father's ultimate success, he had never parted with that flat. It had been a sprawl of dilapidated rooms in an unfashionable quarter of London when he married my mother, and it had improved in proportion with his success, also in pace with the upgrading of the unfashionable quarter into a much sought-after district.

This flat was an anchor in my life, so any provisos or threats James MacDonald might have added to his will did not worry me unduly. Once I had become fully acquainted with Glenrannoch, I would then decide whether to go or to remain, but my home in London I would not yet part with. I had a feeling I might need it as a bolt-hole.

After all, I slept; restlessly, fitfully, jerking awake every now and then as if expecting the midnight walker to return, then sinking into a state of semi-consciousness in which Duncan's personality took over again. I had liked him from our first moment of meeting, when he came towards me in the airport building, hand extended, saying, 'You must be Lavinia. Only a successful dress designer could look like that, and only a MacDonald wear that tartan so well.' Womanlike, I had warmed to him instantly, forgetting the underlying apprehension I had felt during the hour's flight from London.

Shyness with strangers was not a thing I normally experienced. Gregarious parents and a job which brought me in touch with all sorts of people had made me socially confident, but when it came to meeting my unknown relatives, uneasiness had set in. Duncan Campbell changed all that with his friendliness which, I was to discover later, held the warmth which characterized his mother.

His lilting Scots voice, which I had heard when discussing preliminaries on the telephone, also reassured me as we drove through the drab, built-up areas of Glasgow and along the banks of the Clyde until both the city and the great shipping river dropped behind and we were skirting the banks of Loch Long.

He was an easy man to talk to, and after outlining in general the terms of my grandfather's will, he pointed out places of interest along the route, names well known to me from history books and from my father. At Tarbet we stopped for lunch, and the breeze off Loch Lomond seemed to carry the fragrance of heather from distant moors, then we were on our way again, through Glen Falloch, onwards and upwards until Ben More and Ben Lui loomed darkly against the late afternoon sky.

Ahead lay the boundaries of Perthshire and Argyllshire, and then the long climb to Rannoch Moor, every twist and turn revealing higher and wilder hills until the bleak stretch of moorland opened out before us. Beyond it, the desolate mountains were bare of vegetation, due to arctic winter conditions, and that was the moment when I felt, for the first time, that I was heading into the unknown, and apprehension shivered down my spine.

Winter lingered in these parts long after it had given way

14

to spring and even to summer in southern England, snow sometimes mantling the mountains of Glencoe even in May, and to my heightened sensitivity the bleak maw of the glen was eerie.

'Is it true that Glencoe is haunted?' I asked as we skirted the foot of Buchaille Etive Mor, its face granite-sliced, with lavas and dyke-swarms complicating the structure.

Duncan's attention seemed to be solely on the road at that point, the point at which we began the thousand-foot descent from 'the watershed', with the River Coe hurtling down its defile towards Loch Leven and the sea. By the time he spoke we were entering the very heart of Glencoe with, to our right, the sheer escarpment of Aonach Eagach towering three thousand feet above us. Here the MacDonalds had fled eastwards before the advance of the treacherous Campbells, their kilts swinging in the blizzard on that terrible February night in the seventeenth century.

Then Duncan answered, 'Some people believe it to be. Superstition has woven itself into the lives of the people here. Many claim that spectres of warriors roam the hills, clad in boots capped with rawhide and studded with iron, brandishing their swords as they rage through the glen, but when you see the place tomorrow you won't believe such tales. Glencoe is one of the most peaceful places on earth. Only tourists driving through the pass disturb it, but even the sheep ignore them.'

The glen road snaked eastwards down to Ballachulish and Loch Leven, with the last and smallest bastion of all, the Pap of Glencoe, overlooking the loch and the peaks of Mamore beyond. The view was spectacular, and at one point I glimpsed an island in the middle of the water. There was something about it which caught my attention. Lonely as it was, small as it was and obviously uninhabited, I sensed a feeling of life about it even at this distance, as if it had a spirit of its own which lived and breathed. I asked Duncan for its name, and learned that it was Eilean Munde, a burial isle, still considered holy because it had been sanctified by the Christian saint, Fintan Mundus.

'Small islands were, and still are, popular as burial places in Scotland. Eilean Munde was mainly shared by the Camerons and Stewarts and MacIains.'

I knew, of course, that the MacIains were the early MacDonalds of Glencoe, 'slaughtered under trust' following the fall of the Lordship of the Isles and the introduction of the feudal system. I had learned the story in a cold factual way at school, but in a more personal and emotional way from my father. Courageous, proud and stubborn, the clan had clung to their ancient way of life, to their personal laws and beliefs, to their sentiment and traditions, raiding and plundering in time of famine, and at other times too, if history was to be believed. From this wild race I had sprung, and I felt a sudden stirring of pride because their blood was in me. Like them, I was independent. Like them, I would never be dictated to.

'The burial enclosure of the MacIains is still marked and funerals still cross to the island, though less frequently than in the past. It is said to be haunted by the spirit of the last soul to be carried there, whose task is to guard the graves until the next one arrives. It's all nonsense, of course. You must visit Eilean Munde some time and see the burial spot of your ancestors. It's a peaceful place; pretty, too. After that, you won't believe the legend any more than I do.'

In the darkness of my room I remembered Duncan's reassuring smile; nevertheless, I shivered and was glad that my windows faced south and that I could not see the haunted island, as rooms on the northern side did. But I had only to draw back my curtains and look towards the wild hills of the glen to imagine those ghostly warriors returning from the past, storming the rock faces in their boots capped with rawhide and studded with iron, as sure-footed as the midnight walker of Glenrannoch.

By dawn I knew that sleep had gone. For a while I lay watching the misty light beyond a gap in the curtains, then, suddenly impatient with my imaginings and fears, I took a brisk shower, dressed, flung on a warm mohair coat and went quietly downstairs. The best way to deal with a fit of the fancies was to come to grips with it, I told myself sternly. I would go out into the cold morning light and learn for myself how harmless the glen was and that all these wild tales of hauntings were based merely on superstition.

The great door of Glenrannoch swung open silently on well-oiled hinges. Everything about this house was well run, due to Brenda MacDonald's efficient supervision. Having lived with Brenda and Mary for the last three days, I really had no need to speculate on how the situation between them had been handled, and who had enabled it to survive. Brenda, undoubtedly. She was a generous-hearted person; Mary, inhibited and cold. The lines imprinted on my aunt's face must have been a long time growing; the lines on Brenda's likewise, except that they were of a different type, the uplifting lines of friendliness which makes a person ageless.

As I closed the studded door behind me I noticed how well preserved the wood was and that no sign of rust disfigured the large iron hinges, obviously cleaned and cared for regularly. I stood for a moment at the top of the steps, admiring the fine and ancient woodwork, then my glance wandered over the façade of the house, appreciating the thick walls of well-kept stone. No doubt my grandfather had taken great pride in his house, and this pride his wife had shared.

I felt guilty for ousting her from possession and embarrassed because I had been put in such a position. To bequeath his home away from a loyal and diligent wife had been a heartless thing for a man to do. She must have felt so too, despite the generous financial provision made for her, and yet she had gone out of her way to make me welcome.

Tying a scarf over my hair I descended the steps and headed down the curving drive. Early morning mist swirled amongst the trees, ebbing and flowing from the loch. I was confident that soon it would lift and I would be able to see more than the thirty yards or so which now opened out before me, so I thrust my hands deep into my coat pockets and stepped out briskly, gravel crunching beneath my feet. Particles of granite and slate were mixed with it, and there were even tiny sparkling stones, pieces of minute lava threaded with quartz, gleaming every now and then as the morning light lifted and a watery sun tried to pierce the mist.

They were valueless, these chippings mingled with the local gravel, but on some of the hillsides prettier stones could occasionally be picked up. Aunt Mary had shown me samples. Villagers who found them sold them to her for use in craft jewellery, which she made on behalf of local charities. Apparently they went well at Christmas bazaars and summer fêtes, but the supply of stones here was very meagre compared with the Cairngorms.

I was half-way down the drive, the house hidden by the curve behind me, when instead of lifting the mist suddenly closed in, obliterating the tall, wrought-iron gates which lay ahead. One moment I glimpsed them, and the next they were gone. I hesitated, wondered whether to go back, then decided to press on. These Scottish mists could clear as swiftly as they descended. I had only to go forward and after a few yards the gates would reappear.

I was right. The outlines of their fine wrought-iron work slowly emerged. Beyond them was the road which led to Carnoch, thence to Ballachulish.

A few more steps and I was reaching towards the gates, but suddenly, hand outstretched, I stood frozen as one of them swung open silently and a giant figure loomed in the aperture.

CHAPTER TWO

The figure stretched a powerful arm towards me and, panic-stricken, I jerked to life, whirled away and raced blindly back the way I had come. Terror spurred me forward as the echo of iron-studded boots lumbered in my wake. My throat felt dry and my limbs numb, but somehow I ran, as in a nightmare, feeling that I was treading the same spot and getting nowhere. Then suddenly my footsteps were silenced and the ground was soft beneath my feet. I had stumbled from the gravel on to turf.

I must have reached the curve in the drive and, instead of following it, had run straight on to the surrounding verge.

I stood still at once and peered back down the drive. All I could see was thickening fog, but through it I could hear the echo of metal studs on gravel, rapidly approaching. My brain raced. If I could not see him, he could not see me, and since the only sound now came from him, I had the advantage. I held my breath as I stood there, automatically groping through the enveloping shroud until I touched the solid bulk of a tree. I could not have prayed for better concealment and crept round it carefully until reaching the opposite side.

The girth of the trunk was wide, screening me completely as the lumbering figure passed. I saw his shadow retreating through the mist, but made no move until the heavy footfall had faded into silence. I knew then that it had been cut off by the curve of the drive and, my whole body shaking, groped my way back towards the gates.

A sense of direction can be misleading in fog, but I felt instinctively that I was heading the right way and that soon I would gain the road outside. I didn't stop to question whether it was wise or foolish to make for it. All I knew was that I had to get away from the grounds of this house and from the man who prowled there.

Once I reached the road I would feel safe. I would knock at the first house I came to and ask for shelter until the fog lifted. All this spun through my mind as I stumbled uncertainly over the turf, confident that I was skirting the gravel because every now and then sweeping branches of the rhododendron bushes brushed against me, the famous rhododendrons which lined Glenrannoch's drive. Again I was right, for suddenly I came up full tilt against the stone wall which surrounded the estate.

Somewhere, to left or right, were the gates. A second's breathless hesitation and I was groping to the left, my hands following the rough stone – but for too long, and too far. Suddenly frantic, I groped my way back, every snapping twig sounding like a pistol shot, until my right hand fell abruptly through space and my left touched a stone pillar.

The space was a gap between iron scrolls, part of the ornamentation on Glenrannoch's monumental entrance. And there was a greater gap beside me, for the gates stood open as the giant figure had left them, and in a flash I was out and running frantically down the road.

I gasped as I ran, but nothing would stop me now. Panic had given way to relief, but I knew that escape could be short-lived if my pursuer guessed what I had done, and came after me. And so I ran blindly, my breathing loud in my ears; so loud that for a full moment I was unaware of another sound, muffled at first by fog and then suddenly roaring out of the silence.

It was the throb of an engine, and with it came the penetrating beam of a fog lamp. Then the outline of an advancing car emerged and I staggered to a stop, planting myself in front of it. Immediately there was a screech of brakes and a man's voice shouting. 'What the hell . . .?'

A door opened and slammed. The driver came towards me and in the beam of diffused light we looked at each other. I tried to speak, and failed. I could only stand there, out of breath, mouthing foolishly.

Suddenly the man burst out, 'Are you out of your mind? Do you want to be killed?'

I clutched his sleeve. '*Please* – ' I was breathing more easily now, but couldn't hide the relief in my voice.

He stared down at me for a brief second, then took my arm and led me to the car. 'Get in,' he commanded, and I fell thankfully into the passenger seat. Then he was at the wheel and the engine slipped into gear.

'I don't know where you're heading for,' he said brusquely, 'but wherever it is you won't get there yet. You'll have to come to my place at Invercoe and wait until this blasted fog lifts. And that won't be soon. When it crosses the loch from the Mamore hills at this hour of the day, it lingers, as anyone from these parts knows. Which means you're a stranger around here, or you wouldn't be so insane as to be out in it.'

I was breathing more normally now and my nerves had steadied. Goaded by his manner I retorted, 'Then you must be equally insane, or you wouldn't be out in it either.'

He gave a bark of a laugh. 'You're right there. Only a madman would practise as a vet in this part of the world.'

But somehow I felt he didn't mean it. The tough solidity

of him seemed very much in harmony with the surrounding landscape. It had the same granite quality. In the dimness I saw rugged features and wasn't surprised. They were in keeping with the deep voice and what had appeared to be breadth of shoulder when he stood looking down at me in the glow of the fog lamp. But his appearance was hard to judge in circumstances like these, muffled as he was in a great coat with upturned collar. From beneath a tweed deer-stalker cap I saw thick hair which looked dark in this uncertain light.

'You've been out on an early call?' I asked.

'No, an all-night one, and a fine time for a heifer to choose for a first delivery. A pedigree heifer, at that, which made her even more valuable. And what brought *you* out?'

I hesitated, then said lamely, 'An early morning walk.'

This time his laughter was loud and I found myself joining in, conscious of my own absurdity. After a while he said, 'That proves you're a foreigner. I'll take a level bet you're English, not only because of your accent. The English have a mania for early morning walks.'

'This one hasn't. The great distance I walk in the morning is as far as the Underground, a hundred yards away.'

'But something happens to the English when they come to Western Scotland. They tramp for miles, or go climbing without training and get lost, and then the Mountain Rescue Team has to be called out.'

'That's an exaggeration. You get some of our best climbers both here and in the Cairngorms.'

He made a grudging acknowledgment, but I scarcely heard it for at that precise moment I began to shiver and huddled deeper into my coat. Whether it was due to cold or merely to reaction from terror I had no idea, but I was aware of his sideways glance.

'We'll soon be at my place,' he said reassuringly, and didn't speak again until he had nosed the car up a short drive. Then he said, 'Well, we've made it,' and, leaning across, opened the door for me. I heard lapping water nearby and realized that we were close beside the loch.

A sudden gap in the fog revealed a compact stone house and, fleetingly, I thought it could be almost as old as

Glenrannoch; a converted farm cottage, perhaps. The interior confirmed this, but I was suddenly too tired to spare my surroundings more than a passing glance. The door opened straight into a sitting-room and I had a swift impression of comfortable clutter and a wealth of books as I sank into an arm-chair beside the hearth.

The man kicked smouldering logs to life and with a crackle and a roar flames shot up the chimney sending out a welcoming warmth. I shed my mohair coat and murmured something about being grateful.

He brushed it aside. 'Coffee coming up,' he said. 'Meanwhile, relax and get warm.'

He had flung his greatcoat and deer-stalker on to a chair beside the door and now the leaping fire lit up the sandy tones of his hair. I was right about his size and breadth, but not about his darkness.

As his tall figure headed towards the kitchen I kicked off my shoes and warmed my toes by the fire. Soon he returned with an electric percolator which he plugged in beside the hearth, then he placed a couple of large mugs on a low table and took a bottle of scotch from a cupboard.

'And now,' he said, settling opposite me, 'tell me what you were running away from. You were frightened, and not by the fog.'

I didn't find it easy to answer, and he didn't hurry me. I leaned back, listening to the bubbling of the percolator and feeling the warmth from the fire spreading through me. How could I tell this stranger that I had been frightened by a monster in the grounds of a house which was now my own? It sounded ridiculous, the ravings of someone over-imaginative or prone to self-dramatization.

He poured the coffee, laced it with scotch, and handed me a cup. 'My name is Hamish Cameron. And yours?'

It seemed that he was not going to pursue his earlier question. I was glad.

'Lavinia MacDonald.'

His cup was half-way to his mouth. It stopped there. I saw his sandy brows raise and eyes of a quite startling blue stare at me with surprised interest.

'Are you now?' he said slowly. 'Daughter of the errant son. I've heard of you, of course. Everyone has, and everyone is agog to see you. Mrs McPherson, for one.'

'Mrs McPherson?'

'She comes to "do" for me. She remembers your father well.'

I felt a quickening of excitement.

'I would like to meet her.'

'You will. She'll be here, whatever the weather. A bit later than usual, perhaps, because she'll have to walk instead of cycling, but she knows every step of the way from her cottage to this house. And now tell me what you were running away from.'

I looked at him and knew that what this man wanted to find out, he would find out. I took a sip of the coffee: it was strong, and lit with the fire of whisky. The stimulation and warmth of it helped me to say, 'I had reached the gates of Glenrannoch when they suddenly opened and a huge figure stood there. He reached out for me. I can see him now, looming up out of the fog and standing there with one hand on the gates and the other stretching towards me . . .'

My voice shook. So did my hands. Hamish Cameron reached across and took my cup.

'Did you see what he looked like?'

I shook my head. 'Just big and wild-looking. I ran and he came after me. He wore heavy boots, studded I think. He was – terrifying.'

'He would be, seen for the first time in conditions like that. I take it you've not met Luke Fyfe yet?'

'Luke!' I was startled. 'Flora Fyfe's son?'

He nodded.

'Luke is retarded, but not physically. A giant of a man, as you say, but harmless as a fly. He cleans those gates every morning before the world is astir, and the iron-work on the great front door as well. It was a fetish of James MacDonald's that these jobs should be done at that ridiculous hour. He couldn't abide servants and all work had to be carried out when he was not around. It's hard to make poor Luke understand that cleaning the gates is a waste of time in bad weather. I've tried once or twice, when I've been called to Glenrannoch to attend the old man's horses, but the message just doesn't get through.'

He handed the coffee back and ordered me to drink up.

'And you can rid your mind of any fear as far as poor Luke is concerned. His instinct would be protective, nothing more. He probably wanted to lead you safely back to the house.'

For the second time that morning, I felt foolish. I had not even thought of Luke, nor had it occurred to me that the figure could merely be that of a burly handyman. Now I remembered the immaculate condition of the front door and they way in which I had admired the well-kept iron hinges and studs, how free from rust they were despite Highland mists and damp air from the loch. And I remembered something else which had barely registered at the time, but which had subconsciously added to my fear. As poor Luke stretched out his great arm towards me, he had made guttural sounds which I scarcely heard, muffled as they were by the fog-laden air. He had been trying to speak, poor fellow, and all I had done was turn my back on him.

'Is he mute?' I asked.

'He has a speech impediment caused by a cleft in the roof of the mouth, but he is not deaf and can understand something of what others say. More than we realize, perhaps.'

Ashamed, I said, 'Then I shall apologize to him as soon as I see him again.'

It wasn't until after my return to Glenrannoch that I recalled the midnight walker and wondered whether it had been Luke. That heavy tread and the ring of metal on stone were reminiscent of the man's gait on the gravel drive, but the recollection of those same steps approaching my bedroom door, followed by the furtive lifting of the latch, was not so acceptable, although it could have been the action of an inquisitive but harmless servant who knew his way around the house and, now that his intimidating master had gone, yielded to a desire to examine the room which he had occupied.

So it could have been curiosity, nothing more.

Or could it have been the threat of a dangerous mentality combined with a giant physique?

But Hamish Cameron claimed that Luke was harmless,

and Hamish Cameron was the sort of person one believed. He spoke with an air of authority backed by knowledge; he carried conviction.

The fog had lifted after breakfast; a substantial Scots breakfast cooked for us by Mrs McPherson. I gathered from her that such quick evaporation of fog was unusual for heavy morning mists of this type. The woman knew every quirk of local weather, every warning wind.

'Born and bred in these parts,' she told me with pride, 'just as your father was. I remember him well, and liked him well, as did everyone. The best-looking MacDonald of the lot, he was. No Matheson could ever hold a candle to him. The only good-looker the Mathesons ever produced was Miss Isabel – Mrs Forsythe as she became – and now Malcolm, the nephew who lives with her. About your age he'll be, Miss MacDonald, or maybe a year or two older. His father was Miss Isabel's brother, killed in the war. When his mother married again and went to the States, young Malcolm went too, but was sent back to Edinburgh to be educated, then trained to take his place at the mills. There always has to be a Matheson there, same as with the MacDonalds.'

'So I understand.'

She gave me a knowing glance. 'But the Mathesons are one step ahead of the MacDonalds now, having a man to put into the business, and the direct line of the Macdonalds having only a girl – begging your pardon, and no reflection on you, miss.'

I smiled, grateful to the garrulous woman for putting me so effectively in the picture. I began to see the workings of my grandfather's scheming mind. Malcolm Matheson would be the one lined up for me, the one whose name would be linked with mine. Since there was now no male MacDonald stemming directly from James, the next best thing was to tie up his grand-daughter, a girl who could marry and produce children – boys in all probability for the MacDonalds were, on the whole, breeders of men. I could see it all now, hence the proviso regarding the retention of my name.

And, like all the other provisos, it was cunningly laid. I was to live at Glenrannoch for ever and to bring up my children there. Henceforth I was to live in the Mac-Donald tradition without a backward glance, and to take my rightful place in the family business. This final clause set me thinking. What was my 'rightful place' at the Mactweed Mills? What scheme had been in my grand-father's mind in that direction? There had to be a clue somewhere, but his will contained none. Apparently I was expected to work it out for myself.

After breakfast, Hamish Cameron drove me home, and in the clear air which superseded the fog the beauty of the loch and the splendour of Glencoe were breathtaking.

For the first time I felt a stirring of wonder, coupled with an unexpected feeling of pride because I belonged here. Half of my being sprang from this earth, and the tie could be strong.

Suddenly Cameron pointed towards the distant slope of Aonach Dubh. About half-way down, a projecting shoulder thrust menacingly outwards.

'See that vertical cleft in the rock? That is Ossian's Cave, named after a sainted bard who, legend has it, wrote his most noble poetry there, but little is actually known about Ossian, so I wouldn't swear that this is true.'

I gazed towards the challenging overhang. Even at this distance I could discern the shadow of the cleft, with smaller ones at lower and easier levels. I had a sudden urge to explore, to see as much as possible of this unique slice of Scotland before I went away.

If I went away . . .

'We turn off here,' Hamish Cameron said.

We had reached the point where the river began to flow westwards, and I remembered something my father had told me about this very spot.

'Where is Signal Rock?' I asked eagerly, and Cameron pointed again.

'Up there – above the farmhouse of Achnacon.'

I stared and realized that from that very rock the signal to start the infamous massacre had been given. It looked up the glen towards the watershed and down to Carnoch at the mouth. A beacon lit on Signal Rock could without doubt have warned the whole glen of the call to arms.

'Was that the farm where the Chief of the clan was murdered?'

'No. The site now accepted by most people is a mile and a half away, up in Gleann Muidhe. There's a ruined foundation there of a fairly large house with a gable and a fireplace at each end. A memorial slab has been put up there, for the benefit of sightseers.'

'You sound as if you doubt the truth of it.'

'Many people, especially historians, doubt the truth of it. It is more likely to be the site of McIain's summer shieling. The clan used to move up into the hills for better grazing during the short summer season, but in the winter Carnoch or Invercoe would be more accessible, the hills being cut off by snow, and it was during the winter that the massacre took place. There are ruins in a wood about half-way between Clachaig and Leac an Tuim which some claim to have been the home of McIain the Twelfth; others favour other sites, and who is to prove them wrong in a place where ruins lie half buried almost everywhere? You can come across the remains of demolished byres and crofts throughout the glen, if you look for them. All are overgrown.' He added deliberately, 'Nothing can be proved, so take no heed when people claim to know the actual site of the Chief's tragic home.'

I felt as if he were trying to warn me of something, but when I looked at him his face was expressionless.

As we drove round the curving drive of Glenrannoch the great front door opened and Duncan stood there. It seemed to me that he stared at my companion in brief surprise and very little pleasure, but the next moment he was hurrying down the steps to meet us. The ancient Bentley had scarcely stopped before he opened the door beside me, giving its owner no chance to.

'Thank heaven you're back, Lavinia. You've had us all worried. When you didn't come down for breakfast my mother sent Flora to see if you were unwell. The woman found your room empty, so we searched the house for you. We didn't dream you'd gone out in a mist as heavy as this morning's.'

'It was stupid to go walking at such an hour and in

27

such weather,' I admitted. 'Luckily, Mr Cameron found me . . .'

My words died as I saw Duncan's glance flicker to Hamish Cameron and away again, and I wondered if the resentment I detected was a figment of my imagination, for the next moment he was thanking Hamish cordially and inviting him in.

'If Miss MacDonald wants me to.'

There was a dry note in Cameron's voice, subtly stressing that I was now the one to issue invitations at Glenrannoch.

'Of course I do.'

I spoke swiftly, annoyed with the implied snub towards Duncan, especially when I saw a faint flush touch his face and realized that the subtle hint had gone home. He turned to me in apology, but before he could speak I slipped an arm through his and drew him up the wide stone steps towards the front door, talking lightly as we went.

Thus it was that Duncan and I entered the house arm in arm, and somehow I could feel Hamish Cameron's quizzical glance upon us as he followed.

Aunt Mary was in the great hall. The shadowy place made her appear even more gaunt, but a high aureole window spotlighted her thin face and showed up the sudden sharpening of her expression, also the disapproval in it. But it was not for Duncan and myself. Our closeness brought no more than a faint lift of her eyebrows, which said expressively enough, *'Already?'* It was the man behind us who sparked her animosity.

'Well, Hamish, so you've met my niece.'

I don't know why the words suggested that he had wasted no time in doing so, but the tight closing of her lips seemed to imply a great deal more which I could not understand, but was obviously detrimental.

I felt uncomfortable as well as annoyed, for the man had not only looked after me but brought me safely home. But for him I would have been lost out there in the fog. From being vexed by his pointed remark to Duncan, I suddenly swung round in his defence and said deliberately, 'I am in Mr Cameron's debt, Aunt Mary.'

'You're in no debt at all.'

The man's voice was almost gruff, and I noticed that although he spoke to me he was looking at my aunt. His expression held a touch of indignation, but it held amusement too.

I said swiftly, 'Then at least let me be grateful, as I am sure my aunt is. But for you, I could have wandered for hours and still be trying to find my way back.'

'We are all grateful to you, Hamish.'

Duncan's friendly smile eased the moment, and he continued to talk as I walked across the hall to the morning-room, where I rang for Flora. As I turned I saw the two men standing aside for Mary to enter before them. She marched in, stiff as a ramrod, disapproval in every line of her. Apparently she didn't like the idea of her niece being picked up by a man, fog or no fog. I wondered ironically if she would have preferred my rescuer to be a stranger instead of someone known to the family, and felt with momentary despair that I would never be able to follow the workings of my aunt's mind. The gap between us was wider than a generation; she was prematurely aged, much older than her forty-six years.

'And why are you ringing that bell?' she demanded.

I sensed the amusement of the two men. This was really the only attitude to take towards Mary, the only way to withstand irritation.

I told her that I was about to order coffee.

'It was served with breakfast, over an hour ago. The time is now ten o'clock. Flora will serve coffee as usual at eleven.'

'But Mr Cameron has been up all night and I have been out since six. We had an early breakfast. Coffee will be welcome now.'

I spoke with deliberate patience and realized that I was trying to make the point which Hamish had emphasized to Duncan – that I was now mistress here.

It was the first time I had asserted myself since arriving at Glenrannoch. I had fallen in with the ways and customs of the household because it was natural to do so. Until this moment I had felt no more than a visitor, but in ringing for Flora I had made a tacit acknowledgment to myself that I was curtailing my probationary period and taking over the reins.

Before Aunt Mary could reply, Flora tapped on the door and entered. She was a large, heavily built woman, and for a moment I caught a brief glimpse of the girl she had once been – strapping, buxom, even handsome in a way, but had she, even then, had that assessing shrewdness in her eye which seemed to be defensively summing up the world and everyone in it? And had she been silent then, as now, a woman of few words who rarely volunteered a remark unless spoken to?

An unapproachable sort of woman, barricaded by taciturnity. I wondered if this guard had been erected when poor Luke was born, or when it became apparent that her child was not normal. Some women withdrew from others when shame or heartbreak touched them, and in this isolated part of the world, with its ancient beliefs, an abnormal child would indeed be an object of shame to Flora's generation. The sins of the fathers, they called it. A punishment on the parents as well as the child. For what? I wondered compassionately. And how could people be so inhuman as to view an unfortunate child as a disgrace?

These thoughts ran through my mind in the short measure of time in which we looked at each other across the room, and with them I felt a sudden desire to make friends with Flora Fyfe, to get to know her, to help her if she needed help. Until now I had seen her only as an able servant in the background, but as she stood there waiting I saw her as a human being who had kept her tragic child beside her always. Others would have got rid of him, shutting him out of their lives by sending him to a State institution. At least dour Flora had not done that.

I don't know why she looked straight at me when she entered, but now, as if remembering herself, she turned to my aunt and said, 'You rang, Miss Mary?'

'No, Flora. My niece did.'

Deep in the housekeeper's guarded eyes there was a reaction of some sort. Surprise, satisfaction, pleasure? It was hard to tell, and when the woman turned to me I saw no more than the usual impassive respect.

'Coffee, please, Flora. For all of us.'

'Not for me,' Mary interrupted sharply. '*I* don't make demands at inconvenient times, or upset kitchen routine.'

I felt a bristling annoyance, but checked it. 'Then coffee for three, Flora.'

The woman answered courteously that she would be pleased to oblige. This was something my aunt had not expected. It appeared to annoy her as much as the break in routine and almost as much as my assumption of authority.

Flora was turning to the door when Hamish inquired after her son.

The solid shoulders rose and fell in a resigned shrug.

'Luke's well enough, sir. Thank you, sir.'

I put in quickly, 'I think I saw him down by the gates this morning. I didn't realize it was him – '

'Aye, so he told me. He can make himself understood to me, but to few else. I'll make sure he keeps out of your way in future, Miss Lavinia.'

'Please don't. Glenrannoch is his home. I don't want him to feel a prisoner here.'

'He has always been a prisoner; prisoned up in his mind like. That's trying for other people, so I do my best to keep him out of sight.'

She turned the handle of the door, but I couldn't let her go like that.

'Wait! I don't want him treated that way, and I don't want him working out of doors in the early hours of the morning when the weather is bad.'

Her thick-featured face stared at me. Then she bobbed her head abruptly, almost painfully. 'That's good of you, Miss Lavinia, but the late master always insisted that such jobs should be done before the house was astir, in all seasons.'

'The late master is no longer here.'

I heard a gasp from my aunt, as if I had uttered a blasphemy. I spun round and said, 'You'll have to face facts, Aunt Mary. If my grandfather were alive now, I wouldn't be here, but I *am* here and I don't agree with many of his decisions. That one, in particular. Nor does Mr Cameron. Isn't that so?' I finished, turning to him.

'Absolutely.'

'And what concern is it of yours, Hamish?' Mary asked icily.

'I feel the same concern for Luke that I feel for any human being in need of care.'

'Let me remind you that *you* are an animal doctor.'

'Which alters in no way my concern for the human race. I told your father more than once that it was not only a waste of effort for Luke to clean those gates in bad weather, but the size of them takes up so much time that by the end of an hour he's coughing up his lungs in fog or damp. I was never averse to speaking my mind to James MacDonald. Sometimes, but not always, he listened.'

Beneath the man's words ran the hot current with which I was already becoming familiar. Hamish Cameron was not an even-tempered man.

There was a movement from the door; Flora shifting from one heavy foot to the other.

'Well?' my aunt demanded of her. 'What are you waiting for?'

'To thank Mr Cameron, if I may, ma'am. I know he's tried to help my Luke more than once.' The sullen light in Flora's eyes faded slightly as she turned to him and added, 'Of course, Luke's never understood, sir. To him, an order's an order and has to be obeyed. But, well, I'd like you to know that I appreciate your thought for him.'

Her heavily-accented Scots voice seemed to have thickened with emotion which she was ashamed of showing. She glanced hastily and apprehensively at my aunt, then turned to me and mumbled that she would see to the coffee immediately. She was half-way through the door when I called after her, 'There'll be no more gate-cleaning in the early hours if fogs rise like this morning, and if your son won't accept that, make him understand it is a new order, will you, Flora? From me.'

Her answering glance was concealed by the closing door. I was the only one who saw the mute gratitude in it, and the resolution. She knew how to handle her son, how to get things through to him, and from now on poor Luke would not be coughing out there before the world was astir.

As soon as the door closed Aunt Mary said with some asperity, 'May I point out, my dear niece, that you are not yet mistress here? My father's affairs have to be finally settled.'

Duncan brushed that aside. 'A mere formality.'

'Nevertheless, I consider that until then my stepmother is still in authority, and after her, myself.'

'Things won't take long to settle now,' Duncan pointed out. 'There are no snags, no possible hitches. Probate has been filed and will be granted by September. I think it's a good thing for Lavinia to start taking over.'

'That wasn't my intention – ' I began, but was interrupted by a voice from the door saying, 'I agree with Duncan.'

It was Brenda. She had entered in time to hear her son's words, but I wondered if she had also caught an echo of my aunt's. I saw Mary's face flush painfully. Earlier, it had been flushed with annoyance, but this was different. She had been put down, and was embarrassed.

'My dear Mary, don't look like that.' There was understanding in Brenda's voice. 'We just think, Duncan and I, that the earlier Lavinia learns to handle the ropes, the better. She is young, and a young mistress at Glenrannoch is badly needed. The old place has become gloomy through the years; it has been inhabited by older people for too long. And just think how nice it will be for us to be free of responsibility.'

'Looking after Glenrannoch is no responsibility. It is a task any true MacDonald woman is proud to undertake.'

'And I,' Brenda answered quietly, 'am not a true MacDonald.' She spoke as if she had been reminded of the fact many times. 'On the other hand, Lavinia is. She is the daughter of James's only son – your brother. She couldn't be more of a MacDonald than that, so I am sure you must be glad, as I am, that someone so directly in line is taking over. And I'm sure you'll be glad to help her – as I will, if she wants me to.'

'*I'd* be glad!' I declared. 'I don't want to oust anyone. And how can I be expected to supervise a place this size *and* take my part in the family business? What sort of a part, I have yet to find out.'

'You will,' Hamish Cameron said drily. 'You'll find out soon enough.'

'And how do *you* know what my father had in mind for Lavinia?' my aunt demanded. There was still a faint truculence in her tone, although Brenda partially pacified her.

'Hamish was a close friend of James,' Duncan put in. 'You know that, Mary.'

'A good one, too,' his mother added. Her liking for Hamish was apparent. 'I shall always be grateful for the hours he spent playing chess with my husband during the last months of his life. It must have been – trying.'

I was surprised to learn of his friendship with my grandfather and, illogically, disappointed. My own view of James MacDonald did not endear me to a man who was his ally. It suggested that they had a lot in common, which meant that Hamish Cameron had nothing in common with me.

Brenda laughed indulgently. 'Oh yes, James hated to be beaten. I suspect you humoured him, but not always. When he lost he was always in a tearing rage.'

'I've no doubt of that. *And* that he accused me of cheating the moment I'd gone.' He laughed tolerantly, and Brenda said, 'One had to forgive his little foibles.'

I smothered a temptation to ask if it was merely one of his little foibles to reject his own son. The man was dead and Brenda was a kind woman whom I had no desire to hurt or embarrass.

A tap on the door, and Jeannie, one of the two girls under Flora, entered with a tray. Automatically she placed it before Brenda, who looked faintly surprised and said, 'You're early with coffee this morning, my dear.'

Jeannie's russet-apple face beamed. She was a beaming girl; beaming upon the world and everyone in it. I liked her and thought she must be a ray of light in Glenrannoch's vast and gloomy kitchen.

'Lavinia ordered it,' Mary announced. 'I told her that we never have it before eleven.'

I heard an impatient sound nearby. Whether it came from Hamish or Duncan I couldn't tell, but I did see the expression on Brenda's face and guessed she was about to

34

say that surely coffee could be served any time one wanted it. Instead she remarked that there were only three cups.

'Naturally,' rasped Aunt Mary. '*I* am not having any.'

'Then bring another cup for me, please, Jeannie.'

The girl beamed and bobbed and bounced away, and suddenly I wanted to laugh at the absurdity of it all. My aunt's head must be full of trivialities to make such a mountain out of a molehill.

The coffee was good and as I drank it Brenda asked where I had roamed so early in the morning. 'We were very concerned when we found you were missing, but couldn't believe you had actually gone out in that heavy mist.'

'I did – idiotically. It was lucky for me that Mr Cameron was also out at that hour.'

'Luckier still that I missed running you down,' he said with wry humour.

'And he's Hamish to everyone,' Brenda added as beaming Jeannie returned with another cup and bounced away again. 'But what made you leave the house, my dear? It must have been very early, for no one heard you go.'

I filled the cup and handed it to her, saying that it was around six and that no doubt everyone had been asleep.

'And footsteps can't be heard in a place this size,' Duncan put in.

'Oh, but they can. That was why I couldn't sleep. They wakened me, coming directly to my door around midnight.'

There was a taut silence, then my aunt demanded shrilly, 'What sort of footsteps?'

'Heavy ones, with an iron ring about them. I heard them the two previous nights, outside on the terrace.'

'Also at midnight?' she gasped.

'As a matter of fact, yes.' I added lightly, 'Who *is* the midnight walker in this house?'

Duncan began, 'There's no such – ' but Mary cut right across his words.

'There is – and you know there is! You know *who* it is, too, and what it means when he comes.'

Hamish Cameron put down his cup with a sharp clatter, and burst out, 'For God's sake, Mary, don't resurrect that ridiculous legend! You know there's nothing in it.'

'*You* may think so,' she snapped back, 'but *you* don't belong in Glencoe. You're still a stranger here.'

'After three years?' He laughed. 'Thank God others don't think so, or I'd have no practice at all.'

'But what do you know of our legends, and how do you know they are false? Legends are based on truth – '

'Not always,' Duncan put in.

I felt that he, like Hamish, was anxious to silence Mary, but my curiosity wouldn't allow it.

'Tell me the legend,' I insisted. 'I'd like to hear it.'

Brenda protested, agreeing with Hamish that the story hadn't a grain of truth in it and that I shouldn't listen, but this made Mary even more determined.

'You of all people, Brenda, know it is true. Father heard the footsteps, and what happened? He died, inevitably.'

CHAPTER THREE

I froze.

'What do you mean – "inevitably"?'

I was hardly aware that I spoke, but the words echoed in my ears and I knew it was I who uttered them and that no matter how chilled I was by fear, I had to know the truth.

Before my aunt could answer, Duncan cut in, 'Mary, be sensible and drop all this talk. You'll frighten Lavinia.'

Hamish Cameron burst out, '*Will* frighten her? The girl's frightened already, and no wonder. Who wouldn't be, after hearing a statement like that? Anyone would think a murderer stalked the place!'

Aunt Mary protested, 'Oh, not a real murderer! I didn't mean that, of course. But it's the legend, and it always comes true. Everyone knows that.'

'Except me,' I answered steadily, 'so you may as well go ahead and put me in the picture.'

'Then mind you pay no heed to it,' Hamish warned. 'It's a lot of damned rubbish.'

Mary shot him a venomous glance, then turned to me and said, 'It's McIain, Twelfth Chief of the Clan Donald. He was murdered, but still comes back.'

'Comes – back?' I echoed. 'To Glenrannoch? But how can he come back since he was never here?'

'Ah, but he was! He lived on this very spot. He was murdered here, and his spirit refuses to leave the place, even though his house was burned to the ground and Glenrannoch built on the site a century later.'

Duncan ordered quietly, 'That's enough, Mary. Drop it.'

'But she hasn't heard the legend! She won't understand until she does. You see, Lavinia, the story is that when MacIain returns he does so three times; three consecutive visits on three separate occasions. My father heard him three months before his death, exactly as you did – the first and second times on the terrace, where he paused beneath his window, and the third, coming directly to his door. The second triple visit was a month later, and the third a month after that when he came again on the three consecutive nights preceding Father's death. Sometimes the visits are spread over a longer time; no one but MacIain knows when they will be. Sometimes they are months apart, but always the last one coincides with the three nights preceding a person's death. He marks the victim by halting beneath their window when he walks the terrace, and finally comes into the house and to their room. It's a kind of warning, a prediction. And it always comes true.'

I could feel my hands tightly clutching the arms of my chair, their palms damp, then suddenly Hamish Cameron was leaning over me and saying with some force, 'You are not to heed a single word of it. Understand? If there were a particle of truth in it, MacIain would be haunting all the other places in the glen which are reputed to mark the site of his death. Doesn't that prove what a pack of nonsense the legend is?'

I didn't answer. I couldn't. I had heard the footsteps on three consecutive nights, exactly as my aunt had described.

Brenda said, with a sharpness which I would never have expected of her, 'Sometimes, Mary, you are a very stupid woman.'

'And a damned cruel one,' Hamish flared.

They were all angry with her, and Duncan with double reason. 'You do realize, don't you,' he said heatedly, 'that you have reminded my mother all too painfully of her husband's death? And now you're distressing Lavinia into the bargain. We'll hear no more about the midnight walker.'

Aunt Mary became tearful, babbling that it was right that I should know, that it was her duty to tell me. After all, I had heard the footsteps myself, hadn't I, so shouldn't I be warned?

'So that I know I'm to be the next victim?' I retorted with an attempt at lightness. 'But isn't it obvious that I'm healthy, sound in wind and limb, and young enough to live for a very long time yet?' I even managed a laugh. 'Poor old MacIain is going to have a tough time trying to get rid of me! I'm not ill, like my grandfather was.'

Duncan said with approval that that was the sensible attitude to take, and added, 'Now forget the whole thing, but if you feel uneasy in that room, move into another.'

I reached to the table beside me for a cigarette and Hamish stooped above me with a light. His fingers closed over my hand to steady it and I was grateful for that. I had spoken convincingly enough, but a trembling hand would betray me. I glanced up in thanks, and saw concern in his eyes. I might have misled the others, but not him.

I drew on the cigarette thankfully. Normally I was not a smoker, and to anyone who knew me well the fact that I now needed one would have been a clear indication of tenseness in me. But I had not been at Glenrannoch long enough for anyone to know me well, which proved that Hamish Cameron must be intuitive where I was concerned.

The moment was shattered by a sudden outburst from Mary. 'You're all against me!' she cried. 'No one believes a word I say, but it's all true, *true*!'

She rushed from the room, slamming the door behind her. Brenda gave a great sigh, and I saw that, despite her façade of unconcern, her face was white. I felt sorry for her, inheriting a prematurely ageing stepdaughter and one as neurotic as my aunt. The thought momentarily distracted me from my own emotional state, and when she said to me, 'Lavinia dear, what Mary said about your grandfather hearing the footsteps is quite untrue. You do believe that, don't you?' I agreed despite the fact that I felt she was lying for my sake. Only this macabre reminder of her husband's death could have been responsible for her pallor.

I saw her lovely face turn towards her son. At every angle, her features were flawless and more than ever I was convinced that jealousy of her stepmother must have been a contribution to Mary's bitterness and a sore trial in Brenda's life. But mercifully she had kept a sense of humour. She said to Duncan now, with a shaky little laugh, 'What *I* need, my son, isn't coffee but a good stiff drink, despite the hour. But don't let Mary know, will you? The poor dear would never recover from such a break in routine!'

By lunch I was feeling the effects of my disturbed night and early rising, but coupled with fatigue was the terror which the legend of Glenrannoch had planted in me. It was there, no matter how hard I tried to suppress it. The sinister portent of the legend haunted me, and I could hardly dismiss it since I had heard those footsteps myself before I even knew that Glenrannoch possessed a legend.

The significance of that was alarming. Even more alarming was the fact that the midnight walker had visited me on my first three nights in this house.

MacIain had wasted no time, I thought with bitter humour as I toyed with lunch. I had no appetite and soon made an excuse to leave the table. There were only the three of us, Brenda, Aunt Mary, and myself, Duncan having gone to the mills, and as I pushed back my chair I saw Brenda's grey eyes looking at me in concern.

'You're tired, Lavinia, and no wonder. Why don't you catch up on some sleep this afternoon?'

I said it was a good idea, although secretly I doubted whether I should sleep at all in that vast and uneasy room in which my grandfather before me had heard MacIain's tread and, knowing the legend as I had not, had also known its significance. How had a sick old man reacted when that sinister approach halted beneath his window on two successive nights? Had he lain there, a dying man, imagining the ghost of MacIain pointing upwards, foretelling his doom? And on the final night had he listened to the steps coming to his door, as I had done, and experienced greater terror than I because he knew he would never hear them in this world again?

Somehow I managed to hide my tension from Brenda. She herself had been upset by Mary's thoughtlessness — if thoughtlessness it was to remind a woman recently widowed, of a macabre incident associated with her husband's death. Brenda might insist that it was all untrue, but I still felt that she lied for my sake.

As I left the table I glanced at Aunt Mary and marvelled at what I saw. She was eating heartily, as she always did, helping herself liberally to a second slice of Flora's lemon meringue pie as if nothing had sent her storming from the room in a flood of tears and temper. For her, the incident was over and forgotten. Had she also forgotten that she had sent currents of fear darting across the room straight into my unsuspecting mind?

I left the room abruptly, not trusting myself to look any more at those bony hands shovelling food voraciously into her tight-lipped mouth. At that moment she had no thought for anyone but herself and her own satisfaction. Greedy, that's what she is, I thought in disgust as I mounted the right wing of stairs. These rose from either side of the great hall, curving upwards to the minstrels' gallery which, also curved, linked the two staircases at the top like a great horseshoe.

Originally the great hall had been designed for banqueting, subsequently being used as a ballroom, but those days of gaiety and splendour had gone. The magnificence was still there, plus the wealth which former MacDonalds had spent on priceless furniture and antiques to grace their mansion, but I had a feeling that Glenrannoch had been asleep now for a long time, and that the dark portraits of former generations had hung in silence for many years.

These portraits lined not only the panelled walls of the hall, but flanked both staircases, with an overflow on the gallery. They were set with pride and lit with care, and in the majority I could see the similarity of features which marked this branch of the family, particularly its menfolk. The only deviation was in an occasional portrait of a woman, obviously a bride brought to Glenrannoch, but soon any likeness to the women was subjugated in their children by the strong MacDonald strain.

I mounted the stairs slowly, reluctant to go to my solitary room. Change to another, Duncan had advised, but what difference would that make? If the legend was true, the footsteps would find whichever window concealed me, whichever door.

I jerked my mind away from the thought, deliberately studying the portraits to give myself something else to think about. On the whole, they were a handsome lot, and undoubtedly my father had resembled them. I saw his finely bridged nose, well shaped mouth, and determined chin repeated over and over again, century after century, unmistakable despite changing fashions in hair and clothes.

For the most part the male MacDonalds had not been fashion-conscious; there was a similarity in their masculine disregard for foppery. They were well but soberly dressed, except when clad in Highland regalia. Then they stood out, handsome as peacocks against the darkly panelled walls, elegant in velvet and tartan, with lace at wrist and throat, elaborate silver buttons, and handsome brooches fastening the plaid at the shoulder. Then their pride and arrogance seemed emphasized and I felt a stirring in my heart as I studied them.

For all their arrogance, they had been strong, they had been men, and their characteristics had been in my father too; determination, stubbornness, and unrelenting pride which set son against father and father against son, preventing either from giving in.

The same stubbornness was in me, and I knew it. I had worked as unremittingly at my job as my father had worked in his. He had set his course and stuck to it; I had done the same.

My father's creative talent had manifested itself in me in a different way, a feminine way. After an art training I had taken my diploma in dress design and then worked my way from the ground up, starting on the cutting-room floor, going through every department and every stage of the business until at last I was at the drawing

41

board professionally and Lavinia MacDonald designs slowly became known. The day they began to be featured in the glossy magazines put the seal on my success.

I could go back to London any time and continue where I had left off, and there was no reason why I shouldn't do so now. I could run away from the menace of Glenrannoch to the familiar safety of my London flat, haunted by no ancient superstitions. It was, I decided, the most sensible thing to do, but it *would* be running away, and what would suit Aunt Mary better than that? She was one of the inheritors if I decamped.

The thought startled me so much that I halted in my tracks. Could that be what she wanted? Behind her prattle, could there be a purpose? Was she a devious, scheming person instead of the unhappy, embittered creature she appeared to be? Had she told that story solely to frighten me away?

A sound from below interrupted my thoughts. It was Brenda, crossing the hall from the dining-room and following me upstairs. Her serene face glanced up at me and I relaxed at once. She had a soothing personality and, as I waited for her, I looked down on her smooth brown hair and classic features, which would still be classic even in old age. It was all due to bone structure; when the flesh hung loosely the symmetry of those bones would be more finely etched but equally striking.

'I was coming to see if you were all right. I thought you would be in your room by now.'

I told her I had been studying the portraits, and that I didn't know I had so many ancestors.

'These, and more besides. Only those who distinguished themselves were painted for posterity, James once told me.'

I glanced along the gallery and down the stairs. 'Then I presume his portrait must be in the hall below, and I overlooked it.'

She gave a little laugh. 'My dear, no one would be able to overlook James. He was the most striking of them all.'

'And I've never even seen a photograph of him . . .'

'I will show you something better. He wasn't photogenic, but the artist who painted him brought him to life.

42

The portrait hangs in my room. I had it removed after his death, but of course, if you think it should go back to its original place in the hall, I will give it up.'

I protested at once. 'Why should you? And why should *I* dictate? As Aunt Mary pointed out, I'm not yet really mistress of Glenrannoch – and perhaps never will be.'

'But you've decided to stay, I hope? I meant it when I said that this house needs new life, young life. I think James realized that too. Once upon a time the place was filled with it; now, all family life has gone.'

'So you also visualize my marrying and filling the house with little MacDonalds? Or perhaps I should say Mac-Donald-Mathesons?'

She laughed. 'Well, I'm sure that would please James, but remember, *he* didn't marry a Matheson when he married me.'

'That wasn't so essential, was it? If you had given him children the name of MacDonald would have been preserved, not watered down with someone else's.'

She nodded. 'I was thirty-six, and many women well past that age have had children. However, I didn't, and if it had been so essential to James, wouldn't he have sought an even younger bride?'

I apologized somewhat awkwardly, but she brushed it aside.

'Everyone was surprised by our marriage, of course, but none of their speculations was right. James married me, as I married him, for one reason only. He loved me, as I loved him. At sixty-four the age gap didn't seem very great; he was a vigorous man, youthful for his years. We were right for each other, and we knew it as soon as we met. He didn't waste time, either. We were introduced at a local ball and after about five minutes he asked outright where my husband was. "If you had one, he would be here," he said. "No man who owned a woman like you would let her out of his sight. Are you a widow?" You should have heard the hope in his voice and the disappointment when I said no. Then I admitted I was divorced and had been for some years. I was afraid of marrying again. It had been an unhappy experience, but with James, it was not. I loved him until the day he died.'

43

We had reached her room, which was at the end of a long corridor leading to the north side of the house, far away from my own with its short approach from the minstrels' gallery.

Brenda opened her door. 'And now,' she said, 'you can see him.'

The portrait dominated the room, set alone upon a wall and directly facing the four-poster bed. It had a spotlight above it, but at this hour no spotlight was needed to emphasize those strong, handsome features. I saw the hard eyes, the relentless mouth, the ruthless chin – all exactly as I had imagined. The white hair flowed back from a fine, broad brow set above a large and sharply bridged nose. That a woman such as Brenda could have fallen in love with such a man, and remained in love, was hard to credit.

I remained staring at the portrait, and the cold eyes stared back at me. I could almost feel our wills clashing.

'You are disappointed. You don't like what you see,' Brenda said quietly.

'Not disappointed, nor even surprised. He is exactly as I pictured him.'

'Which means you are reading into the portrait the things you expected to see. You have grown up with an adverse impression of your grandfather – '

'Are you surprised?' I was unable to keep a defensive note from my voice.

'I suppose I shouldn't be. I only know your grandfather's side of the story, as you only know your father's. I imagine that James and Andrew must have been very alike.'

'In features perhaps, but had he lived to be an old man my father would never have looked like *him*.' I nodded towards the picture. 'Look at the coldness in those eyes, the iron jaw, the relentless mouth . . .'

'Those eyes could be warm, the mouth tender. That was the James MacDonald I knew.'

'Then why keep this chilling picture beside you, especially if it is so misleading? And can it be so misleading, since you say the artist brought him to life?'

Brenda smiled. 'He brought to life the man the world saw, the man James wanted to appear. It was painted originally for the boardroom at the mills and this was

44

what I called his "business face". He would never sit for another portrait, the whole procedure bored him, and as I lived with the subject, he said, why did I want a mere picture? Finally I persuaded him to have a copy taken to hang at the mills, so that the original could come here. He let me have my way and the portrait hung downstairs until after his death. It is the only picture of him that I have, and so I must be content with it. Besides, it rather amuses me. When I look at that stern face I want to smile because *I* know that the "public face" is a mask. I see the real James behind it, and I can imagine him laughing too. His bark never frightened me, and what was tyranny to others was no more than possessiveness to me.'

'And you didn't mind being possessed?'

'My dear, I loved it. I'm that kind of a woman. To me, a man's possessiveness is a protection, a form of cherishing. I had never experienced it before. My first husband was no good at all; unreliable and dishonest. I was thankful to be freed from the anxiety he caused me, and particularly from any influence he might have had over our son. Duncan was ten at the time; an impressionable age. I was glad to be able to bring him up alone.'

Well, I thought, taking one last glance at the portrait and still seeing it as hard and unyielding, at least you made someone happy in your lifetime, Grandfather MacDonald.

I turned my back on him and looked straight out of the windows towards the loch and a full view of Eilean Munde.

'Lovely, isn't it?' Brenda said. 'This room has one of the best views at Glenrannoch.'

I studied the island with interest. There seemed nothing eerie about it, apart from a ruined chapel. Brenda followed my glance and said, 'You must visit the island some time. It's enchanting; interesting too, with ancient graves inside the ruins of the chapel and two Celtic stones still in existence – one within the chapel on the eastern side, unfortunately broken when a stone fell from the gable end. It's the original chapel built by St Mundus when he settled there, and was still in use in 1485, eight centuries later. Some say that Mass was served there until it was destroyed by invaders around 1573, when it was burned down and robbed of all sacred relics.'

'Duncan told me it was the burial place of the Mac-
Iains, so I suppose some of my ancestors lie there. My
grandfather too?'

'No. The family tomb is beneath the chapel here. If
you haven't seen Glenrannoch's chapel, you must. It is
charming. Small, of course, and family services haven't
been held there for many a year because personal chap-
lains to families ceased long ago. But ours is a peacful
chapel; full of light and well preserved. One can imagine
parents, children, and servants all worshipping there together
in days gone by. And now, I really think you should take
that rest. I'll bring you a cup of tea at four.'

As I crossed to the door I noticed the beauty of Brenda's
room, with its soft colours and its serene atmosphere.
Somehow it was typical of her, but to me the one jarring
note was that portrait; the hard man hanging in pride
of place, surveying the room and everything in it with
stern authority. I marvelled that this very feminine woman
could have loved such a man, and that she could see in his
portrait a totally unevidenced side of his character.

Or perhaps, as she said, it was I who attributed to it
only the qualities I wanted or expected to see.

'I'm glad you were happy with him,' I said. 'But what
about Mary? She couldn't have made things easy for you.'

'I didn't really expect her to. My only hope was that,
being practically the same age, we could achieve a sisterly
relationship and get on together. When I met her, I still
thought it could be possible. At thirty-four she was good-
looking and, on the surface, amiable.'

'My father always said she was pretty. It seems hard to
believe.'

'There are photographs which prove that she was, but
she has locked them all away. Poor Mary. She feels that
life has cheated her. She was young when her mother
died, and she couldn't marry the man she was in love
with.'

'Don't tell me my grandfather interfered with *her* marriage
too!'

'He did not. Something went wrong, I don't know what.
I don't even know who the man was. But it all fell through

and Mary stayed at home with her father.'

'She must have resented your coming. You hadn't much chance of establishing a sisterly relationship, had you?'

'Alas, no. And the years haven't been easier. I have just had to accept her – as, of course, she has had to accept me. I remember that, when I am tempted to lose patience with her.' Brenda suddenly pleaded, 'You won't leave here, will you, Lavinia? Please don't be frightend away by Mary's silly story. You must realize that she is a little unbalanced.' When I hesitated, Brenda went on anxiously, 'I feel you want to go, and that distresses me. Your grandfather was anxious that you should come to Glenrannoch.'

'He wasn't in the least anxious that my parents should!'

'I think he was, but his pride was as stiff-necked as Andrew's.'

'My mother had pride too. She was a wonderful person and more forgiving than I can be. Had my grandfather chosen to get in touch with them, her response would have been quicker than my father's. She wanted the rift to be healed, but she knew how her husband felt, and the hurt his father had inflicted. She shared my father's pride. It was up to James to make the first move; he had been the one to order Andrew out of Glenrannoch.'

'How alike they were!'

I didn't want to believe that. I merely said, 'I have no doubt that my grandfather expected me to come running for my inheritance. I think even your son was surprised when I said I would think things over and didn't want to hear further details until I had made up my mind whether to come to Glencoe or not. Anyway, I couldn't walk out of my job at a moment's notice. I had a contract, terminable by three months on either side. Duncan was understanding and didn't press me, but he did explain that the execution of the will would naturally proceed. I could do what I liked – accept my inheritance or reject it. Whichever way, it would make no difference to the execution of the will and wouldn't hold things up. Now I understand why. Rejection on my part would automatically pass on the estate to the next in line.'

'Which means Mary and myself. Can you wonder I am anxious for you to stay? I couldn't face a lifetime alone with my stepdaughter, and Duncan will ultimately marry.'

I had no answer to that, and Brenda continued, 'Personally, I doubted whether you would even visit us. What made you? You are successful and could be more so. Riches aren't likely to tempt a girl whose prospects could equal Mary Quant's. Nor a girl with your character. So why did you come?'

'Curiosity. I wanted to see my father's home, and his background. And I did leave the door open. I made sure of a renewed contract if I do eventually go back.'

Brenda's smile flashed. 'There's a strong touch of the MacDonalds about you, Lavinia, whether you like the idea or not.'

'If you mean businesswise, my father always said it was essential to stand on one's own feet.'

'Which you are well capable of doing, my dear, so you can afford to take us on probation a while longer, can't you? Give us a fair chance. And you haven't seen the mills yet. They are part of your background and your heritage. You shouldn't run away without seeing them.'

I wondered later, in the privacy of my room, if Brenda was something of a psychologist. To accuse me of wanting to run away was a definite challenge, and as I closed my door I mentally picked up the gauntlet.

As I did so, I looked around, still disliking the room. I didn't like the shadows which even the sun failed to abolish entirely, but something about Glenrannoch reached out to me. I could see what it had once been like, and what it could be like again.

The luxury of everything was impressive, but the atmosphere sombre, for some previous generation with a taste for dark and serviceable colours had ruined the natural beauty of the panelling by staining it almost black, the smoke from open fires throughout the years making it even blacker. To restore the wood to its original colour would be a long and expensive process, but worth it. The money was there, saved by thrifty MacDonalds who also bought precious antiques because they were a good investment, amassing a secondary fortune for the future.

But by far the worst area of the house was the kitchen

wing. The gauntness of those rambling quarters had struck a chill into me at first sight, although I realized that the butter churns, the tub measures of iron-banded wood, the cauldrons and skillets, the great iron fire-dogs which had once been used to stack logs above an open 'down hearth', were all interesting antiquities. The wall behind the great inglenook was protected by a wrought-iron fireback, as elaborately ornamented as the fire-dogs, but I doubted if the cooks of days gone by had appreciated its decoration as they sweated over their stewpots.

Flora and the girls being busy in other parts of the house, and Luke outdoors, I had been able to study the kitchen quarters at leisure. Mercifully, an up-to-date electric cooker and other modern amenities had been installed, plus some comfortable chairs for the staff, but a great deal more was needed to improve the sprawling domestic wing, with its sculleries, stillroom, buttery, bakehouse, dairy and brewery, all in varying stages of disuse and neglect.

All in all, I thought now as I dropped upon my bed, there was a lot to be done to this ancient house. It could be brought alive again, and if I could chase away the gloom and the shadows, I would chase away its horrible legend. Meanwhile, I refused to be frightened away by it, or by any devious desire in Aunt Mary's unhappy mind.

I would show her how little I cared by staying firmly at Glenrannoch. And this room would remain mine. I would fight against fear and cock a snook at superstition.

CHAPTER FOUR

Unexpectedly, I slept, waking only when Brenda arrived with the promised tea. After drinking it, I had an urge to get out in the fresh air and decided to explore the grounds, of which I had seen little as yet. It would also be a good opportunity to visit the family chapel, and after being directed by Brenda I left her sitting on the south side of the terrace, sunning herself. The morning mist had heralded a bright day after all.

49

The tiny stone chapel was exactly as Brenda described it, light and peaceful. The walls were covered with tablets dedicated to bygone MacDonalds, and the floor with commemorative slabs to those who lay in the family tomb beneath, but its air of loneliness was sad, and the fresh flowers upon the altar added a forlorn touch. I wondered who put them there. Luke might be responsible for keeping the place clean, but his clumsy hands had never arranged those flowers.

Emerging into the sunshine again I took a path which opened on to a wide stretch of lawn sweeping towards a tall beech hedge on the far side. In the centre of the hedge was a gap, and right at this moment a woman was walking through it. She was tall, white-haired, and elegant in a suit of Mactweed. I recognized the weave at once, a mixture of heather tones which I had used for some of my own creations. The mills turned out many varieties of tweeds, as well as tartans in wool, silk, and taffetas.

I went to meet the visitor. At close quarters she proved to be younger than I had imagined from the distant impression of white hair. Her face was comparatively unlined and I judged her to be in her early forties. She had a good figure, a good skin, and a very likeable face.

She said without preamble, 'You must be Lavinia. You're like Andrew quite a bit, but not entirely. I'm Isabel Forsythe and I've been wanting to meet you ever since I heard you had come. Naturally I was curious because I'm the girl — was the girl — your father rejected for your mother.' She said it with an engaging smile. 'Perhaps he never mentioned me and I doubt if he ever thought of me. I was Isabel Matheson in those days. I'm not embarrassing you, am I?'

'Not in the least, and of course I've heard of you.'

'Well, I'm glad he remembered me, although Andrew and I fought even as children, and didn't improve all that much when we grew up. Marriage between us would have been disastrous. Of course I was furious when he threw me over, but when the fury subsided, which was quite soon, I realized that only my pride had been hurt. I felt insulted. No girl likes to be rejected. She considers it *her* prerogative to the throwing-over, so I felt cheated too.

That, to my silly young mind, was the unforgivable thing!'

I burst out laughing and held out my hand. 'I wish my grandfather had shared your attitude, Mrs Forsythe.'

'Isabel, please. Well, he did share it in a way. Piqued, that was how he felt. Cheated out of his plans. When I told him so, he was furious – a chit of a girl telling a man of his age that he felt peeved for the same kind of reason as her own! Of course, it wasn't quite the same kind, but more or less; the same indignation because he, as I, wanted to call the tune and Andrew called it instead. But no one dreamed that it would lead to a rift between them which would never be bridged. For my part, I would have welcomed Andrew back, but not as a potential husband. I'm glad he did well in the career he chose. I knew he would. Pushing him into the mills after an art training was folly. He could never fit in.'

We were strolling across the lawn to the high beech hedge. I said, 'Tell me about him. I'm sure you know lots which he never told me. Apart from talking about Glencoe from time to time – I think he was sometimes nostalgic for the glen – he didn't often refer to his life here. He was the kind of man who rarely looked back. He said it was a waste of time and that if one did, one would never go forward.'

'That sounds just like Andrew. He lived only for the present – and the future, of course, once he met your mother. Apart from feeling she had put my nose out of joint, I remember I thought even her name prettier than mine. Vanessa. Isabel is almost commonplace in Scotland.' She led me through a gap in the hedge, still talking. 'This is a short cut from Glenrannoch to Kyleven, which has been my home all my life. When my parents died I inherited it. That was in 1948 and it came to me because my elder brother, Alistair, was killed during the latter part of the war. When we were young the four of us – Andrew, Mary, Alistair and I – made this gap in the hedge as a short cut between our two homes, otherwise it meant going round by a lane on the far side of Glenrannoch, and that took ages. As a result, we broke the hedge down so much that this part had to be removed and ever since then the path between it has remained. I hope you'll use it a lot, Lavinia. Come to Kyleven whenever you feel like dropping in.'

I thanked her, and said I should like that.

Once on her own side of the hedge we walked through an overgrown shrubbery on to lawns far less well-kept than Glenrannoch's. Also the grounds were smaller, as was the house which stood squarely towards Loch Leven. Where Glenrannoch was a rambling mansion, Kyleven was a solid, square-built manor with traces of long-lost dignity. Neglected paintwork, unkempt gardens, and in-effective attempts to keep at bay the gradual encroach-ment of age told a story of either indifference or lack of means.

It was the same inside. In comparison with its size, the house was furnished scantily, and there were faded patches on the walls where once various items of furniture had stood, but despite all this the atmosphere was pleasant.

Isabel said airily, 'Take no notice of the shabbiness – we just never get around to doing anything about it! Ian, my husband, is always too busy with his antiques business – he has a shop in Perth and another in Edinburgh, using this house as a sort of repository for goods in transit. Purchases from sales and elsewhere are stored here until there is space for them at one or other of the shops, so we're either living in overcrowded splendour or compara-tive bareness, as at the moment. Next time you come you may find yourself surrounded by Chippendale, and the next by a mixture of Sheraton or Hepplewhite or goodness knows what. When your grandfather visited us he used to look around in horror, but personally it doesn't worry me. I'm at the mills most of the time – I work in Adminis-tration – so, like Ian, I have little time to attend to things here.' She glanced at her watch. 'Six o'clock already. What will you drink?'

I chose scotch and as she poured for both of us Isabel chattered on, 'I know this place needs re-decorating, but what's the use when furniture is constantly being changed around, or coming and going? We had an ancient Court Cupboard standing over there for a long time, and when it finally went, the wallpaper all around had faded, leav-ing a great dark patch behind. So in a burst of guilt or enthusiasm, I'm not sure which, I had the room done over, and along came a load of Regency and smaller stuff, which ultimately left their own dark patches as one by one they went to Ian's shops.'

She shrugged in a happy-go-lucky fashion which seemed characteristic of her and I didn't like to suggest that to choose fade-resistant decorations might have been a good idea. I could imagine her picking something at random and telling the decorator to go ahead and slap it on.

Almost as if she read my thoughts she continued indifferently. 'What's the use? I expect your father could have come up with some sound ideas, but Ian's head is full of his business and mine is full of my job, which I love; surroundings don't bother me. Of course, Ian is fussy about the décor of his shops. It's only Moira who grumbles about the house from time to time, but she's at the age when most girls are anti-home and anti-parents and anti the whole domestic set-up, so I take no notice.'

'Moira?'

'My daughter. She's nineteen and trying to be a hippy. She'll get over it.'

A male voice from the door said cheerfully, 'Isabel does prattle on, doesn't she? All ad lib, too. My aunt is God's gift to deadly dinner parties – with her around there are never any long silences while the poor hostess wonders how to get the conversation ball rolling. Dear old Isabel does it solo while everyone else gets on with the business of eating. That's why she's so slim. Nothing fat-and-forty about you, is there, my angel-aunt?'

I guessed at once that the handsome youth strolling across the room was the nephew Mrs McPherson had told me about. I looked at him with interest, aware that this could be the Matheson my grandfather had earmarked for me.

There was a touch of the trans-Atlantic about his accent and more than a little American energy beneath his indolent guise. He smiled at me amiably and said, 'I guess you must be Lavinia. Isabel's been longing to meet you. I had a bet with Moira that she'd do it within twenty-four hours, which means I'll now have to hand over a pound to the brat. You've not been quite so quick off the mark as

I expected, Isabel.'

'You must be Malcolm,' I said.

Pouring a drink, he answered, 'Someone been telling you about me?'

'Mrs McPherson.'

Isabel interjected in surprise, 'You mean Hamish's domestic help? How did that woman manage to meet you before I did? And Hamish – I take it you've met him also? And he didn't even tell me!'

'Been holding out on you, has he – he from whom you have no secrets?' Malcolm raised his glass to the pair of us, but I sensed a faint mockery both in his tone and in the glance he turned upon his aunt. This, however, left her unperturbed.

'He certainly didn't mention it when he drove me to the mills this morning. My car wouldn't start so I begged him for a lift. Luckily, he happened to be going that way.'

'Happened?' Malcolm queried suggestively, but his smile was indulgent.

Isabel answered lazily, 'Everyone knows he goes to Fort William to attend the animal clinic on Tuesdays, so naturally I rang him.'

'You ought to turn in that old crock of yours. If my uncle can have a great new Renault Estate, why should you put up with an elderly Vauxhall?'

'Ian needs a good car for his business. He covers miles going to auctions, and he needs something spacious for transporting things.'

'You spoil him. You spoil us, bless you. Particularly that daughter of yours. Where is she, by the way?'

'She was bored, she said, hanging around at home. I'll be glad when the summer vacation is over. She went to Oban with her father to attend a sale.'

'Don't let her know that Cameron drove you to the mills, and presumably waited to bring you back, or she'll be as jealous as hell. She's mad about the man.'

'Puppy love – or should I say kitten?' Isabel answered mildly.

'Neither. She's fascinated by his past.'

'Malcolm!' His aunt's tone was unexpectedly sharp.

'Sorry, but you know what kids are like. Particularly

54

girls. They go for age and experience, especially if there's a spot of murk about it.'

Isabel looked annoyed. I felt she only checked a retort because I was present. As for myself, I was well aware that throughout this conversation Malcolm had been watching for my reactions. I wondered why, and was glad I had revealed none. If this likeable but rather brash young man imagined that I was naïve enough to be intrigued by innuendo, he was wrong. In the rag trade I had grown accustomed to malicious thrust and parry running through sophisticated backchat. In contrast, this family game of verbal bat and ball seemed no more than good-natured badinage, although my curiosity was aroused by the references to Hamish Cameron.

Malcolm took our glasses to refill and as he did so Isabel said a shade to casually, 'Of course, if you had been at your desk this afternoon, as you should have been, *you* could have driven me home. What was it today? The golf course?'

He turned and smiled disarmingly. 'Can you blame me, my sweet aunt, on such a day as this turned out to be? And my Scots blood will out. Don't forget it *was* the Scots who invented the Royal and Ancient game.'

She laughed, and reached out for her refilled glass. 'Why can't I be angry with you for long?'

'Why can't you be angry with me ever?' he answered engagingly, adding to me: 'Isabel gets moments when she feels that, in the absence of my mother, she isn't doing her parental duty unless she utters a reproach or two.'

'You wouldn't have dared to play truant when James MacDonald was alive,' his aunt said severely.

'Don't you believe it – I did, many times, using one of the company cars, too. Of course I took good care not to be found out. It isn't only the MacDonalds who have cunning.' He winked at me hugely, and I laughed. The idea of this young man bamboozling my grandfather appealed to me.

'And I suppose you used a company car today?' Isabel remarked tolerantly.

'I've no other choice until my new Pontiac comes from the States. Delivery any moment now. The agents tell me it has already arrived at Glasgow and will be on its way to Fort William immediately.'

Isabel then asked when I planned to visit the mills and I told her that Duncan was taking me tomorrow. She seemed pleased, and added that she liked the idea of my joining the family business.

'It was my grandfather's idea, not mine.'

'Then I hope you go along with it, and I won't be surprised if you find the textile business is in your blood, as in any MacDonald or Matheson. Well, almost,' she added, obviously remembering my father's rejection of the family-ordained career.

'You didn't tell me more about him – my father, I mean. You were saying that because he had an art training he could never fit in at the mills, but part of that training was textile design. He would have been good on that side.'

Malcolm replied before Isabel had a chance to. 'I'll bet he was put through the whole dreary business, whether he liked it or not. He'd have to learn to work the frames so that he could understand how they operated and be able to judge when weavers weren't getting the greatest productivity out of them. And even if he didn't actually work with the rag-pullers, he would have to know how the messy job should be handled. Can you wonder I play hookey when I can?'

His aunt protested. 'My dear Malcolm, you're no rag puller or labourer, so don't exaggerate. We've *all* had to get a theoretical knowledge of the processes. Can you imagine what the workers would think if we, the bosses, revealed ignorance when we talked to them? They respect only those who know the business thoroughly; they're loyal, but only to hard workers like themselves. So keep the golf course and the car-racing circuit for week-ends, or the whispering at the mills will grow louder.'

The reproach in her tone was not harsh, but it was there, and I caught a glimpse of the business woman beneath her ease of manner. I also judged that the firmness was needed because Malcolm answered indifferently, 'Don't worry, darling, the din of the looms will drown critical voices, and when Lavinia joins us perhaps I'll be more willing to stay nose to desk. She'll be a decorative addition to the establishment. You know,' he finished to me, 'I can sympathize with your father's desire to get away from the place. A man with artistic ability would be like a fish out of water in a textile mill like ours. Tartans are tartans and tweeds are tweeds, but they have their limitations in design and weave; there's no scope for creative art there. What surprises me is that he was even allowed to have an art training of any kind.'

'That was due to his mother's influence,' Isabel explained. 'She was a wise woman. I remember her well – a typical Scotswoman running her home and family with unquestioned authority and keeping her nose out of her husband's affairs. For the most part, Scottish home-life is matriachal, but only as far as the hearth. Beyond the realms of domesticity the husband is boss, the patriarch who earns the bread, dictates on education, and plans the future for his children. It was particularly so in the old days.'

Malcolm gave a sudden laugh. 'The ancient definition of a Scotsman's need for a wife was "to fill his belly and his bed", wasn't it?' He caught Isabel's eye and coughed apologetically. 'Sorry if I sound crude.'

'Then stop being so and let me finish,' his aunt reprimanded mildly. 'I was about to add that Jessie MacDonald not only understood her husband, but her children too, and was prepared to fight for them. She recognized Andrew's talent, whereas his father refused to. It was she who finally persuaded James to let the boy have an art training in Edinburgh, but James agreed only on one condition – that Andrew toed the line and entered the mills, keeping "all that nonsense" as his hobby. Inevitably, like everything else between James and his son, it didn't work out. At the College of Art Andrew's flair for interior design was quickly discovered. He qualified highly in that field, so he had it to fall back on when the break-up came. And the break-up would have come whether he had fallen in love with his Vanessa or not. The pull of the work he was really cut out for would have won in the end.'

'And how did his prejudiced father feel about his success?' Malcolm asked. 'I presume he knew about it?'

'He couldn't fail to. Andrew won a measure of fame

in his particular sphere; his name was quoted frequently in the Press. But apart from that, Lavinia's grandfather kept tabs on everyone.'

But not in touch with them, I thought sadly as I finished my drink and rose.

I was about to take my leave when the sound of footsteps came through the open window and Malcolm, glancing outside, gave a mock groan.

'Here comes Florence Nightingale, looking self-martyred as ever. She's inspecting the weeds in the gravel drive. I wonder they don't shrivel at her glance.'

Isabel said, 'Poor Mary – be nice to her.'

'Aren't I always?' His mischievous eyes regarded us with mock innocence.

Isabel went to meet Mary, but I remained where I was, feeling in no mood for another encounter.

'Perhaps my aunt will invite her no further than the hall,' Malcolm said comfortingly.

But my luck was out. I heard her saying, 'I was on my way over with this herbal rub for Craig when I saw the chapel door open. Has he been there, Isabel? If so, he must have been responsible for leaving it unlocked. You do understand that he is at liberty to go there only if he leaves the place exactly as found, the door closed and the key on the hook behind the porch wall? Otherwise, we will have to withdraw the concession. It *is* our family chapel, you know.'

'Who is Craig?' I whispered, and Malcolm told me he was the Forsythe gardener, bent double with arthritis.

'He's also fanatically devout, and because he can't walk to and from the village church whenever the mood takes him, Brenda lets him use the old MacDonald chapel. Now it sounds as if he's in trouble with Eagle-Eye . . .'

Swiftly, I was in the hall.

'It was I, Aunt Mary. I was exploring the chapel before I came here and must have forgotten to close the door.'

Her surprise was obvious, not because of what I said, but because she didn't expect to see me here.

'And the key was in the lock when I opened it,' I went on, 'so naturally I left it there.'

Isabel pointed out gently that perhaps Mary herself

had forgotten to put the key away after doing the flowers.

Mary's answering glance said eloquently that she would never forget to put anything in its place, but Isabel added that everyone could be forgetful sometimes.

'And Craig will be so grateful for your herbal rub, Mary dear. I'll see that he has it without delay. Won't you have a sherry or something before you go?'

'Thank you, no. Duncan is already back and we always have drinks at Glenrannoch prompt at six-thirty.'

Another routine, I thought, stifling a desire to laugh.

'So you've already found the gap in the hedge,' Mary remarked as we left the house and I headed towards it automatically.

'I met Isabel coming through. It's a nice idea, this easy communication between the two houses.'

Mary sighed nostalgically. 'It was, when we were children, and I suppose it has its uses now. When Alistair was alive it was in much use. He came to Glenrannoch a lot. It was home from home to him, he always said, and he still said it when he returned on leave during the war. He volunteered just as soon as he was old enough.'

I thought her voice shook a little, but it was steady again as she continued. 'Before he was posted overseas he managed to get home most week-ends. He was with a Highland regiment, based in Stirling, so it was easy for him. Kyleven was such a different place then, well cared for, as it should be still – and could be, if Isabel weren't such an indifferent mistress. And Alistair's parents were so charming, always making me welcome . . .'

'They were Isabel's parents too,' I pointed out, but Mary went on as if she hadn't heard, '. . . and they never minded when he hurried over to Glenrannoch almost as soon as he was back. He used to come striding through the gap in the beech hedge, so alive, so gay – ' This time she couldn't hide the catch in her voice. 'It seemed impossible that so much vitality should be destroyed, and so terrible that it should happen only a few weeks before the war ended.'

'Terrible for his wife,' I commented. 'They couldn't have been married very long.'

'They married on his final leave. A few months later he was posted overseas – and never came back.'

'So he never saw his son?' I asked in distress.

'Never. But Margaret, his wife, soon found another husband; an American major. Six months after Alistair's son was born, she remarried and took baby Malcolm to the States.'

'How old was she?'

'Twenty-one.'

'Then surely it was understandable? So young, and so alone – '

Aunt Mary turned on me almost fiercely. 'Some people remain alone for ever!'

So it was Alistair whom she had loved; Alistair whom she had wanted to marry . . .

To change the subject, I said the first thing which came into my head. 'Duncan is taking me to the mills tomorrow.'

'I wonder Isabel didn't offer to.'

'Why?'

'Because she'll go out of her way to be charming to you.'

'I imagine she is like that with everyone.'

'But she'll be particularly nice to you, because she hates you.'

I stopped dead in my tracks. 'Isabel hates me? Why?'

'Because your are the daughter of the woman who took Andrew from her.'

'You're wrong, Aunt Mary. Isabel was never in love with my father – she told me so.'

'That's what she always says, but it isn't true. She married poor Ian on the rebound, and has never been a good wife to him. She still likes to exercise her power over men. One in particular.'

I said somewhat sharply, 'Don't talk like that. I don't like it.'

'There are lots of things and lots of people we don't like in this world, but refusing to heed them doesn't help. Mark my words, Lavinia – Isabel will try to drive you away. Somehow. Anyhow.'

CHAPTER FIVE

On my first visit to the mills I watched not only weaving, but dyeing, bleaching, wool-combing, fabric testing and baling. At the end of the tour Duncan took one look at me and said, 'What you need is a drink,' and carried me off to the directors' dining-room, where I flopped into a chair and accepted a glass gratefully, marvelling that from this room we could hear no sound of the machines.

'That's because your grandfather spent a small fortune on making the works as sound-proof as possible, likewise this room because he liked to lunch in peace. The same applies to the boardroom next door. Come and see it.'

It was typical of its kind, with panelled walls lined with portraits of past chairmen and Managing Directors. Prominent amongst them was the copy of my grandfather's portrait. The strange thing was that against the boardroom background it looked less forbidding than in Brenda's room; the austerity was there, but the eyes seemed more proud than cold, the beaked nose more authoritative than arrogant.

'You can tell the Mathesons from the MacDonalds, can't you?' Duncan remarked. 'I sometimes feel their portraits are here as a concession.'

I smiled, but secretly thought it might be true. The unmistakable MacDonald features were certainly dominant.

'Your grandfather once proposed that the portraits of all Chairmen should hang at the top end of the room and Managing Directors at the lower end. It was a subtle distinction between the two families. The board over-ruled him.'

'So he didn't get his way in everything!'

'He managed to in most things, especially important ones. And now I want to show you something more.'

He opened a door leading straight into an adjoining office. I knew at once that it had been my grandfather's, for the vast desk, deeply piled carpet, floor-to-ceiling curtains in dark velvet, costly leather upholstery, all confirmed that this had been the great man's sanctum. So strong was the impression of his personality that it almost seemed as if he had just walked out of the room.

Duncan slid back a wall panel, revealing a safe from which he took a roll of papers and two books. The papers he spread on the desk, saying, 'Take a look at these. They are blueprints of the mills, plus an expansion which James began to visualize a few years ago. The drawings were completed shortly before his death and I had instructions to show them to you when, and if, you came to Glenrannoch.'

I studied them with interest. All departments were clearly marked, but extending from the north side was the outline of an area as yet undetailed, but some words scrawled beneath caught my attention at once. *Lavinia MacDonald's studio and workroom.* My head jerked up.

'Did he write that?'

Duncan nodded. 'And this will tell you why.'

He opened one of the books and laid it before me. It was full of Press cuttings about myself, starting from the first small notice in a textile magazine which described me as a promising young dress designer who should be watched, a girl who had qualified at the Royal College of Art and then had the good sense to accept employment in a wholesale dress warehouse in order to learn production from the ground up.

Slowly, I turned the pages. Apart from Press reports there were photographs of my designs cut from trade publications, then an item covering my transfer to a bigger house, followed by tear-sheets from the glossy magazines depicting the whole range of my designs in Mactweed tartans and weaves.

But the most significant item of all was a report drawn up here at the mills, detailing the bulk of materials in which my designs had resulted, and the total profit they had meant for the company. The sum was substantial.

I closed the book slowly. Now I know what my grandfather had in mind when stipulating that I should take my place in the family business. There was only one place I could fill; a new place created solely for me and to be established by me.

'The artful old man,' I said softly. 'All these years, he kept tabs on me . . .'

'Not only on you. The other book is a record of your father's career. James MacDonald kept that one solely through pride and sentiment, but for you, yes, he had definite ideas.'

I took the second book, glanced inside, then shut it quickly. This was something to be looked at alone; to be treasured and perhaps wept over a little. I looked up at Duncan and warmed to the sympathy and understanding in his eyes.

'It is yours, of course,' he said, and I held the second book close because suddenly it seemed the most treasured thing in the world. The fact that my grandfather had compiled it secretly throughout the years couldn't fail to move me.

'The proud, stubborn, stupid man,' I said with a catch in my voice. 'Incapable of bending, incapable of forgiving . . .'

'Which was why he had to console himself as best he might. Can you wonder my mother loved and humoured him?'

I said nothing to that. The belief of a lifetime could not be entirely swept away in one moment of pity; the fact remained that he had rejected his only son and refused to meet my mother. But now I discovered that it was possible to pity someone without understanding him.

Even this pity was tempered by the knowledge that, as far as myself was concerned, the canny streak in my grandfather had dominated. I could almost hear him thinking, This girl is a MacDonald and can do for the family business all she is doing for that London dress manufacturer. She has a flair for using our fabrics, so she must come and use them here. Mactweed dresswear must be ours exclusively.

And it wasn't any use trying to resist the idea, for it had taken hold of me at once. The thought of having my own studio, a free hand, complete authority, the chance to specialize and to work exclusively with the materials I liked best, was a chance no designer would have been able to resist. I pulled the blueprint towards me and above

my grandfather's words I wrote decisively: DESIGN DEPART-
MENT. DRESSWEAR.

You've won, Grandfather, I thought. You'll have your
way, you canny old man. But I knew that it was my way
too, and inside me was an excitement which could not be
stilled.

'How long will the extension take to build?' I asked
eagerly. 'And until it is, where can I work? I want to
start at once.'

Isabel was enthusiastic about the scheme. So was the
Managing Director, Angus Matheson, a white-haired, be-
nign man, amply possessed of native shrewdness. I knew
that he was already viewing me as a valuable asset to the
firm, and when I repeated my demand for a room in which
to work, Isabel showed me one next to her own, at present
used for storage but ideal for a studio.

'I'll want shelves,' I said. 'Stacks of them. And archi-
tect's drawers to hold my designs, and a large cutting
table as well as a designer's desk. And a sky-light, the
bigger the better.'

'There's nothing to prevent that.' Isabel was caught up
in my enthusiasm. 'This is the single-storey wing which
your grandfather planned to extend for your department.
I've seen the drawings – he showed them to me. That was
why I hoped you would come and why I hoped even
more that you would stay.'

Her delight pleased me, but to my surprise I felt something beneath it. Gratitude. And that I couldn't understand, because gratitude was only felt by someone in need.

Or by someone lonely.

Duncan had arranged for me to be driven home after
lunch in one of the company cars, but when I emerged
into the main courtyard I saw Malcolm standing beside a
sleek golden Pontiac Firebird with power and luxury in
every line of it. He opened the passenger door with a
flourish and announced that he had dismissed the company
car and was driving me instead.

I looked at the magnificent monster and asked if it had
been tamed yet.

He laughed, patted it with pride, told me he had taken delivery only this morning, and that I was to have the honour of sharing its maiden run, then he handed me into one of the deep bucket seats and a moment later the Fire-bird was zooming out into the main road while Malcolm enthusiastically listed its vital statistics.

'It's the F400 – all-American, with a 6,500 cc. V8 engine and 330 brake horse power. It reaches sixty in six and a half seconds and a hundred in sixteen point four. How's that for power?'

'Impressive. And how quickly to take-off?'

He laughed again and went on listing the car's virtues as the acceleration hummed and we headed south. In no time at all Fort William was behind us, with Malcolm still talking about Turbo-Hydramatic transmission, manual over-ride, kick-down, and an idling capacity of one thousand revs per minute. But in my opinion a car six feet two inches wide, with left-hand steering and a driving compartment which felt more like a cockpit, was not ideal for Highland roads. When I said so, he shrugged.

'They ought to widen them. Better still, abolish them and build good motorways.'

'And ruin the Highlands? Over my dead body – which it might well become at this speed!'

But Malcolm was a good driver; we reached the loch in record time and joined the queue of cars closely tucked in to the left of the short curve leading down from this side of the ferry. The golden monster left little room for other cars to pass and created a sensation when driven aboard.

As we crossed the loch I stepped out on deck and as I did so I had a sudden sensation of stepping back into the past. Across this stretch of water, at this very point of the narrows of Ballachulish, soldiers had been rowed across from Carness nearly three hundred years ago, their pikes aslant and the barrels of their muskets burnished, with the boar's head badge on their bonnets which marked them as men of the Earl of Argyll's Regiment of Foot, while ahead, out of sight beyond the mouth of the glen, Alasdair MacDonald, Twelfth MacIain of Glencoe, was in his house, unsuspecting, unaware . . .

I shivered. For a whole day I had not thought of the legendary Highland chief, nor even last night when I slept soundly in undisturbed peace, and the interest and excitement of my visit to the mills had obliterated from my mind Aunt Mary's frightening story. In Fort William I had stepped back into normal, everyday life; now I seemed to have left it behind in that rather ugly little town on the shores of Loch Linnhe with the towering slopes of Ben Nevis rising well over four thousand feet into the sky behind it, and the hive of aluminium works, pulp mills, and other industries anchoring the town firmly in the twentieth century.

But here, crossing the water to the village of Ballachulish with its derelict slate quarries at the foot of towering Ben Vair, the twentieth century seemed to drop away again and the bloody whisperings of 1692 echoed on the breeze from the loch and amongst the rustling of trees on its shore.

Without warning, the faint shivering I had felt became violent and convulsive.

Malcolm put an arm about my shoulders, and with a deliberate effort I pulled myself back to the present.

'Cold?' he asked.

I pretended to be.

'There's a nip in the air,' I said.

'The breeze off the loch is always fresh. We'll be ashore in a minute or two.'

I glanced at my watch. It was scarcely four o'clock. 'You should be back at your desk, but I suspect you've no intention of going there.'

His good-natured face smiled down at me. 'You suspect right. I aim to see how fast Firebird can speed to Glasgow and back.'

'That's quite a trip.'

'And this is quite a car. How about coming with me? We could dine at the Central and be back by midnight.'

A teeming city, a first-class hotel, dinner in a sophisticated restaurant instead of round the family table at Glenrannoch. Lights and gaiety instead of sombre shadows. Malcolm's light-hearted company instead of Aunt Mary's sourness. It was a temptation until I thought of Duncan and realized that I wanted to be there with him.

But when I let myself into the house I half wished I had accepted Malcolm's invitation after all. The heavy front door closed behind me with an imprisoning thud. The great hall was empty, and so were the rooms leading from it. I switched on lamps to dispel the gloom; even at this hour they were needed if only to make the place more cheerful. I thought of ringing for some tea, then changed my mind. I would go for a walk instead. I had explored little of Glencoe as yet.

I ran lightly upstairs. If Aunt Mary were around and heard my step I would not be able to escape her, but no one appeared and within a matter of minutes I had discarded my dress for trews and a sweater and was on my way out again. Glancing towards the garages, I saw that Brenda's Singer was absent, and so was the Mini which Aunt Mary drove. The Busy-Mini, I mentally called it, imagining her scuttling round the village and hamlets of the glen on her committee meetings and charity works.

I stepped out briskly, heading for the pass. The air was fresh and invigorating, totally banishing the sensation which I had felt so acutely as we crossed the loch, that feeling of being carried back into a dreadful past. Now even the shadowy impact of Glenrannoch was forgotten. I was alive and young, invigorated by the prospect of a new and challenging job, with no room in my mind for flights of fancy or imagined menace.

Crossing the Coe by the small bridge not far from Clachaig Gully, I saw the winding pass stretching ahead, deserted except for quietly cropping sheep and a disappearing tourist coach. When it had gone there was no one in sight, no sound to disturb the engulfing silence. I saw a trail of smoke rising from a distant croft, and the massive bulk of Aonach Eagach stretching its five miles towards The Devil's Staircase. I could also see the rocky slopes of The Three Sisters towering above The Meeting of the Waters, the point where the Coe and its tributaries met, and the nearest of these slopes was Aonach Dubh.

It was a moment in time which I was never to forget, a rare moment when this particular stretch of glen seemed cut off from civilization. I experienced a feeling of awe, and an even greater feeling that throughout my life my footsteps had been heading for this place. The silence wrapped itself about me and I stood alone in the Glen of Weeping.

Perhaps that was why the sound was so startling, a sudden cry which sent a chill running through me. I spun round, but no one was there. The hills of Glencoe towered ahead, above and around me, immovable in their timeless strength. The sound, I told myself, could only be a distant wind wailing about their peaks.

But I knew it was not. It came from somewhere much closer, and as if in confirmation it echoed again – an agonized, bodiless voice crying in the wilderness.

CHAPTER SIX

Logic argued that no voice could be bodiless, that it had to come from something or someone, either animal or human, but logic could not dispel the eeriness of that moment and it wasn't until the roar of a motor-cycle crashed into the silence that I jerked back to reality. The machine came pelting round the bend from the hamlet of Achtriochton, followed by a car trailing a caravan and then another coachload of tourists. This short spate of traffic banished every other sound and enabled me to get a grip on myself, but when the vehicles had disappeared silence dropped like a curtain, and again I heard the cry.

I knew then that it had been neither a figment of my imagination nor an eerie manifestation. It was the cry of a creature in distress, the whimper of an animal in pain. I was annoyed with myself for not realizing it at once.

I stood still, trying to get the direction of the sound. It seemed to come from above and ahead of me, so I went towards the lower slope of Aonach Dubh, where I again stood still and listened. The cry was nearer now and seemed to come from the right, but still above me.

The late afternoon was clear, the sun brilliant; I had to shade my eyes against it as I scanned the mass of scrub and scree. Here and there rocky projections stood out and leading up to them was a rough path. Higher still, I could see the dark gash which marked Ossian's Cave.

Obeying an instinct, I followed the path, and as I climbed the cry became closer. I sounded like the pathetic whine of a dog and minutes later I saw the poor thing perched precariously upon a sharp ledge of rock, too terrified to move and wailing piteously as it dangled a wounded paw. It was no more than a pup and when I called to it, it whinnied with sharp and helpless appeal, then began to cry again, aggravated and frightened by pain.

I looked around, taking my bearings. The ledge was well away from the path and above a steep pitch which would have to be crossed sideways; not an easy manoeuvre, but somehow I had to do it. I couldn't abandon the poor creature even to go in search of help. That badly gashed paw needed urgent attention, so I began to slide crab-wise towards him, slipping every now and then and clutching wildly for hand-holds, digging my feet hard into the rough earth to brace against a fall, and all the time calling in reassurance to the terrified animal. The stretch of earth between us was wider than I realized, but it was better to go on than go back. When a quick glance revealed that I was more than half-way there I paused for breath, then continued to inch sideways until I was able to reach out for him.

My clothes were torn and my hands badly grazed; a falling stone had struck my face and I tasted blood at the corner of my mouth, but when at last I held the trembling puppy I was conscious only of relief and pity. Blood from his wound had already matted the fur around the paw, and now smeared my sweater as I cradled him with one arm and began the slow and careful trek back. It was more difficult this time, with only one hand to guide me, but eventually I reached safety, scrambled down to the pass and carried the puppy to a shallow part of the Coe. There I washed his injured paw; the gash was deep and would have to be stitched, so without delay I hurried to Hamish Cameron's house.

The pup was a long-haired collie no more than a few

weeks old. His coat was a warm shade of chestnut, but darker on his back, with a black tip to his silky tail and a white patch beneath his chin. I loved him at once. At the moment his velvet eyes were dulled with pain, but they looked up at Hamish with mute trust while he examined the wound. I was relieved to learn that the paw was uncrushed and no bones broken.

'He must have cut it when climbing,' I said. 'The rock he was perched on was jagged.'

'That could have done it, poor little devil.' Hamish fondled the silky head. 'I'll have to stitch it. I can see he doesn't want to be parted from you, so hold him securely while I give him an injection.'

The puppy's dark eyes turned to him, and a feeble tongue came out to lick his hand, then the small head dropped back, like that of a tired child, into the crook of my arm.

When the job was done Hamish gave me a searching glance. 'You look as if you could do with a bit of attention yourself.'

I glanced down at my clothes; they were a sorry sight, but my hands were worse and after treating them Hamish delivered some stern advice about S.O.S.'ing for help next time I saw a creature in distress, instead of risking my neck. My protest that the dog was too small to climb far merely earned the comment that he had been sufficiently agile to land himself in a tricky spot.

'They're wiry little creatures, these Highland pups. Every time a litter is born around here at least one strays and gets lost. Like people, an animal can get into difficulties very quickly in this wild country.' Hamish glanced at the unconscious dog. 'He'll be round soon. I see he's wearing no collar or identity tab, so I'll take care of him until the owner is traced or turns up to claim him. Everyone comes to me if they lose a pet or one of their stock although the Police or Mountain Rescue Team can be more useful in finding them. Meanwhile, I'll find out if anyone has lost a member of a new litter.'

'And meanwhile I intend to keep him. I did find him, you know. Tell me if there's anything special I should do.'

'No more than feed him and look after him in the normal way. He won't be anxious to put that paw on the ground

70

for a few days, but you'll be surprised at how rapidly he'll pick up. I'll give you some tablets to crush into a drink for him tonight, and in a day or two I'll drop by to take a look at those stitches.' He studied me for a moment and then said, 'I'm more concerned about you. This little incident seems to have shaken you – unless something else has happened?' He finished casually, 'No more footsteps in the night?'

I shook my head.

'And no more frightening stories from your eccentric aunt?'

'None – except that Isabel Forsythe is likely to be my enemy rather than my friend.'

He answered indignantly, 'That's not true. Isabel is one of the best people around here.'

His swift defence reminded me of Malcolm's inference that between his aunt and this man there was a strong friendship '. . . *he from whom you have no secrets*'. That was how he had referred to Hamish. The words took on an uneasy significance, and as if to add to it I heard Aunt Mary saying again, '*She has never been a good wife to Ian. She likes to exercise her power over men; one in particular . . .*'

I felt disturbed, which was unreasonable since this man meant nothing to me and Isabel's affairs were her own.

I was thankful when I saw the puppy's eyelids flicker, and shortly afterwards I was sitting with him on my lap, being driven once again in Hamish Cameron's ancient Bentley back to Glenrannoch.

But this time I felt self-conscious with him. I was aware of his glance once or twice, and each time turned my attention to the puppy. I couldn't analyse my embarrassment; it amounted almost to shyness, which was something I never experienced with men. I stared through the window all the way home, but saw nothing; my mind was dwelling not only on the innuendo about Isabel and Hamish, but on Malcolm's reference to the man's past, and that was definitely no concern of mine.

As I walked up the steps of Glenrannoch I was aware of him standing below, watching me, but I didn't look back.

I went straight to the kitchen, but found it empty. I could

hear Flora scolding someone in a distant scullery and hoped it wasn't Jeannie; the girl's good humour was needed in this gloomy place. I shivered slightly although the room was warm, and wondered why Brenda had done no more with these quarters than add a few items of modern equipment. It seemed uncharacteristic of a woman who was normally thoughtful for others.

I called Flora's name, but my voice echoed round the stone walls and came back to me. These walls were so thick than anyone working in the rooms beyond could not hear a thing, so I stood alone in the empty kitchen, wondering where I might find a box in which to make the puppy comfortable, and as I stood there I suddenly had the uncanny feeling that I wasn't alone.

A small sound, like the scraping of a boot on the stone floor, made me spin round. I was facing the enormous fireplace, looking straight at a figure seated within the inglenook. It rose slowly, so big that it had to stoop to avoid the blackened ceiling, then stood shuffling its feet awkwardly, as if afraid to come nearer.

I knew at once that it was Luke.

This was the first time I had seen him since our foggy encounter, and even now the sight of that abnormally huge figure was startling, but there was a pathos about him, standing there looking down at his great feet, engulfed in an agony of shyness.

I said gently, 'You must be Luke,' and he lifted his untidy head and looked at me. The matted hair was tow-coloured, the forehead bulging, the mouth hung open loosely above a square jowl, and his hands were immense. In the whole face there was not one redeeming feature to lessen the overall impression of ugliness – until I looked into the vacant eyes and saw in their depths such gentleness that I knew Hamish Cameron spoke nothing but the truth when he said that this great fellow would not hurt a fly.

I indicated the puppy and said, 'Look what I found, lost in the glen.'

Luke made an inarticulate noise and came out of the inglenook in one great clumsy movement, his boots echoing just as they had echoed when I had run from him in terror. But now I felt no fear, only overriding pity as one great hand reached out and shyly touched the animal's head.

I could never have believed that a hand so large could have been so gentle; it looked strong enough to break the animal's body with one stroke, and yet its touch upon the silky head was so light that the sleepy-eyed dog was scarcely aware of it.

'I'm calling him Jock,' I said, wondering if the poor man understood what I said. Apparently he did because the huge head nodded and the mouth shaped the sound in a distorted echo, then a smile spread across the tragic face as Jock turned and licked his hand.

'He likes you, Luke. He likes you very much.'

A gurgle of pleasure came from Luke's thick throat. He was like a lonely child welcoming a playfellow, and on an impulse I held out the puppy for him to hold. For a moment the vacant eyes stared at me, doubtful, disbelieving, so I nodded and smiled and went on holding out the puppy until at last Luke was confident enough to take him.

Jock gave a sharp whimper of pain and I said quickly, 'It's all right – you didn't hurt him. His paw is injured, but he'll soon be well again.'

The uncomprehending eyes stared down at the bandaged paw and then, slowly, tears trickled down the ugly face. It was a long time since I had witnessed such grief as this; the sudden helpless grief of a child. All I could do was put my hand upon Luke's arm and repeat that Jock would soon be well.

'Mr Cameron has seen to him; he will make him better.'

This evidently meant something to Luke for he smiled again and nodded his two head vigorously. All would be well, the gesture said, if the vet had seen him, the man he knew and trusted. The tears were wiped away with the back of a hairy hand.

Flora's footsteps, coming from the distant scullery, pulled up at the door.

'I'm sorry, Miss Lavinia, I didn't know you were here. Will you be wanting something?'

Then she saw the puppy in Luke's arms and for a moment her face remained in its rigid mould, but gradually her mouth softened. It would have been uncharacteristic of Flora to unbend completely, but I knew then that I would have no opposition from her about a dog around the house.

'Oh, my goodness,' shrilled a voice, 'that'll make a mess about the place!'

I looked beyond Flora and saw Maggie Munro, the other girl employed at Glenrannoch and one entirely lacking Jeannie's good humour.

Flora whipped round on her. 'You keep a still tongue in your head, miss, and get on with peeling those potatoes.'

The girl turned away sullenly, muttering something about 'not trusting an animal with that Luke'. I felt a sharp anger. Stupid Luke might be, but he was aware of the girl's hostility, and hurt by it.

I told her to find a box and something to line it with so that Luke could make the dog comfortable. Her lip curled and she began to protest that the creature was a miserable stray until she saw my glance and was quelled by it. She was rebellious and sullen. I didn't like her, but for Flora's sake I checked a sharp reprimand. Domestic help was hard to get, with the aluminium works at Kinlochleven and the paper and pulp mills at Corpach offering good money if workers were willing to undertake the daily journey. Glenrannoch was under-staffed as it was.

To my surprise Flora announced that she had the very thing – an old dog basket which had been around for years. I detected an excitement in her which she was at pains to conceal.

The basket, lined with an old piece of blanket, was produced from the depths of one of the vast kitchen cupboards, and when Jeannie came bustling into the room, announcing that the dining-table was set for dinner, but Miss Mary said she'd put out the wrong table napkins ('She wants the damask ones tonight, Mrs Fyfe, not the linen.'), Luke and I were already making the dog comfortable.

Jeannie gave a cry of pleasure and fell upon the puppy with enthusiasm.

'Is he yours, Luke? My, but he's bonny! He'll be company for ye.'

Her kindly face beamed into his, but he shook his head, mouthed unintelligibly, and lifted a clumsy hand towards me.

Jeannie sprang to her feet and bobbed deferentially. 'Beg

pardon, Miss Lavinia,' She was ashamed of what she regarded as lack of manners towards the new mistress of the house, and finished apologetically, 'I was carried away, ma'am. Luke here loves animals and I was glad to see he had a pet of his own –'

Her attitude towards Luke was directly opposed to that of Maggie.

'In that case, I don't see why he shouldn't have one,' I said. 'Why doesn't he, Flora?'

'The late master forbade it, Miss Lavinia. He was never fond of animals about the house. That was why young Master Andrew kept that basket down here in the kitchen –'

'You mean my father?'

'Aye, Miss Lavinia.'

I rose. Jock was already curled up in the blanket-lined basket, soothed by its comfort and by the warm friendliness about him. The vast kitchen seemed no longer a gaunt and empty place, and I no longer a stranger in it because, as a boy, my father had kept a pet of his own in this very basket in this very room, slipping down here to feed and play with it unbeknown to his stern parent.

'What sort of dog did he have?'

'A young collie, same as this, Miss Lavinia. Jock, he called him.'

At some time in my life I must have heard my father talk about his dog, which was why the name had sprung instantly to my mind. I looked at Flora and guessed why she had fetched the basket so eagerly. She had been welcoming back the past.

'And you aided and abetted him?' I asked.

'Aye, that I did, Miss Lavinia. A boy should have his pets if he wants them. Leastways, to my way of thinking. Your grandfather had no objection to them provided they were kept in their proper places, which meant outside in kennels, like the horses in their stables. But on cold Highland nights a kitchen's a warm place for a boy to play with a pup for an hour or two before going to bed.'

'But your own boy was denied even that.'

'Oh, no, Miss Lavinia! Master Andrew always let my Luke play with his puppy, even though the poor lad didn't really know how to handle him. Luke was a babe when I came to Glenrannoch, and your father a schoolboy, but he was right kind to the bairn.'

It was obvious that Luke knew how to handle a dog now, so I asked if he could look after Jock when I was at the mills.

Pleasure touched Flora's face. She turned to her son and, using signs supplemented by words, told him what I wanted. I saw dawning delight in the man's vacant eyes and then his huge head nodded eagerly. Jeannie gave a bounce of delight and cried, 'Won't that be nice for ye, Luke, won't that be *nice*?' and we all looked at each other and smiled. Even Flora. I felt it was the first time she had smiled for many a year.

Later, I remembered that the puppy wasn't mine yet, and if Hamish Cameron came along with the news that its owners wanted it back, there would be someone in this house even more disappointed than I. I could imagine Luke retiring to his corner of the inglenook again, hugging his grief in the lost and lonely corners of his mind.

'But you can't keep a stray!' Aunt Mary protested. 'The creature isn't even house-trained.'

'He will be.'

'But you don't know where it has been or what sort of a place it comes from. It might even be carrying something – germs, *anything*!'

I checked my impatience and told her that I had every intention of keeping the puppy until Hamish traced the owner.

'In a way I hope he doesn't. Incidentally, I've called it Jock.'

Briefly, my aunt was silenced, then she gave a short and reminiscent sigh and said, 'Andrew had a collie named Jock. I suppose he told you. I remember how we used to slip down to the kitchen to see him when Father wasn't around, or when he thought we were in bed.'

Her voice trailed off on a sad little note while Brenda, sitting opposite me across the dining-table, warned me not to get too attached to the animal, nor to pin my hopes on being able to keep him. 'Crofters don't part with good collies all that easily. They're as useful as sheep dogs very often.'

76

'Then let's hope Jock was one of a large litter and can be spared, but if the owner won't part with him, I shall get another for Luke's sake.'

'Luke?' Duncan echoed. 'Why Luke?' It seemed to me that there was a hint of anxiety in his voice.

'Because he loves animals. His joy was pathetic when he heard I wanted him to look after Jock when I'm at the mills.'

Brenda's grey eyes looked concerned. She was wearing a dress of vivid green, beautifully cut, expensive, and for the first time I saw that there were green tones in her eyes and that their impression of quiet greyness was misleading. Candlelight picked up the glinting colour and gave a more sophisticated impression of her. For a moment my interest was caught, the interest which is always sparked when an accepted personality, suddenly seems different.

Now she said, 'My dear, do you think that wise? Luke isn't normal, poor man, and apart from that he is physically clumsy.'

'He was never clumsy with Andrew's dog,' Aunt Mary said sharply, glad of an opportunity to disagree with her stepmother.

Brenda pointed out mildly that he had been a child then. 'Now,' she said, 'he has grown to immense physical strength. I'm not saying he would intentionally hurt the puppy, but Luke doesn't realize how strong he is. He could beat any man for miles around at tossing the caber, if he were fit to qualify for a Highland Games team.'

I assured her that if she had seen him with Jock, she wouldn't worry. 'He handled him as gently as a lamb,' I added.

'But there might be moments when he would not,' Duncan spoke reluctantly and I felt he was anxious not to say more.

Aunt Mary rose and pushed back her chair. Once a meal was over she hated to linger. Sitting around idly was a waste of time, she always said, and now she glanced impatiently at the three of us, loitering over dessert. The glance said eloquently enough that it was time we moved into the drawing-room for coffee. I caught the amusement in Duncan's eyes as he told her not to wait for us.

A lifetime of 'correct' routine battled with the lure of a portable work-table which she had set up in the drawing-room before dinner. On it were wires and tools and gem stones, all the equipment for her jewellery-making set out meticulously. Another charity bazaar was coming along and her restless fingers itched to be at work. Nevertheless, she stood there, having a tug-of-war with herself because to leave the dining-table before every member of the family had finished was simply not done.

I had a sudden vision of her as a child, waiting patiently for a signal that she might leave the table, for permission to speak, for paternal authority to acknowledge her right to do whatever it was she wished to do. My father had often told me of his rigid upbringing, looking back upon it with some amusement. Now I realized that he could afford to, for he had escaped. Poor Mary had not.

I felt a stirring of compassion for my embittered aunt; too often her acid tongue nipped in the bud any inclination to it, but that helpless moment of indecision suddenly revealed her as a basically insecure person.

I laid down my dessert fork and said, 'I'll join you, Aunt Mary,' and was immediately sorry because, instead of pleasing her, all I did was give her satisfaction. She had got her own way, and as she marched ahead of me it was I who felt that I had sought and won parental approval. I looked back over my shoulder and caught Duncan smiling broadly, and it was all I could do to stifle my laughter.

The drawing-room had tall windows at each end. At one, they overlooked the stretch of lawns between the old Chapel and the beech hedge which marked the boundary between Glenrannoch and Kyleven. The other faced the front of the house, taking in a sweep of the grounds with the rising peaks of the Three Sisters in the distance. Of the two views, this was the finer, and particularly lovely at this hour. Duncan, Brenda and I always gravitated towards it when sitting here after dinner, but Aunt Mary never did. She would take her coffee to the other window and sit half turned, facing the distant beech hedge.

She had set her table there this evening, and at precisely the same angle, as if it had always been her custom to sit in that particular spot in that particular way. Sometimes I wondered if it was because Alistair Matheson, whom she had loved, used to come striding through that gap . . .

As I poured coffee I saw her rummage in her capacious bag and take a little pile of sugared almonds and set them neatly in a small bowl at hand.

I said jokingly, 'Don't get them muddled with your gem stones, Aunt Mary. Anyone buying a ring set with a sugared almond might feel defrauded!' But she didn't hear. She was staring through the window, and there was a kind of tautness about her which I couldn't understand. I set a coffee cup beside her and followed her glance, and then I knew what was wrong. Isabel, whom she disliked so much, was walking across the lawn, a man beside her and a girl dawdling behind. I wondered if Mary disliked Ian Forsythe as much as his wife and certainly, I thought, she would never approve of a girl like that. I knew at once that it was Moira, the daughter who was trying to be a hippy.

Brenda and Duncan came into the room and I said over my shoulder, 'We've got visitors,' and went to the fire-place to ring for more coffee cups, only to find that Brenda's hand was there before me.

Momentarily, I stared at the finger on the bell push, surprised by the bluntness of it. I had never really noticed Brenda's hands before, but now I was fascinated by the contrast between them and her willowy figure. They were short, square, capable hands, spatula-tipped, stumpy; the kind of hands one might expect in a short, square, thick-set person.

When I glanced up she was smiling at me. 'Don't look upon the Forsythes as "visitors" in the formal sense, Lavinia. Close neighbours like us drop in on each other whenever we feel inclined.'

I was glad, for I liked Isabel and hoped I would like her husband equally. When they entered I saw a convention-ally handsome man in his fifties, whose regular features somehow matched his correct tweeds, and Moira Forsythe was simply a twenty-year-old edition of her mother. It was like looking at the girl whom my father had been expected to marry, except for the clothes.

I had a swift impression that Moira had dressed expressly

to displease her elders; washed-out jeans torn off above the knees, an old blouse tied above a bare midriff and left undone so that when she moved the deep plunge was emphasized. She wore no bra, was barefooted, and her long brown hair trailed from beneath an Indian head band. She looked untidy, almost slatternly, but still the prettiest thing I had seen for a long time.

Aunt Mary threw one glance in her direction, suppressed a shudder, and bent swiftly over her work, apparently too busy to spare more than a brief greeting for any of them. Moira slouched across and leaned over her, watching the long bony fingers manipulating the tools, whereupon my aunt brushed her aside impatiently. 'Get away, child, get away – you're blocking my light.'

The girl shrugged, laughed and turned aside. I had a feeling that if her parents had not been present, some pert reply would have shot back, but she contented herself with a contemptuous glance and strolled over to Duncan, who was pouring brandies. He said something to her and she looked at him coquettishly, the way a young girl looks when a man flatters or teases her. Then I realized that coquettish was the wrong word, outmoded, particularly in regard to Moira Forsythe. Her look was one of blatant sexual awareness.

I heard her father saying, 'I apologize for my daughter's appearance. She refused to come over in anything but that freakish get-up.'

I saw my aunt's flash of agreement, and felt she enjoyed hearing the girl condemned.

'It's fancy dress, isn't it, darling?' Brenda said indulgently.

I wondered why they hadn't the sense to realize that their attitude would only goad the girl further, but Ian Forsythe went on blandly, 'However, she did wash. A concession these days, dirt being more fashionable than make-up apparently. It's probably the newest idea in Women's Lib. "Back to nature and look one's worst!"'

Moira glowered, muttered something beneath her breath, and reached towards a brandy glass.

'Thanks, Duncan – I'll have one of those.'

But the glass was in Duncan's hand before she reached

it, a gesture so quick and so casual that it gave no indication of being deliberate. 'Elders first, baby,' he said, 'and I'm afraid that's the last of the brandy, anyway.'

She shrugged again, but this time not defiantly. She seemed to like being called 'baby' by Duncan because it sounded like an endearment. A faint flush coloured her cheeks and her eyes followed him as he came over to me.

'How about a turn in the garden, Lavinia, before the light goes?'

'I'll come too,' Moira said at once.

'Sorry again. Lavinia and I have things to discuss.'

'Legal stuff, I suppose? Do you *really* want to own this morgue, Lavinia? Malcolm and I were sure you'd head straight back to London as soon as you clapped eyes on it, and now I see you I'm surprised you didn't. You're not the type to settle down at Glenrannoch or anywhere near Glencoe.'

'What makes you think that?'

'You've London stamped all over you. Not beat-London but classy-London – top-restaurant type. I suppose you know this place is haunted?' she added at a tangent. 'Some old boy from the past comes on the prowl periodically, spelling death to the person who hears him.'

'That story is poppycock,' her father said contemptuously.

'But people swear it's true. I should think it's enough to frighten anyone away.'

'But not me,' I told her, and went out into the garden with Duncan. I could hear the girl's voice prattling on behind us, grumbling because everyone was being anti-social this evening – 'and that bastard Malcolm has gone jazzing off somewhere in that fabulous new car of his without even thinking of taking me . . .'

Outside, Duncan gave a sigh of relief. 'Five minutes of Moira is all I can take.' His hand sought and found my own, and we walked away from the house, out of sight of the drawing-room windows. Through the trees I caught a glimpse of the loch and the outline of Eilean Munde.

'That island looks so pretty and so peaceful I just can't believe it's haunted,' I said. 'I keep remembering the story you told me about it when I first came to Glencoe.'

81

He said abruptly, 'Forget it. There's been enough talk of hauntings recently, and it's all superstition. I told you so at the time.' His hold on my hand tightened and, looking up, I saw his fine features etched in the evening light, his face had charm, appeal, and masculinity, all equally blended. It was impossible not to be physically aware of this man. That he was aware of me in the same way I could tell by the tightening of his hand.

Then he seemed deliberately to break the spell. Because it was too soon, too premature? Unwise to rush things? I hoped it was that, but when he spoke his words were the last I expected to hear.

'Lavinia, I want you to promise not to let Luke look after that dog.'

It was an anti-climax, like reaching out for something lovely and finding it wasn't there. Hurt, I withdrew.

'You too?' I said. 'Everyone seems to mistrust poor Luke.'

'We know him, Lavinia. You don't.'

I knew then that Duncan was trying to tell me something and that I didn't want to hear it. I turned away, but he caught my hand and pulled me back.

'If you allow Luke to take care of that dog,' he said with deliberate warning, 'he might kill him. Strangle him. He has done it before.'

CHAPTER SEVEN

When we went back to the house I saw Ian Forsythe standing beside Aunt Mary, admiring her work, and Isabel and Brenda sitting side by side upon a couch, talking, and Moira slumped in a chair looking bored. I saw gratification in Aunt Mary's face because Ian was complimenting her on a stone-studded bracelet, and I went over to join them because I wanted to think of anything but what Duncan had just said.

I picked up a ring and slipped it on my finger; it was large and promptly fell off. I heard my aunt saying that there were smaller ones, and she picked up another with a greenish coloured stone and handed it to me. It fitted well. Ian Forsythe admired the contrast with my amber-toned dress and I asked if I could buy the ring before the charity sale and put the money in the funds, but still my mind ran on Duncan's words.

'*He might kill him. Strangle him. He's done it before.*'

Not great, big, awkward, gentle Luke! I wouldn't believe it. I think I had cried out that I didn't believe it before I turned and ran back to the house, and that Duncan had called after me, but I was too bewildered to be sure. I knew that he was now standing near the fireplace, watching me although pretending to talk to Moira, but I wouldn't look that way. I couldn't.

Luke, a strangler? A man who would take an animal by the throat?

Distractedly, I tried another ring and put it aside again.

'Of course,' Aunt Mary was saying, 'you can reserve anything you want, but you can't have it until after the bazaar. Everything has to be on display so that other people can order similar ones, if they wish. Oh, don't you like that one? Now *I* think that dark blue stone much prettier. It was one of those you found for me, Ian.'

'I must look for more the next time I go near the Cairngorms. I can always turn off at Aviemore and take the chair lift to the White Lady Shieling; it makes an interesting break to lunch up there and then hunt around for stones. A pity there aren't more in Glencoe.'

The conversation was flowing over me. I was only vaguely aware of the words, and of the tinge of pleasure in my aunt's face. I wanted to rush along to the kitchen to see if Jock was all right, although I knew quite well that he was. Flora was there. Luke wasn't alone with him.

The thought shamed me. I remembered tears pouring down the ugly face; gentleness in the vacant eyes; joy when the puppy licked his hand. When and how had such a man turned savage and strangled an animal as mute as himself? I wished now that I had waited to hear the story, instead of pulling free and running away.

'*Luke here loves animals . . .*' The voice of warm-hearted Jeannie suddenly echoed in my mind. For his sake she had been delighted because there was to be a pet about the place.

She saw Luke daily, she knew him well, therefore her opinion was to be heeded and I knew her judgment to be right. Moreover, Luke's attitude to the wounded dog proved that.

So Duncan was wrong. He had made a mistake.

Suddenly I was aware that Moira was beside me.

'I hear Hamish Cameron is going to find out who owns your stray puppy,' she said. 'Brenda's been telling my mother about it.'

I nodded and moved away, but Moira moved with me. I didn't want to talk about Jock any more this evening, but the girl was not to be evaded.

'If Hamish succeeds, I hope to buy it,' I told her. 'If not, I'll keep it.'

'And you're trusting him with Luke. Brenda told us that, too. They're arguing about it, my mother "for" and Brenda "against". But my mother's a bit of a nut, as you've probably gathered. She actually thinks Luke is harmless.'

I took a deep breath. 'And so do I. And so does Hamish Cameron. And since he's a vet he ought to know whether a man can be trusted with animals or not. He says Luke wouldn't hurt a fly.'

Interest sparked in Moira's eyes and I knew then that it was Hamish she was interested in and whom she really wanted to talk about.

'In that,' she said, 'I'm with you. And I'm all for Hamish, although not everyone is – my father, for one, but that's to be expected because Mother sticks up for him, so of course Dad takes the opposite view. They always do. I've never known my parents agree on anything, and certainly not about Hamish Cameron, but personally I think it's a pity he was ever caught.'

Caught? Like a thief, a criminal? I pushed the thought aside and didn't ask what she meant. I didn't want to know, nor did I want to discuss Hamish because he had befriended me, not only on that foggy morning, but again today, and in particular I didn't want to discuss him because I could tell that Moira was avid to do so. Even more, I felt she was eager to reveal something unsavoury or scandalous which to her, gave him an air of glamour.

84

Apart from that, I had heard one disturbing thing tonight and didn't want to hear another. Despite my dismissal of it, I couldn't get Duncan's statement about Luke out of my mind.

I was glad when the Forsythes left. I went straight along to the kitchen and found Jock curled up in his basket, whimpering with pain every now and then. He had been doing so, on and off, all evening, jerking out of sleep continuously, Flora told me, so I crushed one of the tablets Hamish had supplied and put it in some warm milk. Luke stood looking down from his great height and as Jock feebly lapped up the milk I saw the same concern as before in the man's pathetic eyes.

'He'll sleep now, Luke, there's no need to worry,' I said.

For the first night, I had decided that Jock should sleep in my room, so I carried the basket upstairs and set it on the floor not too far distant from my bed, where I could keep an eye on him. He was drowsy by the time we reached the minstrels' gallery, but unaccountably pricked up his ears the moment we entered my room, then he began to whimper and his ears shot back, lying flat against his head as if in fear. I wondered if he was conscious of the smothering weight of this room, as I was; it seemed the only explanation, coupled with the fact that it was also alien territory to him.

But he had shown no fear downstairs in the vast kitchen, which was also alien territory.

I stroked his silky head, glancing around as I did so. The damask curtains were closed tightly over the enormous windows and the massive furniture seemed to cast shadows as deep as those in distant corners. The four-poster bed, topped by a deep canopy and backed by a great headboard of dark linen-fold panelling, seemed to cast additional shadows which the bedside lamps failed to overcome. There were other lighted lamps about the room; on a secretaire set between the windows, beside a tallboy with deep, coffin-like drawers, on a round library table which was a fine specimen of its kind but now seemed over-large, with a deep well of shadows beneath. Against all this the lamps cast no more than small pools of light which only served to emphasize the darkness elsewhere.

The puppy's quivering body was taut beneath my hand,

85

as if he were sensing the unrest which I myself felt the first night I slept here, and which seemed to grow no less. I wondered now if it would have been wiser to leave Jock downstairs, but was reluctant to take him back in case he needed attention during the night.

Despite the tablet I had given him, it was a long time before the puppy finally dropped off. He seemed to fight against sleep, the way a child does when afraid of being left alone in the dark. Every now and then his drooping eyelids would jerk open and dart apprehensively about the room, nostrils quivering and ears flattening. Once he struggled to rise and I felt the hair of his coat prickle beneath my hand. He made a feeble attempt to bare his teeth, as if at some invisible foe, then mercifully the tablet had its effect and oblivion overtook him.

I went then into the bathroom which in itself was large enough to make a second bedroom, but mercifully lacking any shadows due to concealed lighting which ran all round the ceiling. There were also brilliant lights above the mirrors, which were everywhere. They covered the walls around three sides of the sunken bath and were repeated above the double wash-basins and the long built-in toilet table which still bore my grandfather's brushes, electric razor, after-shave lotion, and toiletries.

Presumably, Brenda had forgotten to remove them. She had completely cleared the feminine part of the bathroom, which was partially screen by a mirrored wall so that it formed a kind of boudoir equipped with every kind of luxury. The locked door from the outer passage was in this section, but undetectable because that, too, was covered by floor-to-ceiling mirror.

James MacDonald might have insisted upon the bedroom retaining its antique splendour, but he had certainly made concessions here. My bare feet sank into the thick pile of oyster carpeting, the towels were enormous and deeply soft, and everything blended into a colour scheme of oyster, flame, and gold, which was beautiful but oddly sensuous. It made me think of exotic tiger-lilies and it struck a bizarre note in this ancient house. Such ornateness seemed not only out of tune, but also out of character with the former occupants of the suite.

But what did I really know of my grandfather's character, or of his widow's? Behind closed doors people were often very different . . .

My thoughts broke off at the sounds of footsteps in the corridor outside. My heart jerked, then steadied, for these were not the footsteps I had heard on my first three nights at Glenrannoch. These were brisk, and I immediately recognized them as Duncan's.

I pulled on a robe and went to answer his rap on the bedroom door. Now that Jock had fallen asleep I didn't want him wakened, so put a warning finger to my lips.

'I had to come along,' he said. 'I upset you out there in the garden and want to put things right.'

In his sleep, Jock stirred, and Duncan's glance went across the room. 'I see you've brought him up here – I'm glad. I thought he might be sleeping in Luke's room.'

'If he were, he would be safe, I'm sure, but when he is well he can sleep in the kitchen at nights.'

Duncan said with a touch of pleading, 'Lavinia – ' but I interrupted quickly.

'If you're going to say again that Luke is dangerous, please don't. And I don't want to hear any ugly stories about him.'

'Better now than when it is too late. I don't want anything to happen which would hurt or shock you. Luke is harmless enough in the usual way, but he does have bouts of abnormality, although they are accepted as emotional traumas. It is then that his behaviour can be unpredictable.'

Jock whimpered again and I hurried to him and knelt beside the basket. Once more his tiny body was taut and quivering.

'He's afraid,' I whispered. 'He's been afraid ever since I brought him into this room.'

Duncan studied him carefully, then said, 'Poor little chap, he's had the fright of his life, getting lost and then gashing his paw into the bargain. He's having a bit of a nightmare as a result of it all. Nothing to worry about.'

I hoped that was all it was, and said no more. I drew the blanket lightly over the puppy and Duncan went back to the door, but before he left he said again, 'I want to put things right between us. I hated upsetting you like that, but I'd hate even more to see you distressed by the loss of that puppy. You've become attached to him so quickly, and for this reason if anything did happen to him you'd feel it even more. I'm not saying Luke would *deliberately* hurt him – '

'You said kill. Strangle. Those were the words you used.'

'And that was what he did to a mountain rescue dog a couple of winters ago. It was out with its handler on training exercises. It was a valuable Alsatian and his training was going well.'

'Too well, perhaps? Did he attack Luke?'

'They are taught to rescue, never to attack. Luke shouldn't have been up there on the slopes when exercises were in progress.'

'How was he to know that?'

'He'd been told, not only by his mother, but by me. And he'd grasped the point all right. Even allowing for the fact that his simple mind forgot it and that Flora should have been diligent in keeping him at home, what he did was a terrible thing and proved that he shouldn't be allowed near animals. I saw it myself, Lavinia, and it was horrible.'

I found that I was holding my robe close about my throat, shivering a little despite the warmth of the room, but I said steadily, 'Having told me so much, you'd better tell me the rest. It was what you came for, wasn't it?'

'Only because I hated the way we parted, the way you ran away from me. You didn't give me a chance to explain, or put things right. Do you think I wanted to upset you? Can't you realize I was thinking of you and only of you? I can't bear the thought of your being distressed in any way.'

I softened at once, and apologized for having left him so abruptly. 'I shouldn't have run away,' I admitted. 'I should have faced up to it, so I'll do so now. Tell me the rest.'

'Only the handlers and those acting as victims were up there. The victims have to be buried in the snow and then, at a sign from their handlers, the dogs have to go in search of them and dig them out. This Alsation had just received the command and was heading straight for target when Luke suddenly rose up from behind a rock and stood in front of him, making those inarticulate noises which can be frightening to someone unacquainted with him. He terrified the animal, so of course it leapt. Any average man goes down beneath a leaping Alsatian, but not a man so abnormally strong as Luke. He seized the dog by the throat and strangled him. It was over quickly; so quickly that no one could stop him.'

I shuddered, and Duncan's arms went round me. I could feel the litheness of his body through the paisley dressing-gown and his hands caressing me through the flimsiness of my own.

'He did it in self-defence,' I said, trying to control my shaking voice.

Duncan went on holding me, but made no answer.

'It *must* have been self-defence,' I insisted, drawing away and looking up at him. 'He must have thought the Alsatian was attacking him. He probably meant to hold him off, no more than that, but he's so strong . . . '

'And even stronger when these bouts occur.'

'You make him sound – certifiable.'

'Some people think he is. The odd thing was that your grandfather didn't. Of course, in Flora he had a valuable housekeeper and such are hard to come by in remote parts like this. One sure way of keeping her was to allow her son to remain. She wanted a home for him. She has always refused to be parted from Luke, which is commendable, perhaps, but foolish. And I admit he's harmless enough so long as he's confined to simple jobs about the place and not allowed to wander into the rest of the house from the kitchen quarters. We're all sorry for him, of course. Who couldn't be? But you do understtand now why I think it unwise to let him care for this puppy?'

I made one last, desperate protest. 'Hamish Cameron swears he is harmless.'

'Hamish Cameron doesn't know him as we do. He hasn't been in Glencoe long enough.' Duncan seemed about to say something else, then changed his mind. Instead, he touched my cheek gently.

'Go to bed now, and don't hate me for what I've told you. Understand why I had to. I can't run the risk of your suffering any distress.'

✳

Next day, Hamish called to tell me he had traced Jock's owners, crofters not far from the spot where I had found him.

I remembered wood smoke rising from a single-storey cottage nestled in a distant fold of hillside.

'Their bitch had a litter a week or so ago – quite a number, so they scarcely missed this poor little devil,' Hamish said.

'They'll sell him?' I asked eagerly.

'They've already done so. He's a present from me to you.'

I was touched, and said I couldn't think of a nicer gift. 'And I've already christened him. His name is Jock.'

Hamish ruffled the puppy's head. 'Suits him well, and I must say he's looking better than when you brought him to me. How did he sleep last night?'

'Restlessly. I had him in my room. He didn't seem to like it very much.'

'He would have spent a restless night anywhere.'

Of course, I thought sensibly. It had nothing to do with the room.

I had carried Jock's basket out on to the terrace and he lay contentedly in the sun. I was glad I had come to Glencoe in the summer, when the landscape was less stark. In the winter, Duncan told me, people from the hamlets ski down to Ballachulish for supplies and mail. It would be a beautiful world under its tremendous mantle of snow, but a bitter one. Right now the sun shone, and a gentle breeze fanned from the loch.

Hamish stayed for tea and we had it alone, Brenda having gone to her Bridge Club in Fort William, and Aunt Mary scuttling off somewhere in Busy-Mini. Hamish seemed in no hurry to leave and I was unreasonably glad of that. I told myself that I was averse to being alone at Glenrannoch, but knew this to be untrue, for despite my first impression of the place I was beginning to feel a growing kinship with it.

Somewhere in the house I could hear Jeannie singing, and from the distant kitchens the smell of Fora's baking was wafted on the breeze. The sound of hedge-clippers came to us intermittently, and I knew it must be Luke because the heavy electric cutter was reserved for Fergus, the gardener who lived in the Lodge. He treasured that implement as a connoisseur might treasure a masterpiece. No hands but his must touch it, much less a great clumsy fellow like Luke.

I said abruptly, 'I've arranged for Luke to take care of Jock when I'm not here. Everyone is against the idea. I hope you're not.'

Hamish answered in that explosive way of his, 'Why the hell should I be?'

'They seem to think he might hurt him – accidentally, of course.'

Hamish cursed in a thorough and fruity fashion.

'People are fools,' he scoffed. 'Thank God, you're not.' His keen blue eyes surveyed me with approval, then he added, 'I hear you're starting a new department at the mills. That means you're staying.'

'Who told you?'

'Isabel, of course.'

Isabel, of course . . .

I stooped and picked up Jock. 'It should be interesting,' I said. 'I'd be bored if I weren't occupied.'

'Is that the only reason? Sure it hasn't anything to do with your grandfather's stipulations?'

'And what do you know of my grandfather's stipulations?'

'As much as anyone else. Perhaps more.'

'Which means that the whole neighbourhood has been gossiping about the will?'

'Inevitably. It's been the greatest excitement in these parts since your father turned his back on Glenrannoch.'

I made an exasperated movement. 'I suppose small communities always gossip, but I should have thought it would be no more than a nine days' wonder.'

'True. But no one has been certain, until now, that you would remain.'

'It would have made little difference had I gone. Life would have proceeded as before, and the household would have been unchanged.'

Hamish studied me thoughtfully for a moment, then said, 'You weren't here for the reading of the will, were you?'

'It wasn't necessary.'

'But customary.'

91

'I couldn't make it. Duncan asked me to come because I was a beneficiary, but I was busy with new designs for the autumn collection and couldn't be spared. Besides, I didn't expect to inherit much, and to tell the truth I was surprised to learn that I was to inherit anything at all. So it was agreed that the will should be read in my absence and that I would come as soon as I was able. After the contents were disclosed to the family, I heard the details.'

'Then you knew about the codicil.'

Of course I knew about the codicil. It was this which carried the stipulations governing my inheritance. I wondered how this man knew about it and with that disconcerting ability of his to read my thoughts he explained, 'I witnessed it. Your grandfather telephoned me one day and asked me to come to Glenrannoch. When I arrived that was the reason.'

'I see.'

An uncommunicative silence fell upon us, during which Hamish leaned over Jock and studied him.

'I told you he'd recover quickly, didn't I? Another day or two and those stitches will be out. He'll be frisking all over the place.'

Shortly after that, Hamish left. I watched his ancient Bentley soar down the drive and when it had disappeared I put Jock back in his basket and wandered aimlessly indoors. I couldn't understand either my restlessness or my uneasiness, and I was faintly worried by the man's questions about the will. I wished now that I had told him that Duncan had shown me both the document and the codicil, insisting that I should be fully acquainted with every detail.

Suddenly I wondered if Hamish had hoped that Isabel might be a beneficiary.

The thought troubled me. Everything troubled me. The whole atmosphere of this place troubled me. I wished Duncan had not been unexpectedly called to London this morning. I needed his reassuring personality right now.

Then I wondered why my grandfather should have asked Hamish Cameron to witness the codicil. There must have been other people available. Angus Matheson, Managing Director of the mills, for one. Ian Forsythe, nearby at Kyleven, for another. Why call the local vet, friendly as the two had apparently been? And that was another inexplicable thing, the friendship between a man like Hamish Cameron and the autocratic James MacDonald.

Wandering out on the terrace again, I saw Jock struggling to his feet, and succeeding. He looked so proud of himself, and so comical wobbling on three legs, that I laughed aloud and promptly felt happier. A few more tries and he would be carrying that wounded paw around like a shopping basket.

I sat on the balustrade of the terrace, and as I did so I heard the shrill sound of Busy-Mini coming up the drive. A few minutes later Aunt Mary was walking up the steps to the terrace, taking in the tea things at a glance and saying, 'You've had company, I see. Who was it?'

'Hamish Cameron.'

She didn't sniff audibly. She merely looked as if she wanted to.

'And what did *he* call for?'

'To tell me that Jock is mine. He bought him from the owners.'

'And you accepted the gift? My dear, was that wise? You know what kind of a man Hamish Cameron is.'

'But I don't. I only know he has been friendly and kind.'

'Then don't let him be *too* friendly. He's a very undesirable type.' She felt the teapot and added, 'Cold, of course,' as if it should have been kept hot for her specially.

'I'll make some fresh.'

'That's Flora's job.'

Impatiently, I picked up the teapot. 'Does everyone around here expect to be waited on? Can't anyone undertake a simple job of making tea? What happens when Flora is off duty?'

'Then one of the girls makes it.'

'Great heaven, what age are we living in – the Victorian?'

'My dear Lavinia!'

'I am *not* your dear Lavinia. You've made that plain enough since I came.'

I felt my temper rising, and knew I had to check it. There would be five minutes' explosion and instead of feeling better after it, I would feel worse. I always did. Anger was rarely a safety valve for me.

So I marched off to the kitchen with the teapot, and when I returned Aunt Mary, to my astonishment, was cradling Jock, but the scene did nothing to pacify me.

'Don't make a lap-dog of him,' I said.

She raised her eyebrows.

'You sound like your father, my dear. He used to fly off the handle like that, suddenly and without warning and always without apparent reason.'

'Well, I *have* reason. I'm a MacDonald as much as you are, and whether you want me in this house or not, here I am and here I mean to stay, and that goes for anyone else who might want me out of the way.'

'And why should anyone want you out of the way?' she queried mildly, whereupon I promptly felt foolish and ashamed and, to my chagrin, burst into tears. I was aware that she jerked to her feet, still holding Jock, her plain face twisted in consternation.

Humiliation and annoyance with myself made me slam down the teapot and run indoors.

I didn't pause until I reached my room. The solid oak door closed with its heavy thud and I flung myself upon the bed. Above me the huge canopy hung like a pall, enveloping, smothering; I had a sudden feeling that I was lying in state, like one of those marble effigies in cathedrals. All I had to do was close my eyes and clasp my hands and I would be silent and still ferever . . .

There was a scratching at the door. The latch lifted and Jock hobbled in. Aunt Mary's gaunt face looked at me anxiously from the aperture.

'He wanted to be with you, Lavinia. He began to whimper as soon as you had gone.' She hesitated, then said uncertainly, 'Is there anything I can do? Don't you feel well, my dear?'

'I feel fine, just fine. Take no notice of me. I'm sorry I blew my top. It's just that – oh, I don't *know*! I don't know how I feel about anything.'

Or anyone, especially an inscrutable Scot with intensely blue eyes and a disturbing curiosity. His past, whatever it was (probably no more than a scandal over some woman) couldn't be the reason for the way I felt. It was simply the man himself and the mere fact that he was around; that he could look into me and through me and seem to know so much more than I knew myself.

I wished again that Duncan would come home. Even Jock's frantic licking at my cheek did little to cheer me. I thrust my legs off the bed and said to Aunt Mary, still hovering by the door, 'I'll take a shower. That will pull me together.'

'I doubt it,' she answered caustically. 'My guess is that Hamish Cameron said something which disturbed you, but if you are wise you'll take no notice of that man. He's not merely undesirable, he's a criminal.'

CHAPTER EIGHT

I stared at her.

'A *criminal?*' Then how was it my grandfather was friendly with him?'

The thin shoulders shrugged, the thin lips tightened.

'Your grandfather, my dear, thought Cameron the best man for miles around when it came to handling horses . . . That was all that mattered to him. In his lifetime, the stables at Glenrannoch were full, but Brenda sold the whole stud shortly before his death. I doubt if my father knew because, towards the end, he wasn't aware of anything very much, but in my opinion she had no right to sell them, although she declared that James had given them to her a long time ago when he was forced to give up riding. But that had never lessened his interest in horse-breeding, and I must say it was very strange of him to make a present of them to Brenda because she never rode and didn't know a thing about horse-flesh – or care. However, I understand she got a very good price for them, although she never revealed how much. Not to me, at any rate.'

I didn't want to listen to any more of my aunt's belittling of Brenda, so reverted to Hamish Cameron.

'I can't imagine a man as shrewd as my grandfather placing any trust in a criminal,' I declared, resisting the temptation to ask what the man had done. Any story Aunt Mary related was likely to be garbled and prejudiced.

'Your grandfather,' she said tartly, 'was a law unto himself. No one questioned what he did, or what he thought, or what he decided, and it isn't for us to do so now.'

'We hardly can, since he isn't here,' I answered drily.

She lifted pious eyes to heaven, and departed. I wanted to laugh, but only a faint giggle escaped me. It echoed in the distant corners of the room, like a mocking whisper. Jock hobbled to the door, casting begging glances over his shoulder as if asking to be let out, but when I opened the door he refused to go. He just stood there, a three-legged bundle of pleading.

I told him firmly, 'I can't trot around with you everywhere, my boy. You've got to learn to find your own way about.'

Like me, I thought. People might show me the house and the mills, teach me how to supervise the estate and the household, but no one could point the way to what would happen next, or guide my steps to avert disaster.

Jock gave a short, demanding little bark, jerking me out of introspection and a dangerous, nonsensical feeling of fear.

'All right,' I said, 'if you won't go, you'll have to wait here while I take that shower.'

He sat as close to the door as possible and all the time I was showering I heard him barking anxiously in the bedroom. I paid little heed because my own thoughts were troublesome enough. A criminal, Aunt Mary had called Hamish. But anyone who didn't conform, or who failed to tread the staight-and-narrow, would be a criminal of some sort in her bigoted mind.

Personally, I think it's a pity he was ever caught.

I turned off the shower, wrapped myself in an immense towel, and rubbed myself vigorously. Damn Moira, I thought furiously. Damn that stupid, prattling girl. I doubted if a word of truth or sense ever came out of her. And yet I liked her. I couldn't help it.

In the ancestral gallery of portraits of Glenrannoch was one which partcularly fascinated me. It was of a young woman seated side-saddle on a chestnut mare, her tartan riding skirt hitched above a shining black boot and on her head a glengarry bonnet with streamers flying. I wondered who she was, and admired the jaunty air of her and the defiance in her eye.

Every time I passed this portrait something compelled me to study it, and one day, coming upon me there, Brenda said, 'That was Shuna MacDonald, an early mistress here. She came from Inverness and was one of the beauties of her day. Also one of the most unconventional. The neighbourhood didn't wholly approve of her, but men adored her.'

'She certainly had a fashion sense.'

'Like you, my dear,' Brenda looked at the picture and then at me. 'You're very similar in looks, too – the same tilt to the nose, the same lift of the head, the same warm copper tones of the hair, and the wide, smiling mouth, as if the world amused her. You looked like that when you came to Glenrannoch, ready to laugh at anything, but now you don't smile so much. Aren't you happy here, Lavinia?'

I didn't answer, because truthfully I didn't know. If I wasn't smiling so much these days it was because I was beginning to feel unsure of myself, as if I were obscurely threatened but unable to break away and return to the old life. This feeling of impending threat was unreasonable because nothing had happened to provoke it since my early arrival here; life had settled into a pattern so serene that I even wondered if I had heard the midnight walker in anything but my dreams. Ever since then my nights had been undisturbed.

'I'll be happier when I'm working again,' I said restlessly. 'I'm not used to idleness.'

'So of course you find it frustrating, but it won't last much longer.' Brenda glanced once more at the portrait of Shuna MacDonald and went on listing comparisons. 'Your eyes are the same colour, too – that distinctive hazel which Highland women sometimes have. Time seems to have skipped the centuries and reincarnated the legendary Shuna in you.'

I was flattered, but couldn't believe that this was true. In one thing Brenda was right, however – idleness was frustrating. I was impatient to see my studio finished and irked because I had not transport of my own to get to the mills to see how it was progressing. I had ordered a Triumph

G
D

G.T.6 Mark III and now awaited delivery impatiently. I disliked having to rely on others when I wanted to go farther afield than Glencoe.

I was glad when Isabel came to see me one afternoon and hoped it was to report progress. I was sitting on the side of the terrace which overlooked the wide lawns spreading as far as the dividing hedge between our two homes, and I thought how nice she looked as she strolled through the gap. She had a good figure and held herself well.

I found myself wondering if it were true that she and Ian Forsythe didn't get along together. According to their daughter they disagreed on almost everything, but on my first visit to Kyleven I had found the atmosphere easy to relax in. Disharmony in a household usually left a feeling of tension about the place.

A Great Dane loped at her heels and, seeing Jock, she called, 'Goliath won't eat him, I promise. He's nothing but a great big soft-hearted baby!'

The two dogs assessed each other, then decided to be friends, Goliath flopping down beside the puppy like a protective guard dog. Isabel reported that my studio was coming on well, and offered to run me over to see it. When finished, work would then go ahead on rooms for cutters, machinists, fitters, and finishers.

'Thank goodness!' I said fervently. 'You don't know how frustrated I am, doing nothing. I miss my work very much.'

We settled for two days hence, and I strolled back with her across the lawn, the dogs beside us. Jock's paw was healing well. He could even put it to the ground very gingerly.

Suddenly he made a comical attempt at running; it was no more than a three-legged wobble but was prompted by such eagerness that I looked round to see what caused it.

It was Luke. He was coming from the direction of the chapel, carrying a broom in his hand. Part of his duties was to keep the place clean and this task he carried out with the laborious diligence which typified everything he did.

At the sight of Jock's eager attempts to run, the man's tragic face broke into a broad smile, and Isabel said, 'The kindest thing you ever did was to let the poor man have a share in looking after Jock. You've proved them wrong, all those who said it would be folly.'

I had indeed. I watched Luke drop his broom and lumber towards the welcoming puppy, then pick him up in his great hands and fondle him with such gentleness that I knew he could never have been capable of attacking that Alsatian except in self-defence.

A strangler? Never. And if Isabel knew of the tale, I felt she would share my opinion. I looked at her, liking her, glad to have her as a friend. The sun shone on her white hair, and the frame of it enhanced her very charming face. I noticed her hands, too. One was idly plucking a sprig of Veronica and twirling it between long, slender fingers.

Just as idly she said, 'Moira tells me that Hamish gave you the puppy as a gift.'

I admitted this was true, and that I thought it kind of him, but added no more because I felt that although her comment was uttered indifferently, she didn't feel that way. At once I recalled Aunt Mary's hints about Isabel's partiality for one particular man, and Malcolm's reference to their close friendship, and Moira's statement that her mother always stuck up for Hamish despite her father's opposition. Even more vividly I recalled Hamish's swift defence of Isabel; his refusal to hear any criticism of her.

After that, a restraint fell upon me. I could think of no more to say and was thankful when Hamish himself unexpectedly appeared on the terrace, announcing that Flora had told him I was out there and that he had come to remove the stitches from Jock's paw.

Isabel took hold of Goliath's collar and led him away.

'He'll howl his great silly head off if Jock so much as whimpers,' she said. 'I told you he was a soft-hearted baby.'

She smiled at us and went towards the beech hedge again, turning to wave before finally disappearing, but somehow I felt her smile and her wave were particularly for Hamish, and I saw the answering affection in his glance before turning his attention to Jock.

'We'll take him indoors,' he said. 'I must scrub up first.'

I reached for the puppy, then paused. Luke's eyes were full of pleading and I lacked the heart to take the animal from him. Instead, I asked him to carry Jock for me, and this he did with inarticulate gratitude.

Afterwards, Hamish said, 'You're helping poor Luke more than anyone has ever done.'

'With the exception of yourself. It was you who made me understand him. As harmless as a fly, with an instinct purely protective – that was how you described him. You told me to rid my mind of any fear of him, and I have. It was easy. I could never mistrust a great simple fellow like Luke.'

Soon afterwards, Hamish left, telling me that all would now be well with Jock's paw but to keep a careful eye on it until completely healed. He promised to look in from time to time, and the thought of him doing so gave me unexpected pleasure. I realized that I would be sorry when Jock needed his attention no more.

I was pleased with the studio, and particularly with the increased light. When I had last seen the room it had been a dark and cluttered store. Now the place was transformed.

I shed my coat and stood in the middle of the room with Angus Matheson and Isabel. I could tell that my delight pleased them, also Duncan who looked in briefly, then drove off to catch a plane to London. His office there seemed to be making increased demands on his time, but when Brenda suggested that it might be a good idea if he operated mainly from there, handling MacDonald-Matheson's account as that of any other client, he had firmly refused. He disliked London and wanted to be based at home.

I became aware that white-haired Angus Matheson was saying benignly, 'I'm glad you're pleased with the studio, my dear. As you can see, only half the glass is in the sky-light as yet, temporarily fixed. When the rest is in place, the whole lot will be fixed permanently. Until then, for safety's sake, I've given orders that no one is to come in here.'

Isabel assured him that no one was likely to, except the workmen. 'When they've gone off duty I keep the door locked, and when I go home I hand the key over to the night porter, who gives it to them when they arrive early next morning.'

I spent the rest of the morning looking at fabrics in the stock-room, and making a selection of those most suitable for the designs I had in mind. I was still there when Malcolm thrust his head round the door and announced that he had come to carry me off for lunch. 'But *not* in that prosaic directors' dining-room. I know a good pub in Fort William.'

As he spoke, the lunch siren sounded throughout the mills and there was a sudden cessation of noise as the machines hummed to a standstill. I heard the march of hundreds of feet heading towards canteens, and through the windows of the stock-room, which looked out on to the area which would eventually accommodate the extensions to my studio, I saw the builders climb down from the roof and go tramping across the yard.

I told Malcolm I would meet him in the main hall, and went along the corridor to get my coat, which I had left in the studio. As I approached the door I saw that it had been left ajar, and as I walked through I paused to see what further progress had been made. Tall ladders reached up to the sky-light, which was still only partly glazed.

I stood directly beneath it, looking up. A breeze blew down through the open part, fanning my hair and my face. I was glad of it, for the stock-room had been hot. My hands were soiled in a rather oily way which much handling of textile produces, especially wool. A fresh-up was badly needed and, I suddenly realized, so was that lunch.

I moved away, searching for my coat, and as I did so a fierce draught from the corridor crashed the door behind me. The impact was so violent that a louder crash immediately followed and I flung myself face downwards as a shower of broken glass pelted me from above.

Instinct made me cover the back of my neck and head, but I felt the sharp prick of fragments against my hands and on one of my legs. Terrified, I lay rigid on the floor, conscious in the horrified depths of my mind that only just in time had I moved away from the centre of the room.

I heard the sound of running feet; voices; the crunch of footfalls on broken glass; exclamations, alarm, horror, all inextricably mixed, and through them Isabel's anxious voice as someone picked me up and carried me into her office next door.

I had been lucky. If I had been directly beneath that crashing sky-light my neck could have been severed. I could have been killed.

The staff medical officer attended to my cuts, which were fortunately minor, and needed no stitching, after which Isabel insisted on my having strong tea with plenty of sugar; the best treatment for shock, she said, and I certainly felt better for it. Angus Matheson, who had carried me into her office, fussed a lot, demanding to know how it had happened, but all I could remember was a sudden surge of wind along the corridor and the heavy slamming of the door.

Isabel was upset because she had been delayed by a telephone call and so had failed to lock up the studio when the workmen knocked off.

'But what made you go back there?' she asked.

'To get my coat. I'd left it behind.'

She opened a cupboard and took my coat from a hanger.

'I noticed you'd forgotten it, and I couldn't leave it lying around while the men were at work, so I took care of it for you.'

As she spoke, Ian Forsythe walked in. I saw Isabel's pleasure at the sight of him, and couldn't believe that it was anything but genuine. He had come to join her for lunch, he said, but she insisted that he should take me home instead.

Malcolm was sulking in the main hall as we departed, like a spoiled boy cheated out of a treat. In other circumstances I would have been amused, but not now. I was in no mood for Malcolm, nor for the well-catering pub, and was much more appreciative of Ian's quiet solicitude. This was the first time I had been alone with the man, and found him both likeable and kind. When he pulled up at the steps of Glenrannoch he seemed reluctant to let me go without summoning either Brenda or Mary to look after me, but this I would not hear of. There had been enough fuss and I wanted no more.

Luke was in the great hall, stacking logs in the Gothic fireplaces at each end. When he saw my bandages he came shambling towards me, making inarticuate sounds of concern. I knew he was asking what had gone wrong and, in his helpless way, if there was anything he could do.

'Just bring Jock to me,' I said, adding that I would like

to see his mother too. He seemed to understand what I said for he nodded eagerly and shuffled off at an ungainly trot which echoed loudly between the high walls.

Aunt Mary thrust her head through the door of the morning-room and demanded sharply, 'Was that Luke? What was he doing in this part of the house? Good gracious, Lavinia, what *have* you been up to?'

'I've been up to nothing, Aunt Mary, and yes that was Luke. It's his job to bring in the logs. I discovered the other day that the girls have always done it and that seems senseless to me. Why should women carry heavy loads when there's a man to do it? Besides, I think Luke should be given work around the house. It helps to make him feel trusted.'

She shook her head at me. She had started doing that lately instead of her earlier sniffs of disapproval.

'I think it unwise, my dear, but I won't argue with you just now.' Her pale eyes studied my bandages. 'Both hands, *and* your leg. What caused it? An accident?'

I told her what had happened, hoping that once her curiosity was satisfied she would leave me alone, but I was totally unprepared for the calm, calculated statement she came out with.

'That was no accident, Lavinia. It was deliberate, and Isabel would be responsible. Her office is right next to that room – oh, don't imagine I'm not acquainted with the layout of the mills, even though I don't work there. Many's the time I've visited them, and at one time I helped my father secretarially, but we didn't get on. We *could* have got on, if Brenda hadn't suggested he needed someone younger – '

I passed a bandaged hand across my forehead, wearily. I was in no mood for Aunt Mary's acrimony and only too thankful when Flora appeared. Behind her was Luke, with Jock trotting at his heels.

I said I would like some lunch; something light on a tray in the library. When I walked away, Jock followed, but so did Aunt Mary, saying crossly, 'You weren't listening to what I said, Lavinia.'

'Yes, I was. You said you used to be grandfather's secretary.'

'Not *that* – what I said before. About Isabel. I warned

you she'd do anything to get rid of you, didn't I? How do you know she didn't see you go past her office and into that half-finished room? How do you know she didn't slam the door on you – '

I interrupted impatiently, 'It was caused by a draught. I felt it sweep along the passage outside.'

'Then she probably went along to the end, opened the swing doors into the main hall, and caused the draught deliberately, knowing it would create a current of air through the studio door and the sky-light. Lunch-time, you said? Office staff going out of the building? The front doors wide open to the courtyard? Really, Lavinia, I was beginning to think you were an intelligent girl, but it seems I was mistaken. I know well enough that those doors from the main hall to the courtyard are fastened back when staff are passing through. So don't you see? All she had to do was open the doors at the end of the passage and cause a terrific draught to sweep along it – and crash goes the door of your studio and crash goes the sky-light above.'

I looked at her aghast. 'How could you think up anything so horrible?'

'I didn't, but I can guess that she did. You don't know Isabel. I do. She'll stop at nothing to get her own way, and that means no rivalry from any other women even in business.'

I refuse to heed the ranting of a neurotic mind. In any case, she was wrong. If Isabel had opened those double doors and held them so that the wind swept through, she would have been seen by Malcolm, who was waiting for me in the main hall. He had been there all the time.

The next few days, while I waited for the studio to be ready, were frustrating, my cut hand preventing me from sketching. I turned to reading as a substitute, dipping into my grandfather's volumes of Scottish history, particularly of the Clan Donald from earliest times.

It had been a proud and contentious tribe, claiming descent from Conn of the Hundred Battles, from Colla, the Prince of the Isles, and from Fergus, the first ruler of the Scoto-Irish Kingdom of Dalriada. I became lost in the stories of Celtic heroes who had fought great battles with the Vikings; men like the giant Coll MacMorna, who had slain Earragan, King of the Norsemen, whose tents had been set up in a field by Laroch, a mile from the mouth of Glencoe.

I read of the coming of the Christians, wandering saints from Ireland and the isles off the western coast; of Mundus, who came from Iona with Columba's blessing and lived on the island in the loch, building the chapel which was now a ruin; of Angus Og, who declared that his proud lineage entitled him to become Lord of the Isles, and finally of his bastard son, Iain Og nan Fraoch – Young John of the Heather – who became the first MacDonald of Glencoe early in the fourteenth century.

It was he who founded the small Clan Donald, here in this glen, the land being a gift from his devoted father. From John of the Heather the Glencoe chiefs took the title MacIain, and immortalized him with their bonnet badge of heather. From him sprang a breed of mighty men; a warrior society, the last chief being the Twelfth MacIain, loved by his people, hated by his enemies, a protective father to his clan, a man of vengeance in the eyes of others. To some, a thief, a marauder, a murderer; to others a man of integrity, honour and courage.

In which character did he stalk this house, the midnight walker of Glenrannoch?

I became obsessed with the desire to learn more about the legendary MacIain and felt sure these bookshelves would yield all I wished to know, but nothing was catalogued and no one seemed to have taken an interest in the library, other than to keep the books dusted. Consequently it was a matter of coming across things accidentally, or by diligent searching.

In between this obsessive reading I helped with household affairs, exercised Jock, and took long walks in and around the glen. It was during one of these walks that I met Ian Forsythe driving through the pass on his way back from a country house auction in Glen Etive. He asked where I was heading and I admitted that I hoped to reach Ossian's Cave.

'You'd be wise not to try it alone for the first time,' he said. 'It's a low-level climb, but not so easy as it looks. I'd be glad to take you; in fact, we could pony-trek, which you'd find less tiring. We've a couple of mountain ponies at Kyleven which Malcolm and Moira sometimes use; if you wait here, I'll fetch them.'

I was delighted by the invitation. My stout shoes and tough trousers were ideal for such a trip, so I sat in the sun by tiny Loch Achtriochton until he appeared about half an hour later, with one pony on a leading rein. He helped me to mount, showed me how to slip-hold the reins, to grip with my thighs and to keep my heels well down in the stirrups with my toes up, then he led me at a gentle pace up the lower slope.

I quickly became accustomed to the saddle and really had nothing to do but follow, the leading rein attached to his mount guiding my own. Every now and then Iain glanced reassuringly over his shoulder and halted once or twice, apparently to point out places of interest but, I suspected, to give me a rest before approaching the steeper stretch ahead, then he showed me how to lean my body forward to keep my balance against the pitch of the horse's as it climbed, and shortened the leading rein in order to keep me closer to his side.

It was during this trip that I took a liking to Ian Forsythe and saw him as something more than a conventionally handsome man. He was kindly, considerate, and interesting to talk to, especially when at last we reached our goal and, after helping me to dismount, he tethered the ponies to an outcrop of rock and led me up the track to the cave, which turned out to be no cave at all but a dark, jagged slit in the hill face, sharply pitching and open to the sky. He helped me up the rocky floor, which was worn smooth by the feet of climbers.

'There's a tin box here containing a visitors' book, liberally filled with signatures. You must add yours, Lavinia – it must be a long time since a MacDonald of Glencoe did so.' As I wrote, he added, 'If Nichol Marquis could return and see this book he'd be amazed to learn how many people have followed in his footsteps.'

'Who was Nichol Marquis?'

'A shepherd who climbed up here in 1868; according to history, the first man ever to do so. At that time this rocky floor was covered with vegetation.'

'I thought Ossian was the first man to come here,' I remarked as we scrambled out of the dark and chilly chasm into the sunlight again. 'I understand that legend claims it to be the place where he wrote his most inspired poetry – hence its name.'

'Legend indeed, but there's no proof of it any more than there is proof of the even more picturesque story of the origin of this so-called cave.'

We sat down on a patch of moss-covered rock, with the glen below sweeping down to the waters of Loch Leven. Eilean Munde, with its adjoining chain of small islands, looked very tiny from this height.

'Tell me the story,' I said.

Ian lit his pipe, puffed it alight, then said, 'Well, long before St Fintan Mundus came here and established his tiny oratory down there on Eilean Munde, another saint passed this way – St Kenneth, a Pict of County Derry, who came on a missionary journey to Alba, as Scotland was then known, about a year before Columba arrived in Iona. In Glencoe, St Kenneth dwelt "in a sunless place under a great mountain" – this one, Aonach Dubh. While at prayer one day, an angel came to him and offered to remove some of the mountain to let in the sunlight, but St Kenneth protested that the task was too great, even for an angel, but the celestial being went to work. By the time St Kenneth persuaded him to stop, the angel had penetrated so deeply into the rock face that the cleft was formed. Not,' Ian finished with a smile, 'that much sunlight seems to have been admitted, but at least poor St Kenneth could see the sky.'

'Glencoe seems to abound in legends,' I said, suppressing a faint shiver which I could not understand.

Ian Forsythe looked at me carefully, his eyes faintly troubled.

'You're not thinking of that nonsense about the midnight walker, I hope? You heard my opinion of that the other night.'

'Perhaps I was, subconsciously.'

'Then don't. We want you to stay here – all of us.' He laid a friendly and reassuring hand on my arm. 'You mustn't be frightened away. Promise not to heed that ridiculous story. And if you're worried by it and feel you'd like to talk to someone, come to me.'

I thanked him, appreciating his fatherly interest and glad to have a friend I could trust. I gazed down on the magnificent view and felt a stirring in my heart.

'This is the land of my ancestors,' I said. 'Nothing and no one is going to drive me away.'

'Good. I knew when I first met you that you were a sensible girl. A true MacDonald, in fact.'

We sat in companionable silence for some time after that, until at last Ian knocked out his pipe and said, 'Time to trek home. I'm sorry. I've enjoyed this afternoon.'

I had too, and said so, but the journey back, taken slowly and carefully on the down-pitch due to sliding stones, was more fatiguing than I expected, and I was more than ready to go to bed early that night. Aunt Mary noticed my tiredness and scolded me slightly for overdoing things so soon after the accident at the mills.

'I'll bring you a tisane,' she offered. 'I make it from an ancient herbal recipe, and I guarantee it will give you a good night's sleep.'

I thanked her, but hoped she would forget. In that, I under-estimated my aunt, for I had scarcely been in bed for more than ten minutes when she arrived with it, insisting that I must drink every drop. I sipped some to humour her, but disliked it and, as soon as she had gone, disposed of the remainder in the bathroom.

Some time later I wakened with a feeling of nausea, and when I opened my eyes the room spun dizzily. In the darkness the even darker shapes of furniture seemed to advance and retreat, the window curtains drifting like menacing ghosts, but most terrifying of all was the sound which penetrated through these whirling sensations – the sound of footsteps on the terrace below; heavy, measured, with a metallic ring about them. Footsteps which paused beneath my window and then went on again, fading gradually into silence while the echoing boom of midnight sounded from the great hall, leaving me in a state of helpless terror.

CHAPTER NINE

In the morning, feeling better, I told myself that it had all been part of a nightmare and that because I had felt unwell I had imagined the whole thing. Mary's old-fashioned herbal recipe had disagreed with me and, hovering between waves of nausea and sleep, I had dreamed of the midnight walker.

But the disturbed night had left its mark and even after I bathed and dressed, taking particular care with my make-up so that the family should detect no signs of strain and choosing one of my slickest outfits to boost my morale, I felt anything but my normal self. Breakfast held no appeal, so I called to Jock and took him for a long walk beside the loch, heedless of time. The day was warm and I lingered beside the water, playing ducks and drakes with flat, slim stones. Jock barked furiously because he was unable to retrieve them.

By the time we returned to Glenrannoch it was mid-morning and the coffee ritual was due, Brenda making it because it was Flora's day off and neither of the two girls knew how to make anything but the instant variety. Brenda was fussy about the way in which coffee should be made. The beans had to be freshly ground, the water correctly measured, the percolation time dead accurate. She had initiated Flora into the routine from the time she had come to Glenrannoch as my grandfather's bride.

It was Saturday and the Forsythes came to join us, including Malcolm. I hadn't seen him since my last visit to the mills and he came to me immediately, asking how I was. Moira, wearing a garment of hessian which looked as if it had been cut with a knife and fork, began to play with Jock, who was particularly frisky this morning.

Duncan drew me to one side. I knew he had noticed the bee-line Malcolm had made for me and I was amused but flattered to think that he could be jealous of the boy, for that was all Malcolm was to me; extrovert and like-able, but decidedely immature for his years. I could enjoy

Malcolm's company up to a point, but Duncan's a great deal more because Duncan was a man with a sense of responsibilty, plus very masculine adulthood.

In casual clothes he looked different from in formal office clothes, and I said so, admiring his well tailored Mactweed jacket worn with a turtle-necked Shetland sweater.

'Some day,' I said, 'the mills ought to branch out into men's wear as well as women's.'

He smiled with a fondness which he was at no pains to conceal from the others, and said indulgently, 'You're getting as bad as your grandfather – obsessed with the family business, or well on the way. I'm glad, of course, because this means there's less likelihood of your leaving Glenrannoch, and I don't mind confessing that I'd hate you to go. By the way, Probate will be granted very soon. Everything has gone smoothly.'

Except for the return visit of the midnight walker, I thought involuntarily.

Jock sprang up against me, demanding attention. I ordered him to be quiet, and, with a protesting whimper, he obeyed, but not for long. A second later he was frisking over to Moira to be made a fuss of, and Aunt Mary, handing round coffee, complained loudly when he almost tripped her up.

She said crossly, 'That dog shouldn't be allowed in here, Lavinia. Put him out into the garden at once, or he'll send someone's coffee spilling on to the carpet.'

I opened the french windows and shooed Jock outside. He barked at me from the terrace, demanding that I should follow, and I picked up a rubber ball which I kept out there and threw it far across the lawn, watching while he scampered after it.

Duncan said beside me, 'Now you've started something. He'll expect you to keep this up all morning. And don't try to evade me, Lavinia. I feel you are, somehow.' His fingers closed over mine. 'Don't you realize how much I want to be with you?'

His calmness was reassuring, so much so that I was on the brink of telling him of my sickness and terror of the night before, and the nightmare I had experienced about the return of the midnight walker, but at that moment Aunt

Mary came out on to the terrace, carrying a tray bearing two cups.

Indicating one she said, 'This is yours, Lavinia – black, with two sugar lumps, they way you like it.'

I picked up the coffee just as Jock came bounding back with the ball, dropped it at my feet, and leapt up against me, begging for it to be re-thrown.

The cup went flying, leaving broken china and a small pool of coffee on the terrace – and my skirt stained. I heard Aunt Mary's cry of dismay, which turned to disgust as Jock eagerly licked up the coffee and then spat distastefully. The noise attracted the others and from the french windows I heard Malcolm say with a laugh, 'Perhaps he only likes it with cream!'

Duncan took out his handkerchief to wipe my skirt, but I stopped him quickly because I knew the only thing to do with this particular type of fabric was to soak it immediately. I went indoors to change, leaving Mary wailing over the broken china, and Brenda trying to pacify her. What a fuss, I thought, as I took off my suit and went into the bathroom to plunge the skirt in water.

The mirrored walls threw back my reflection. Despite careful make-up my eyes were shadowed and my face strained. I wondered if Duncan had observed these signs, and suddenly I felt I could no longer delay in telling him about the return of the midnight walker. I acknowledged now that it had been no nightmare. Through the haze of nausea I had definitely heard the iron ring of MacIain's footsteps.

I chose another dress at random and, as I stepped into it, I heard Jock barking below. Glancing through the window I saw Luke working in a distant shrubbery and Duncan throwing the ball in that direction for Jock to retrieve, but the animal chased it less eagerly. As I zipped up my dress I continued to watch, thinking that even when he reached the ball he merely pushed it around a bit with his nose, whimpering in a plaintive way as if he were tired. At Duncan's commanding whistle, he picked it up and trotted back listlessly.

Duncan ruffled Jock's head and replaced the ball behind

the stone pillar where I kept it, and then I heard everyone saying goodbye. I was glad, because now I would be able to speak to Duncan alone.

I flicked a comb through my hair, aware that Jock's barking was growing fainter and thinking absently that he was probably following the others towards the beech hedge, then forgot all about him as I went downstairs. To my disappointment, Duncan wasn't there.

He had gone over to Kyleven, Aunt Mary told me. Ian had asked him to examine a Deed of Covenant concerning a valuable painting he had been offered, which was part of a Trust invested in a family in Stirling who now wanted to sell.

'Ian wanted Duncan's opinion on the legality of the sale. It seems these Trusts can come up with all sorts of snags.'

So I settled down in a lounger on the terrace to await his return, idly flicking the pages of a magazine but not taking in a word of it. The aftermath of my disturbed night, coupled with suppressed tension, destroyed my concentration. I could only think about the heavy tread of the midnight walker approaching my bedroom window again, halting, and then moving on . . .

The first night of the second visitation. The thought sent a shiver through me, and I went on shivering despite the warmth of the sun.

Duncan seemed to be a long time at Kyleven; so long that after a while I tossed aside the magazine and wondered whether to go over there myself. Anything was better than sitting here waiting, and brooding, and feeling the ragged edges of my nerves fraying more and more as I relived the nightmare of those long dark hours which, if the legend was true, would be repeated tonight.

I swung my legs off the lounger – and there I remained, sitting on the side of it as Luke appeared from across the garden, carrying Jock's limp body in his huge hands.

The puppy's head hung at an unnatural angle, and I knew at once that he was dead.

I don't know how long I stared at the puppy's swollen face, bulging eyes, lolling tongue and limp neck, all of which showed plainly enough that he had been strangled.

Nor do I know how long Luke stood on the lawn below, holding out the limp little body and staring rigidly into space. There were no tears in the man's eyes, no bewilderment. Just complete blankness, like a robot incapable of any feeling. But none of this I recalled until later.

I remembered rising slowly and walking across the terrace, and Luke coming to a halt at the foot of the steps, and both of us remaining like that, he staring into space and I staring at the puppy who had been alive and happy only a few minutes before, and I remembered feeling something more than shock; stunned disbelief that the hideous, distorted little face had ever been alive and good to look at.

It was then that Duncan mercifully reappeared. This angle of the terrace could be seen from the Kyleven boundary and for a moment he stopped dead, then came running. I heard him shout, '*Luke, in God's name, what have you done?*' and the great robot of a man gave a sudden jerk, as if someone had pressed a switch within his uncomprehending mind and sent an electric shock through him.

He dropped the dead puppy and fled.

Duncan stooped over the body lying on the grass and in the shocked recesses of my mind I was glad that Jock had fallen on to soft, warm earth instead of the stone steps, painfully. I couldn't believe even now that he could feel nothing, nor ever would again.

I heard Aunt Mary come out of the house, her footsteps clacking sharply on the stone flags of the terrace, but I didn't turn to look at her, nor did I heed her sudden babbling, which was meaningless. My mind was fixed only on two things – the strangled dog, and the man who had done it.

I realized that, after all, Aunt Mary was not babbling senselessly. She was questioning, demanding, even officious, but Duncan paid her no more heed than I, and now, as he stooped to pick up Jock's body, she said quickly, 'Don't get rid of it, Duncan – it will have to be examined.'

'What will have to be examined?'

The question came from Brenda, and her lovely face creased in puzzlement because she had only just come out to join us and knew nothing of what had occurred, but as she looked from Mary to me, and from me to her son, a dawning comprehension took over and she said quickly, 'Is something wrong? Lavinia dear, you look shocked – '

Duncan told her that Jock was dead, and that he had met with an accident, but no more. It was enough to bring a sick look into his mother's soft grey eyes, but she said shakily, 'I still don't see why the poor thing has to be examined. An accident is an accident,' Her voice cut off, then she added swiftly, 'What sort of an accident?'

When Duncan told her that Jock had been strangled, Brenda's hands flew to her face. It was rare for her to be demonstrative with them, but now the stumpy fingers trembled, and even in my present state of mind I thought how totally out of character they looked against her lovely features.

'*Not by Luke?*' she whispered.

'Who else?' Duncan's voice was regretful.

'Who found him? And where?'

I told her that no one had found him, that Luke had brought him to me, then I burst out, 'He couldn't have known what he was doing! He loved Jock – everyone knows that. He just *couldn't* have known what he was doing!'

It was the only answer. I saw again that great, shambling figure walking like an automaton across the lawn, carrying the tiny, lifeless thing which, a few moments before, he must have been playing with. I saw again the blankness in Luke's eyes, like someone knocked senseless, and then that great jerk to life which Duncan's shout had sent through him. It had been like the spasm created by the shot of a gun.

There had been something else at that moment too, something which hadn't registered then because my whole mind had been focused on Jock, but now it emerged from the back of my consciousness and I saw it clearly – the leaping agony in Luke's face in that one quick flashing moment when he dropped Jock's body on the grass.

It had been the recoil of horror, the sudden penetration of truth, and it was from this that he had fled. Not from Duncan. Not from me.

Did he know then what he had done? Did he suddenly realize that he had killed the puppy he loved? Did he remember his great, clumsy hands fondling the silky neck and perhaps, in a rush of affection, squeezing just that bit too hard?

Or had he been bringing the puppy to me to find out what was wrong, why the tiny head lolled in the broken way?

I heard Brenda saying that she could do with a drink and Aunt Mary snapping back that there was something more important than *that* to think of. Their footsteps disappeared indoors and I sat down, glad to do so. Duncan stood looking at me, his back to the sun. In silhouette I couldn't see his face, but knew there was kindness in it.

'I'm leaving you for a moment, Lavinia, but I'll be back.'

I was glad the sun was behind him, because I couldn't see the bundle in his arms. 'I'm taking him away,' he added, 'and, darling, try not to fret. It must have been over for him in an instant.'

Of course . . . Jock had been so very small . . .

I nodded and Duncan went down the terrace steps and along a gravel path towards the outhouses near the stables. From indoors came the echo of Aunt Mary's voice speaking urgently. I couldn't catch her words, but she was obviously speaking into the telephone.

Duncan returned very soon. He stooped and kissed me, and I was grateful for the warmth and tenderness of it, and for the muttered words which told me how he felt.

The moment was broken when Aunt Mary came marching out again.

She announced briskly, 'He's coming at once. I don't approve of the man and I never will, but he's the right person to handle this job, so I've sent for him.'

'Who?' I asked rather stupidly, wishing she would go away.

'Hamish Cameron, of course. Who else? Duncan says the dog was strangled and from the look of the poor creature I'd say he was right, but it will have to be confirmed because this time Luke will have to be – dealt with.'

Duncan was saying impatiently that he wished she would leave things to him, but I scarcely heard because Aunt Mary's words stirred in me a wild protest. The complete taking-for-granted, on everyone's side, that Luke was to blame, was suddenly more than I could bear and I cried, 'How can you be so *sure*? Perhaps Luke merely found the body and picked it up. You saw the state he was in – stunned out of his wits.'

'Out of his wits, yes,' Duncan agreed, 'but who else in this house would be capable of strangling a puppy, or even want to?'

'Perhaps Jock wasn't strangled. Perhaps he choked on something. A bone he dug up. Anything!'

Duncan looked at me sympathetically. 'In which case,' he said, 'we'll find out as soon as Cameron gets here.'

It wasn't long before he did. I was grateful because he had wasted no time. I couldn't understand why the sight of his ancient car filled me with such relief, because after all he could only confirm that the others were right and I was wrong.

And that he, too, had been wrong when he said that Luke wouldn't hurt a fly.

After Duncan had taken Hamish to the outhouse where he had temporarily put poor Jock, and handed over the body, no one spoke of the incident again. Brenda suggested a run into Oban to do some shopping after lunch, but nothing appealed to me less. The meal was a strain, made even more so by Flora's taut expression as she served. No one had told her about the death of Jock, but somehow she knew, and I could feel her anxiety like a clamped-down spring.

'She'll take it hardly,' said Brenda, 'when he's taken away,' and although she spoke sympathetically I could stand it no longer. I pushed my plate aside, food untouched, and walked out of the room.

Duncan came after me. He took hold of me and made me face him.

'Listen, Lavinia. I know how you feel about poor Luke, but you're deluding yourself if you imagine that he is sane or safe enough to stay at Glenrannoch any longer. As he grows older, he'll grow worse. You didn't believe the story I told you the other day about his strangling an Alsatian because you didn't *want* to believe it, but now you've seen what he's capable of doing you've got to face facts. This sudden lack of control of his will grow more unpredictable and may not stop merely at animals. Human beings have to be protected, too.'

I made a protesting sound and he put an arm about me and led me across the great hall into the room he used as a study. This was his private sanctum; here no one would disturb us. We sat together on a deep, leather-upholstered settee and he kept my hand in his as he went on talking, telling me that I had nothing in the world with which to reproach myself and that no one could have done more to help or encourage the man, but kind as my ideas were, they had been wrong.

I felt too depressed to point out that I wasn't reproaching myself, but everybody else.

'Your grandfather had the right ideas,' Duncan continued. 'So long as Luke was confined to limited jobs, he could be controlled. Let him wander farther afield, and alone, and anything could happen.'

I pushed a weary hand through my hair and said, 'He was allowed to work in the garden, wasn't he? Well, that's what he was doing. I saw him from my window, doing something with a hoe in the shrubbery.'

'He's only allowed to work under supervision, which means beneath the head gardener. That's Fergus, and he's a tough man. Luke had no right to be working in the shrubbery without his instructions, and I doubt if Fergus gave them since he doesn't work on Saturday. Luke was taking advantage of the trust you've placed in him and Fergus will be none too pleased when he hears that Luke helped himself to a hoe from the tool shed.'

'To hell with Fergus! Let him complain to me.'

Duncan smiled. 'That sounds more like you. You must be feeling better.'

I wasn't, but I let him think so.

'What did Aunt Mary mean when she said that Luke would have to be dealt with, and that Hamish was the man to handle the job?' The question forced itself out of me, though I knew the answer.

'Simply that, being a vet, he'll confirm that Jock was strangled.'

'And did he say so, when you handed over the body?'

'He said what I expected him to say – that it certainly looked like it, but he would examine the body to ascertain whether death was due to strangulation or the remote possibility that the animal's neck had been caught in a rabbit trap. But there were no trap marks on the neck and Fergus has set none in the grounds near the house, and since Jock didn't wander farther afield, obviously that can be ruled out.'

This was cold comfort, and I said nothing as Duncan went on, 'The examination won't take long. A formality, no more. And, darling, don't worry. Luke will be taken great care of. Somewhere he'll be happy and protected. A mental home, not a prison.'

Somehow, the rest of the day dragged by. The was no call from Hamish and I was glad. I didn't want that official confirmation to come through. Every time the telephone rang I felt apprehension rise in me, and then subside in relief when it proved to be someone else. One call was from the car dealer, saying my Triumph had come from the manufacturers and would be delivered to Glenrannoch early Monday. Duncan brought me the news, and I could see he expected this to cheer me. All I could say was that I was glad.

Malcolm telephoned to ask if I'd like to run over to Spean Bridge for a game of golf. I was an indifferent player and told him so.

'Thirty-six handicap. What can you expect from a London week-end golfer?' I said lightly.

All his cajolery about helping to improve my game fell on stony ground, and I got rid of him by admitting frankly that I felt in no mood for anyone's company, but didn't say why. So far, the news about Jock, and Luke's involvement, was being kept strictly to Glenrannoch, and I was grateful to the others for tacitly agreeing to this.

Even prattling Aunt Mary didn't refer to the incident again, perhaps because, as far as she was concerned, the matter had been dealt with by placing it in Hamish Cameron's hands and to her, as to the others, his verdict was a foregone conclusion.

Eventually the long day came to an end but, tired as I was, I dreaded going up to that uneasy room of mine. I remembered how Jock had disliked it; he too had felt the restlessness of it. And the menace? Had he felt that too?

His whimpering and whining, his pleading to be let out of the place, his plaintive crying, all echoed in my memory as I opened the heavy oak door and let it close behind me with its usual thud.

The night had come and I had to face it. *The second night of the second visitation?*

I switched on all the lights and left them blazing. I did the same in the bathroom, the mirrored walls sending back brilliant reflections. I decided to leave them on all night, the intervening door open, and if this was giving way to cowardice I was quite ready to give way to it because I couldn't face darkness any more.

I prolonged the ritual of preparing for bed. It was eleven o'clock before I settled down, if leaving all lamps alight and trying to read could be called settling down. Their brilliance from the bathroom streamed in a vivid path across the carpet, but even this didn't reach the furthermost corners of the room where, as always, shadows lurked. The great tester bed faced that way and I could see my grandfather's wardrobe, like a giant sarcophagus spread across one wall. Now it housed my own clothes, but in imagination I pictured the great doors swinging silently open and revealing emptiness; great yawning emptiness ready to swallow me whole.

I flung my book aside furiously. I was behaving like an hysterical fool, no longer the practical, level-headed Lavinia MacDonald who had been taught by her father to stand on her own two feet and to fight for herself, whatever life did to her. I was becoming neurotic, frightened of shadows, haunted by an accident logically accounted for.

And Jock's death? That could be logically accounted for too, according to everyone else in the family. It was only I who refused to accept it, and I, at the moment, was fatigued, irrational, losing my grip.

Eleven-fifteen. Resolutely, I went into the bathroom and switched off the lights. In the bedroom I turned off all lamps except a bedside one to guide me back there. Automatically, I turned the great iron key in the door; this had become a ritual now.

Finally I switched off the bedside lamp, and darkness covered me like a shroud. Now sleep, I commanded myself firmly. For goodness sake, go to sleep and stop thinking. Then you'll hear nothing, nothing . . .

But I was still awake when the footsteps came, and I heard them clearly and unmistakably; the same pace, the same metallic ring, the same heavy tread. From the distance and out of the darkness they came, growing louder, coming nearer, ready at any moment to halt beneath my window. I lay taut and terrified, then action triggered my brain. I leapt out of bed and stumbled blindly to the door, my shaking fingers finding the iron key and turning it violently. I was racing along the minstrels' gallery before the midnight walker even reached my bedroom window.

I had to get to Duncan. His room was on the same floor, but in the opposite wing, and that meant going round three sides of the minstrels' gallery with the yawning chasm of the great hall spread out below. The whole house was in darkness and as I groped my shaking way along the panelled walls, feeling for a light switch, the heavy boom of midnight reverberated from the unseen depths of the hall, and in the echoing silence every stroke sounded like a death knell. Slow, deliberate, crashing through the darkness into my terrified mind.

And then, miraculously, my fingers touched a switch and chandeliers blazed, an endless chain of dazzling light running full circle round the gallery.

In seconds I was rapping on Duncan's door. No reply came, no sound but my own heavy breathing and the erratic echo of my trembling knuckles as they rapped again.

I lifted the ancient latch and the door swung open. Moonlight streamed into an empty room.

I stood there in disbelief. The curtains were not yet drawn. The bed had been turned back, but Duncan was not in it. I saw his pyjamas laid out, ready and waiting for him, and in a remote corner of my mind I wondered why Flora had forgotten to draw the curtains. Then I remembered Duncan once saying that he always slept with them apart.

I shivered in my thin nightdress and my bare feet felt suddenly cold. It was too late now to tell him about the midnight walker, too late to urge him outside to investigate. I turned and walked slowly back along the gallery, and from below his voice called, 'Lavinia! Is something wrong?'

He was standing in the open door of his study, looking up at me in surprise. Behind him I could see his desk, littered with papers, a single lamp burning. He was fully dressed.

He came racing up the right hand sweep of the stairs, peeling off his jacket as he came. When he reached me he wasted no time in questions, but put the jacket round my shoulders and led me down the great staircase into his study. A fire burned. He sat me beside it, but when I tried to speak he stopped me.

'Drink this first, then talk.' He poured a generous tot of scotch and handed it to me, then he stooped, felt my feet, and began to chafe them between his capable hands. Suddenly I felt calm and safe, and my shivering ceased.

He left me there, fetched a dressing-gown from his room, and wrapped me in it. I felt the soft warmth fold me close, and what with that, and the whisky, and the fire, plus his calming personality, I began to feel myself again.

Duncan poured a drink for himself and said, 'I saw the sudden flood of light from the minstrels' gallery. I knew it wasn't from the hall because light from there penetrates strongly beneath this door, but lights from above reflect down the stairs and out of the corner of my eye I saw the pale streak through the gap. Then I heard distant knocking, and your voice — '

I told him I had wanted him urgently, but that it was too late now. 'He'll have gone. The midnight walker, I mean.'

Slowly, Duncan put down his glass and stared at me.

'It's true. I heard him last night and again tonight, out there on the terrace. It was exactly as Aunt Mary said, and exactly as I heard it when I first came here.' I took a gulp of whisky. 'You've got to believe me,' I insisted. 'I didn't imagine it either time, but I was out of my room tonight before he reached my window — '

'So you don't know if he stopped there.'

'No. But he would. Same as before.'

I was glad he didn't brush the whole thing aside, or tell me I'd imagined it, that the day's happenings had disturbed me. He put down his glass and headed for the door.

'I'm going outside to investigate.'

'You didn't hear the footsteps from here?'

'No. This room is on the opposite side of the house.'

'In any case, the midnight walker only haunts his victim!' I was ashamed of the note of hysteria in my voice.

Duncan said calmly, 'There *isn't* any midnight walker, Lavinia. Can't you realize that it must be some practical joker, though who the hell it can be I can't imagine. Not that I don't mean to find out.'

I saw then that he was wearing bedroom slippers, and that a Thermos and empty cup stood on a tray on his desk. I had known him stay up late on work before. When he did, Flora always left a flask of coffee for him. I could have been down here with him all the time, I thought regretfully, sitting by the fire while he worked, and hearing no midnight walker at all.

I waited while he flung on a coat, then collected a powerful quartz-iodine climber's lamp and went outside to investigate. He took a long time over it, and when he came back he reported that there wasn't a sign. Not even a footprint.

'Would there be?'

'If the joker approached the terrace from the garden, yes. There'd be dirt and damp grass; they cling to spiked shoes, and since you say the footsteps sounded like those from metal-studded boots – '

'I didn't. I didn't describe them at all.'

'Not tonight, but the first time. Remember? You said they had an iron ring about them.' He shed his overcoat. 'The obvious deduction is that if this so-called midnight walker didn't approach the terrace from the garden, he went straight from the house, through one of the doors or french windows. And the only people who have metal-studded boots at Glenrannoch are Luke, for outdoor work, and myself, for climbing.'

Which meant, of course, that someone could have borrowed them. Duncan didn't have to say it; I knew it. I didn't believe that those footsteps belonged to the shambling Luke, nor did they belong to Duncan. I knew his step by now; the brisk, quick step which characterized him so well. And practical jokes weren't his line. He was a sound, well-balanced lawyer.

He smiled, reading my thoughts. 'Just in case you should have any doubts, I can assure you I've been hard at work here ever since dinner, and long after the household went to bed. Of course, without a witness that's not a solid alibi, but when a man loves a girl the way I love you, the last thing he's going to do is play practical jokes to scare her out of her wits.'

He didn't come to me, or touch me, but the feeling of closeness was so great that it was almost as if he held me.

'I want to marry you, Lavinia. You know it, don't you? I've tried to hide how I feel, but not very successfully. And of course it wouldn't fit in with your grandfather's plans. He had Malcolm Matheson in mind for you –'

'So I've gathered. But Malcolm is not in my own mind.'

'And I?'

I wanted to say, 'Very much so,' but I didn't trust either the moment or myself. I was aware of him physically, but I had learned in the past not to place too much reliance on physical attraction. There had to be something more than the desire of body for body, and there had to be something more than a reaching out for comfort and reassurance.

Duncan said, 'I don't want to rush you, Lavinia. You've gone through an uprooting in your life which could make you interpret a need for companionship as a need for love. I can give you both, I want you to remember that, also that I've sufficient means to provide well for you even if you didn't want Glenrannoch. I'm successful and mean to be more so. My London partnership is profitable and established. I've no interest in your inheritance and only want you to have it because you are entitled to it and because I don't think your father had a square deal, consequently I don't think either you or your mother had a square deal either. Your grandfather's bequest makes up for that, at any rate partially, but when everything is settled and you've had time to get used to being a fully accepted MacDonald, well then, you'll have time to think about us – you and me.' He added with sudden amusement, 'And I have no objection to preceding the name of Campbell with that of MacDonald. It would be unprecedented in Glencoe, but perhaps a recompense long overdue!'

Then his voice softened. 'But the most important thing,

Lavinia, is that I love you. I want you to remember that.'

I slept long and late the next morning. When I wakened I rang Flora, who brought some breakfast and told me that the family had gone to church. I wanted to ask if Luke was all right, but a shutter seemed to have clamped down upon Flora, rendering her unapproachable.

Shortly after she left me the phone began to ring downstairs in the great hall. I pulled on a dressing-gown and ran to answer it, wishing, not for the first time, that there was an extension to my room.

When I picked up the receiver I heard Hamish Cameron's voice.

'Lavinia? I want to see you urgently. Can you come to my house at once?'

I was still slightly befuddled by sleep, and stammered, 'I'm not yet dressed – '

'Then do it quickly and get here fast.'

The line cleared before I could even suggest that he should come to Glenrannoch. I dropped the receiver back, thinking how characteristic it was of the man to rap out orders and expect people to jump to them. Then I remembered how quickly he had answered Aunt Mary's call yesterday and decided that the least I could do was to reciprocate.

But there was more to my haste than that. There was the sudden remembrance of Jock, and a frightening sort of question at the back of it. If all Hamish had to do was confirm that the puppy had been strangled, why send for me, and so urgently?

The question must have been in my face when he opened his front door. I had borrowed Brenda's Singer and raced there, and as I stepped across the threshold Hamish said without preamble, 'I wanted to tell you away from your family. Jock *was* strangled, but that didn't cause his death. He died of poisoning before it happened.'

CHAPTER TEN

My first reaction was relief because this cleared Luke. He had not killed my puppy and no one would be able to accuse him of it, or take him away, but hard on that thought came another. Poison – and *then* strangling?

Apprehension rose in me again and I asked sharply, 'Couldn't they make that out to be even worse?'

Hamish echoed quickly. 'They?'

'The family. Everyone. They'll see it as a double sign of insanity.'

'In Luke, you mean? And how do they know he did it?'

'They don't. No one does. But it seemed so because he came across the lawn, carrying Jock's body. I was alone on the terrace and he was bringing it to me, I think. I can't be sure because he looked so stunned. Dazed. As if he didn't really know where he was going or what he was carrying. It wasn't until Duncan shouted to him that he was shocked back to his senses.'

I paused. Luke had so few senses. Had he taken leave of even those?

'And then?'

'He dropped it. Jock's dead body. As if he'd only just realized what he was holding. And then he ran. So you see, it did look as if he was guilty. Not deliberately or consciously, but in a blind moment of insanity. That's why they say he'll have to be sent away, especially since this is the second time.'

'So you've heard about the Alsatian.'

'Couldn't it have been self-defence that time?'

'It was, although I was the only one to say so. I was up there, watching the exercises, on call in case of injuries to the rescue dogs. They're valuable beasts, but often highly strung. This one was particularly so, and not yet fully trained. He attacked – he was an ex-police dog, did you know?'

I shook my head.

'It was that fact which helped to exonerate poor Luke,

up to a point. Being on the spot I testified that he acted in self-defence, but I was a newcomer here and people weren't entirely prepared to accept my word at that time. Things are better now. Local inhabitants are less suspicious of me.'

'Why should they ever have been?'

Hamish shrugged. 'The insularity of country folk, their inherent doubt of strangers.' He changed the subject abruptly. 'What did carry weight in Luke's favour was the fact that the Alsatian hadn't forgotten his police training – to attack when necessary. In early rescue exercises no stranger is allowed to cross the snow path between the buried victim and the rescue dog, so Luke's sudden appearance triggered off the animal's suspicion, and Luke defended himself. His abnormal strength did the rest. Unhappily, he has never been exonerated in the eyes of many. This could be prejudicial now.'

I slumped into an arm-chair and said unhappily, 'To everyone at Glenrannoch the deed *is* a repetition. I was even warned – '

I broke off. Somehow I didn't want to bring Duncan into this conversation because of the antagonism I had sensed between these two men right from the beginning. Now I knew the probable cause if it; the incident of the Alsatian, on which they disagreed.

'Aunt Mary says he will have to be "dealt with",' I added. 'That's why she sent for you, for confirmation of death, proof that the dog was strangled. And now it's worse, isn't it? A kind of double death.'

Hamish said with emphasis, 'But no proof that it was done by Luke. He could merely have found the body.'

'I've already thought of that, but proving it is another thing. The man can't defend himself and the evidence seems stacked against him. Who else would have injured the puppy? Who else *could* have? Mary and Brenda were indoors, Duncan was over at the Forsythes, and anyway, none of them would. Jock had become part of the family.' I asked suddenly, 'Poison?' What kind of poison?'

'Arsenic. A minute dose, but enough to kill a tiny creature.'

'But how did he get it?'

'It's contained in certain weed-killers,' Hamish pointed out reluctantly.

And Luke helped in the garden. Rough jobs, like hoeing and pouring diluted weed-killer on brick or gravel paths. And yesterday he had helped himself to one of the gardening tools without permission. Why not to something else? I gave a despairing sigh.

'Or,' Hamish went on, 'it could have been in something Jock drank. Say, for instance, he was given water in an old weed-killer tin and some of the stuff was clinging to it – just a few grains would be enough. Or if an old lid had been abandoned and held rain water. He could have drunk that without anyone knowing. But of course,' he finished significantly, 'there's been no rain for the last three days, and early morning dew evaporates quickly.'

'Not to mention the fact that Fergus is meticulous about disposing of weed-killer containers, liquid or powder form, plus the additional fact that Jock was with me all morning until I went – '

I broke off, and Hamish prompted, 'Went where?'

'To my room to change. Jock had jumped up and sent my coffee flying.'

'Where did this happen?'

'Outside on the terrace. Duncan and I went together and I was throwing Jock's ball for him to retrieve.'

'With a cup of coffee in your other hand?'

'No. Aunt Mary brought out a tray, and as I took my cup Jock brought the ball back and leapt up at me, begging for a re-throw. He was very frisky.'

'So the coffee spilt?'

'Down my skirt. More than that, the cup and saucer went flying, which didn't please Aunt Mary.'

Suddenly intent, Hamish demanded every detail.

'Of the entire morning? How can I remember – '

'No. When the coffee was spilt. I presume it didn't all go down your skirt. There'd be some on the terrace, along with the broken china.'

'Quite a pool.' I broke off again. 'Now look here!' I protested. 'You're not thinking – '

'That the coffee might have been poisoned? Yes, I am.'

'But that's ridiculous! Everyone drank it.'

'But not from your cup. Was there a special one for you?'

'Of course not.'

But there was. Black, for me, with sugar — the way I liked it. I heard Aunt Mary saying the words, saw her indicating the cup and turning the tray round to make sure I took the right one. And Jock licking up the spilled coffee and spitting distastefully. I even heard Malcolm's voice from the open french windows: 'Perhaps he only likes it with cream!'

I jumped up and moved restlessly towards the window, staring out across the loch.

'I don't like what you're hinting,' I said. 'It's ugly.'

'Of course it's ugly. Trying to kill someone always is.'

I spun round, anger blazing. I'd never had any love for the MacDonalds, but suddenly Glenrannoch was home to me and the people in it were no longer strangers, but people to whom I belonged. I was astonished that in so short a time this feeling of intimacy had grown between us, and that a house which could still seem vast, gloomy, and sometimes sinister should have started to bind me close, as if it had tentacles of its own which could reach out and entwine and never let me free.

'Are you trying to suggest that someone at Glenrannoch tried to poison me, and poor little Jock died instead?'

'Yes,' Hamish repeated. 'I am.'

'Then kindly explain how,' I demanded sceptically.

'By adding it to your cup after the coffee was in it, or putting it in the cup before the coffee was added. Then making sure you got the right cup. You wouldn't have died, of course. The dose was too small. But accumulated arsenic poisoning over a period of time can be unsuspected. You'd have bouts of nausea and sickness occasionally and the local doctor would prescribe for stomach upsets . . .' He looked at me hard. 'You're remembering something.'

I was. The tisane. And the nausea following. And the nightmare of the midnight walker as I lay there in the dark.

I sat down again, weakly. I heard myself saying that I didn't believe it, and Hamish asking who made the coffee, and who poured it, and did anyone make sure I got a certain cup. I lied, saying I didn't know, I couldn't remember, and his keen blue eyes looked back at me, their expression saying plainly: *Yes, you do, but you won't admit it.*

Then he asked if I would let him have my skirt. 'I could have the stain analysed. That would prove whether it contained anything besides coffee.'

My heart sank. An overnight soak had washed the stain clean out. Hamish swore soundly, declaring that with that evidence he could have cleared Luke *and* convinced me that his suspicions were correct.

Suddenly, and gladly, I proved him wrong. 'You've forgotten to explain why Jock was strangled! There was no motive behind that, surely?'

Hamish shook his head at me, long and sadly.

'For an intelligent young woman, Lavinia MacDonald, you're being very obtuse, because you don't want to believe what is staring you in the face. The strangling was a cover-up. Someone knew that the coffee Jock licked up contained poison – not enough to kill a human being, but enough to make a dog sufficiently ill for a vet to be called. A fully-grown dog, that is. And a vet might diagnose poison, although he might have difficulty in proving just how it was taken. As it happened, Jock wasn't fully-grown so the dose was enough to kill him. A healthy young pup doesn't drop down dead suddenly, so some other cause had to be suggested. And what more convenient than strangulation, especially when there's a man in the household already known to have strangled an animal in the past? Many a vet would have examined the neck alone, because it was an obvious cause of death. It was expected that I would do the same.'

It all sounded so feasible it was terrifying, and sent my memory winging back to yesterday morning. I was looking out of my bedroom window, zipping up my dress, seeing Luke working in the shrubbery and Jock, suddenly listless, abandoning all attempts to play, obediently trotting back to the terrace, but wearily . . . very wearily. And Duncan putting the ball back behind the stone pillar where I kept it, and then going over to Kyleven with the Forsythes.

So the only ones left behind were Aunt Mary and Brenda. I hadn't looked out of the window again.

Hamish said with conviction, 'Someone wants you out of the way. When they can't frighten you into going, they try other methods.'

'But *why*?'

'You know the answer well enough. Because of the codicil.'

The codicil leaving Glenrannoch to the two women, if in some way the house failed to come to me; fanatical Aunt Mary, with her herbal recipes, her tisanes, her frightening stories of MacIain's ghost returning to predict a person's death, her care that I should take the right coffee cup . . .

And Brenda MacDonald, charming, elegant, friendly . . . with blunt, strong little hands which could encompass a tiny throat.

I drove slowly back to Glenrannoch, and when I reached there I saw Duncan's Jaguar in the garage and knew they had all returned from church.

Again slowly, I went into the house, not wanting to face any of them because I was afraid they might be able to read my face, or that I should be unable to keep my knowledge from them. Hamish had told me that he would telephone his diagnosis, and his call preceded my arrival home. Brenda was just replacing the receiver when I walked in, and her shock was evident.

'The puppy – it was *poisoned*! Poisoned and then strangled . . .' A shudder ran through her slender body and her delicate features paled.

Aunt Mary gave a little cry of horror and prattled something about Deadly Nightshade and other poisonous weeds, and how the postmaster's cat had eaten some and died almost at once, but no one took any notice. Duncan, looking serious, said nothing at all, but I could tell that he was thinking a lot. So was his mother.

She sat down weakly in a high-backed chair, looking as delicate as a piece of Dresden china, the soft skirt of her dress outspread against the rich brocaded upholstery. Then she looked at me compassionately and said, 'Oh, my dear, this makes it all much worse for you. You were convinced that Luke was innocent, weren't you, but how can you be now? Only someone insane would poison an animal and then strangle it. Duncan – you'll have to call Doctor MacFarlane at once. Luke will have to be taken away.'

I was glad when Duncan said that Flora must be consulted first. 'She *is* his mother,' he pointed out. 'She deserves consideration, and she must be present when the doctor sees her son. She's a good woman; we must make things as easy as possible for her.'

But as it happened Doctor MacFarlane had no opportunity to see Luke. Nor had anyone else, because suddenly he disappeared.

If Flora knew what had happened to her son, she wasn't saying. She stood before us, breaking the news in her rigid, phlegmatic way.

'He was in his bed last night. This morning, he was not. That's all I know, sir. Me and the girls have looked everywhere, but there's neither sign nor sound of him.'

There was nothing to do but notify the police. Without transport, Luke couldn't get very far. Inquiries at the ferry and in the local villages confirmed that no one had seen him. After an official search of the house and grounds it was concluded that he must be somewhere in the glen, which he knew like the back of his hand. Search parties were organized, but when darkness fell, they returned with the news that no trace had been found of Luke, and that the search would be renewed tomorrow. To scour the glen and surrounding slopes would take many days, by which time hunger would force the poor man from his hiding place.

Next morning my new car arrived, and Duncan delayed his departure for the mills to accompany me on a trial run and to check that everything was in order. The sun was brilliant, the air stimulating, and we drove much farther than intended – east across Rannoch Moor then south until we reached the Bridge of Orchy. The river sparkled like a silver ribbon wending its way towards Loch Tulla, so that it was inevitable to cross the bridge and follow the road on the opposite bank until we reached the Inveroran Hotel. By that time the morning had gone and we stopped for lunch before returning home.

It was the first outing we had had together since I came to Glenrannoch, and because Duncan avoided any reference to recent events my mind was able to reject them. It was like escaping from a cage of fear into a world of freedom, and our feeling of companionship deepened.

It wasn't until we reluctantly headed for home that reality began to take over, and then not until the dramatic peak of Buchaille Etive Mor pierced the sky from the west, marking the entrance to the pass.

As we descended, fold upon fold of towering hills encompassed us, the atmosphere of the glen reclaimed me, and back came all the fears and unanswered questions, one of which leapt unbidden into my mind. Why had Hamish Cameron in particular been asked to witness the codicil to my grandfather's will?

When I put the question to Duncan, he seemed surprised. 'You didn't ask that when I showed it to you.'

'I didn't glance at the witnesses, and if I had, the names would have meant nothing to me.'

'Then how do you know he was one?'

We were turning the bend in the pass by The Meeting of the Waters. I answered lightly, 'Now you sound just like a lawyer, cross-questioning his client.'

He laughed. 'Sorry, but naturally I wondered.'

'Hamish told me himself. Why are you slowing down?'

He nodded towards the Mountain Rescue Post, where police cars were gathered. 'To find out if there's any news about Luke, although I hardly feel they'd still be gathered there, if there were.'

There was no news, and we drove on towards Clachaig Gully. Soon we would be back at Glenrannoch, and I didn't want to go there. I felt in no mood for either Brenda or Aunt Mary, or to isolate myself in the library. After a morning such as this I wanted to cling to freedom, so I asked Duncan to drive straight on to the mills and to take me with him. He agreed willingly, and it wasn't until we were on the ferry that he asked, 'When did Hamish tell you?'

For a moment I felt mentally out of step, then I realized he was referring to the codicil again.

'The day he came to tell me that Jock was mine.'

'And what brought it up?'

For the life of me, I couldn't remember, nor could I see that it was important. What was important was to conceal the fact that we had discussed it again yesterday, because that would mean revealing Hamish's suspicions and cast a terrible reflection upon Duncan's mother, as well as Aunt Mary. Those suspicions now seemed impossible, although yesterday they had loomed large enough to disturb me.

Duncan said with a smile, 'You can't understand your grandfather's friendship with Hamish Cameron, can you? When my mother first told you, I could see your surprise. Well, I suppose such a friendship *was* surprising, the two men being so different, but it was real enough. James would never hear a word against Cameron.'

'Was there any reason why he should?'

'Some people might think so.'

A criminal, Aunt Mary had called him, and empty-headed Moira had almost confirmed it, but all Duncan said now was, 'Your grandfather had every right to ask anyone he wished to witness his will, or any addition to it.'

That was reasonable enough, and so was Duncan's tone. We didn't mention the matter again as we drove off the ferry and headed towards the mills, where I was delighted by the progress which had been made on my studio. Not only was the big sky-light fixed, but shelves were going up and my long work desk would be ready for use in a day or two. My empty days at Glenrannoch would soon be over.

I killed the remainder of the afternoon by driving through the hitherto unexplored area of Glen Nevis, then returning at five to pick up Duncan and go home.

He took one glance at me and said, 'You look yourself again, the way you looked when you first came to us – alive and wonderful. What is it due to – the prospect of working again, our Highland air, or me?'

'A combination of all three!'

'And to keep it that way I want you to do something – sleep in my room tonight. I'll sleep in yours. And to make sure you get a good night's rest, take one of my mother's sleeping pills.'

It was a kind thought, but I wished he hadn't mentioned it because it brought the legend of Glenrannoch back to my mind, and the awareness that tonight would mark the third of MacIain's second visitation. It was something I neither wanted to think about nor face, so the thought of sleeping in another room held decided appeal. Nevertheless, I said slowly, 'I don't think that's a good idea. The others – your mother and Aunt Mary – will wonder why, and then we'll have to tell them about last night.'

'Not necessarily. We don't all troop off to bed at the same time. There's no reason why they should know.'

'Your mother will wonder why I need sleeping pills. I didn't know she took them.'

'She's been an insomniac for years. That's why she had her own room when your grandfather began to be ill and restless. She'll be sympathetic if I tell her you've been sleeping badly. No one could be more so.'

I agreed to take the sleeping pills, but something stubborn in me insisted that I should race this thing out. If either of the two women was my enemy, it would be wise to pretend ignorance, not to arouse suspicion in any way, although reason argued that the steps of the midnight walker were not those of any woman.

Nor could I really believe that Brenda and Mary would connive together to claim Glenrannoch for themselves when neither could tolerate the other or live happily together. I remembered that Brenda had even begged me to remain in order to spare her from such a situation.

The more I thought about it the more convinced I became that Hamish Cameron's suggestion about the codicil being a motivation was unfounded. I even began to blame him for harbouring the thought. I began to wonder what sort of a man he was, after all. To some, a person to be condemned; to others, like shrewd old James MacDonald, a person to be trusted. And yet again, to a woman like Isabel Forsythe, a man to be loved?

I pushed that final thought aside for I had no proof of the truth of it.

There was still no news of Luke when we reached Glenrannoch, nor by the time we went to bed. Flora was uncommunicative again. When I asked for a glass of hot milk to be put in my room she inclined her head in silent ackowledgement, but Aunt Mary remarked, 'You don't usually drink hot milk when you go to bed, Lavinia. Aren't you sleeping well?' Then she gasped, 'You – you haven't been *disturbed* again, have you?'

I saw exasperation in Duncan's eyes, and heard it in his voice as he rapped back, 'Not in the way you're thinking of, Aunt Mary, but this business of the dog has been distressing for her. That's a great deal more tangible than your unfounded ghost story.'

His tone had the immediate effect of quietening her. I felt she stood a little in awe of Duncan, now the only man in the house.

'I'm sorry,' she said defensively, 'I was concerned for her, that's all. A young person needs plenty of sleep.'

'And tonight she will have it. My mother has some sleeping pills.'

Brenda agreed at once, and went to fetch them, whereupon Aunt Mary, not to be outdone by her stepmother, insisted on bringing the hot milk up to me. I felt there was being a great deal of unnecessary fuss, and said so, but no one took any notice. The result was that I felt somewhat exasperated as I went upstairs, which was a good thing because it overcame my apprehension. I felt eager to get away from my aunt's fussing and Brenda's solicitude; even Duncan's concern, although I had gone racing in search of him last night.

But again I switched on all lamps and welcomed the blaze of light in the bathroom. When I emerged, Aunt Mary was coming along the short passage to my door. She stood there a moment, tut-tutted over such unnecessary extravagance, put the hot milk and a small bottle on my bedside table, and went round turning off all lights but those beside the bed.

She even stood over me as I climbed into it, propped me up with pillows, then picked up the bottle and shook some pills into the palm of her hand.

'Two only, Brenda says, no more than that. Doctor MacFarlane prescribes them and they're very mild, but you're a healthy young woman, Lavinia my dear, and I should have thought one would be ample.'

She was behaving so much like a mother hen that I expected her to start clucking at any moment, and a wild desire to laugh threatened me. I managed to choke it down, accepted the pills, but decided not to take them because suddenly I was afraid to.

135

I sipped the milk slowly, wishing she would go, but she stood over me determinedly. Even when I thanked her and said good night she refused to take the hint. 'It can't be all *that* hot,' she said. 'Drink it up like a good girl, and let me see you swallow those pills. You've looked tired these last two days, and as Duncan rightly says, this business of the dog hasn't helped . . .'

Her voice trailed away, then to my surprise she added sadly, 'Poor Luke – I wonder where he is? I don't like to think of him out there in the glen, hiding in some crevasse or cave, alone and frightened. And the nights are so cold here, even in summer.'

Her gaunt, embittered face looked suddenly soft and compassionate, then she pulled herself together and said briskly, 'But they'll find him and take care of him, I have no doubt.' She jiggled the little bottle impatiently. 'Come along now, my dear, take those pills and lie down and you won't hear a thing until morning.'

I had no choice. She wasn't leaving until I obeyed. When I had swallowed them and the last drop of milk had gone, she tucked me in, and a minute later only the light from the corridor remained.

I remember seeing her angular figure silhouetted against it as she stood in the aperture, looking back at me; I remember seeing her pop a sugared almond into her mouth from her hip bag of *petit-point*, and I remember thinking that as soon as she had gone I must lock the door as usual. I would wait a moment or two then slip out of bed and turn the great iron key . . .

After that, I remember nothing until I wakened with a jerk. The room was dark as pitch, the house silent and, in the passage outside, footsteps were coming directly to my door.

The lifting of the iron latch echoed sharply in the blackness. The door hinges creaked as it swung open. I reached wildly for the bed-lamp and heard scream upon scream piercing my brain.

CHAPTER ELEVEN

Aunt Mary's voice said in distress, 'I only came to see if you had dropped off, my dear.'

A light switched on. She stood there in her dressing-gown, her face creased in concern. In a moment she was beside me, picking up the lamp which, in my panic, I had sent flying, then she was settling me back in bed.

Stroking my hair from my forehead, she said, 'You must have been having a nightmare, poor girl.'

I turned restlessly on the pillow, and saw the small dial of my bedside clock, the fingers pointing clearly to eleven.

My heavy eyelids fell and the wild terror began to ebb away, but at the same time one thought hammered through. An hour to go. One more hour to midnight.

Dimly, I heard Aunt Mary saying how sorry she was to have disturbed me, and that one sleeping pill would certainly have been enough. 'Brenda said two, but I was right . . .'

The voice faded. The stroking ceased. I fought against enveloping sleep, clinging desperately to the thought that as soon as she had gone I had to turn that key. I listened to the departing clip-clop of her slippers, to the click of the light as it went off, to the careful shutting of the door, then blindly, stumblingly, I was dragging myself towards it, hands outstretched, and the big projecting key seemed to thrust itself into my palm. I grasped it, turned it, and groped my way back to bed.

I wakened to sunlight streaming through a gap in the curtains, and Flora rattling the door latch, demanding admittance. My bedside clock said seven-thirty. I had slept the night through and heard nothing.

Flora, bearing morning tea, asked if I would mind not locking my door at nights so that she could bring it straight in, as with the others. I apologized and said it was a habit I had got into, and was about to ask if there was any news of Luke when she turned abruptly and departed, barricaded as before by taciturnity.

A brisk shower cleared the lingering after-effects of the sleeping pills and when I went down to breakfast Duncan gave me an approving glance.

'You look better, and you'll feel better still when you get yourself outside this.' He served me scrambled eggs, topped them with a rasher of bacon, and poured coffee. The two women were not yet down, and I was glad of that. Across the table Duncan smiled and said, 'Obviously, you slept well and didn't hear a thing.'

I had to admit that this was true. After Aunt Mary's second departure I had submerged promptly into sleep.

'Doesn't that prove I was right when I said that the story about the midnight walker was a pack of nonsense?'

To please him, I agreed, but pointed out that I had been heavily knocked out by sleeping pills.

'I thought you said they were mild, but two was one too many for me.'

'Because you're not accustomed to them. All the same, I'm not sorry you had the extra dose, although I'm convinced that if any iron-studded boots had marched to your door, you would have wakened.'

That seemed logical, since Aunt Mary's leather-soled slippers had managed to rouse me, creaking the floorboards outside. I rejected the thought that perhaps I had been drifting only in the shallows of sleep when she came, and that an hour later the pills were having their full effect. All that mattered was that the night had held no further terrors.

I felt rested and energetic, and a morning in the open air completed the cure, although I was not happy after walking to the Mountain Rescue Post. The men in charge of operations seemed less confident; also, for the first time, puzzled. In winter, a person could be buried alive beneath the snow on these hills; in summer, the only danger was from a treacherous fall, and such falls usually left traces leading to the body – articles flung from pockets, sometimes a trail of blood.

There were four teams, aided by volunteers, spread out across the towering walls north and south of the glen, well organized and in touch by walkie-talkie with base headquarters. All had nothing to report.

'It's almost as if the man had gone into hiding, Miss MacDonald, but Luke Fyfe hasn't the intelligence to plan such a thing. He would have to lay in supplies, food, covering for the night.' The superintending officer of Mountain Rescue shook his head. 'Luke has the ability and the strength to climb, and he roams the glen as the MacIains did in days gone by, so he might know, as they did, the hidden passes used as escape routes into Appin and beyond. In that case, he could have wandered far. We'll have to spread the net wider if today yields no results.'

'How about Eilean Munde?' I asked. 'Has that been searched?'

'Thoroughly, by the police. Even the small islands alongside, although there's no hiding place there, and the ruined chapel offers no concealment. It hasn't even a roof to shelter a body.'

Returning to Glenrannoch, the words lingered in my mind. *'It's almost as if the man had gone into hiding.'* Secretly, I was convinced that this was precisely what Luke had done, aided and abetted by his mother. Somehow she had got him away before officialdom stepped in and did it for her, and all the questioning in the world would not prise open her guarded mouth. He was probably well away from Glencoe by now, and I could only hope and pray that he was safe and happy, although I knew that the only guarantee of happiness and care for Luke was beneath his mother's eye at Glenrannoch . . .

I pulled up short. Why hadn't I thought of that? He *had* to be here because she was here. She had kept him beside her all his life, so was she likely to send him away to some alien place where she would be unable to protect him now? If Flora had any relatives, they had turned their backs on her years ago, so they would hardly open their doors to her unwanted son at a time when the police were searching for him. They would say, as others said, that he should be put away.

Thoughtfully, I went up to my room. At this hour of day, with the noon sun high in the sky, it was less sombre, but the distant corners still seemed remote and shadowy. There were many such rooms in a house like this, and all of them empty. Upstairs were endless attics, none of which I had ever entered. What if Luke was in one of them, isolated but safe? What if the searchers, when they combed the place, had somehow missed him? There could be cupboards beneath the eaves, vast enough and dark enough to conceal him while they went their rounds.

There were indeed, but all of them yawned at me, mocking and empty, as I went from room to room, starting with the attics and working down. I knew before I had finished that I was wasting my time. The house had been thoroughly gone over by experts before me and they, like I, had failed.

After nearly an hour of fruitless effort, I stood in the centre of a disused room and sighed. There was no doubt that the house sheltered no refuge.

I moved restlessly across the room, running my hand over the patina of ancient wood, the smoothness of brocade, the softness of velvet. This lovely furniture had been used in bygone days when Glenrannoch had accommodated large MacDonald families and an even larger number of servants to wait upon them, but the difference in furnishings between the attics above and the family rooms below was marked. Up there, truckle beds and bare floors; down here, fine carpets formed a luxurious background for valuable pieces which must now be worth a fortune.

I don't know what made me wonder how long it was since the collection of antiques at Glenrannoch had been valued. I must ask Duncan; he would know. These things had to be kept up-to-date for insurance purposes.

I was about to leave the room when I noticed that the window seat was panelled to the floor, with a hinged lid, forming a deep chest. I felt compelled to open it, although I knew full well that it could not shelter a man of Luke's immense physique, nor that he could survive internment in it.

What it did contain was a store of beautiful gowns, carefully preserved. Tartan taffetas and silks, with billowing skirts, sashes for the tiniest of waists; velvet jackets with lace jabots and cuffs, and even a cloak of peacock satin lined with MacDonald tartan in softest silk. A quickening of excitement told me that these had belonged to one particular person; a vivid person whose portrait challenged me every time I passed it. Shuna MacDonald. It was like meeting her face to face.

I swept a pile into my arms and as I closed the chest my glance strayed through the window, straight towards the disused family chapel. An old man was hobbling away from it towards the gap in the tall beech hedge – Craig, of whom I had heard but not yet met, had apparently been at his devotions. With fleeting amusement I hoped he had put the key back in its place this time, or Aunt Mary would be bustling over to Kyleven to protest again.

Then another thought struck me, and a moment later I was heading downstairs. In my room I tossed the gowns upon my bed, then raced back to the stairs, but on the minstrels' gallery I pulled up short. Brenda and Mary were below in the great hall, their voices rising sharply, Mary's with vexation and Brenda's with restrained impatience.

They were at loggerheads over some household matter, and suddenly Brenda cried, 'Thank heaven there's a new mistress here! You'll have to take your complaints to Lavinia now, not to me, and I'm sure she'll deal with them more firmly than I. I've been too indulgent, too patient with you ever since I came to this house.'

'And what have *I* put up with? Taking second place to a woman who has no idea of thrift or economy, and who high-handedly invites people to dinner without even considering whether *I* enjoy their company or not. You know perfectly well I cannot tolerate Isabel.'

'Then it's about time you learned to,' Brenda answered in a voice which was, for her, sharp with reproof, but Mary blazed on.

'And to order venison – *venison*, when its price is at its highest!'

Her stepmother laughed. 'You'll be even more displeased to hear that Hamish Cameron is coming too. He hasn't dined at Glenrannoch since your father died, and it's time you changed your attitude towards him also. The Camerons of Lochiel were always friends of the MacDonalds, and Hamish stems from a branch of the family.'

'*One* Cameron was no friend!'

I raced softly for the back stairs, determined to avoid the two women, but also wishing that Hamish could have heard their bickering, for nothing could have convinced him more thoroughly that people who got on each other's nerves to such a degree were the last to plot together against the new owner of Glenrannoch in order to get it jointly for themselves.

The back stairs led to a passage which opened at the side of the house. From there I was swiftly at the chapel, where I found the key on its nail behind the porch.

I searched the place thoroughly, but I should have known it would yield nothing. I think I had some vague hope of finding a secret hiding place, like a priest's hole, but apart from the family vault which the police had searched thoroughly, there was none. My fleeting idea that Flora might have concealed her son here was stillborn. The house and estate had been ransacked, so why should I hope to discover something the experts had overlooked?

I went out of the chapel, locked the door, and replaced the key on its hook.

At lunch I feigned ignorance when told about tonight's unexpected dinner party, made noises of agreement with the remarks of both women, and skipped dessert in order to escape. Upstairs I examined Shuna's dresses one by one (to me, they would always be Shuna's whether true or not) and marvelled over the expert handstitching. I tried them all on, and apart from a tightness about the waist, due to the fact that the original wearer was probably laced and I was not, they fitted me well.

Standing before a long cheval mirror I swept up my hair and stood for a moment, startled, for it did seem as if the young woman in the portrait had stepped out of her frame.

An idea seized me. I would wear one of these gowns tonight. I chose a tartan taffeta with long sleeves, full skirt, and lace at wrists and throat, I spent the afternoon letting out the waist and became so absorbed in the task that I forgot my surroundings and my dislike of the room; in some subtle way it even seemed to change, its restlessness giving way to repose because a woman sat quietly sewing.

Had she sat before me, Shuna MacDonald, glancing through the windows every now and then towards the towering peaks of the Glen of Weeping and to the softer, leafier, more fertile area of our gully, and had she responded to the haunting beauty of the place, as I did – Shuna, my lovely ancestor, with her flair for dress, her proud head, her courage and gaiety, all of which some unknown artist had immortalized on canvas? Why not? She, too, had been mistress of Glenrannoch. This would have been the room she shared with her husband.

I felt that from now on her personality would take over from the iron-willed James MacDonald and others like him who had occupied this room, and when I hung her gowns in the vast wardrobe and caught a lingering fragrance from them, I felt that I would no longer be alone here; that a kindred spirit had come to share the room with me.

It seemed less alien from that moment.

There was an abrupt silence as I descended the stairs. Everyone was gathered in the hall and at the echo of my footsteps on the ancient oak treads they looked up in unison. I saw Duncan's admiration, Brenda's surprise, Isabel's pleasure – and, more than all, something in the keen blue eyes of Hamish Cameron. His gaze was unflinching and, before it, my eyes fell, because somehow it said a great deal more than even Duncan's.

Isabel said, 'Lavinia, my dear, you look beautiful! Where did you get that dress?'

Brenda answered before I had the opportunity. 'From a window chest upstairs. They have been preserved throughout the years, but no mistress of Glenrannoch has ever been allowed to wear them.'

'Why ever not?' Malcolm Matheson demanded.

'It was stipulated in the will of a former master of Glenrannoch.'

'I'm sorry,' I said. 'I didn't know.'

I had reached the foot of the stairs and stood there hesitating, wondering whether I ought to go back and take the gown off, then deciding not to. These masters of Glenrannoch seemed too dictatorial, even after death. I had to abide by my grandfather's stipulations, but saw no reason why I should yield to a ridiculous one laid down generations before.

'She looks just like that portrait on the stairs,' Moira

Forsythe piped, 'and I must say that dress is pretty smashing.' She glanced down at her jeans and faded sweater with an expression which clearly said that perhaps it might be fun to dress up.

'I have said all along that Lavinia resembles Shuna MacDonald,' Brenda remarked.

Everyone with the exception of Hamish, who was still watching me silently, and Aunt Mary, who seemed torn between approval and disapproval, looked up at the portrait on the staircase wall. I heard Ian Forsythe and Isabel agreeing with Brenda, and Duncan saying that in his opinion I was even lovelier, and Malcolm adding that Shuna looked as if she'd been quite a girl, but I paid little heed because Hamish's look was disturbing me in a way I refused to analyse.

Then Moira piped up again. 'Isn't she the one – Shuna MacDonald – who disgraced the family?'

Aunt Mary said swiftly, 'We don't talk about it,' and set her lips tightly, as if sealing them forever.

It was then that Flora announced dinner and we all trooped into the dining-room. I saw beaming Jeannie standing proudly by the sideboard, honoured because she was helping tonight, and Ian Forsythe escorting Brenda, Duncan with Isabel, and, at my own side, Hamish Cameron. He said no word, but when he held my chair for me I was still aware of his intent and disturbing glance.

I asked impulsively, 'In what way did Shuna disgrace the family?'

He smiled with unexpected charm and answered, so that only I could hear, 'She fell in love, and ran away. With a Cameron of Lochiel.'

Not until after dinner did Duncan and I really meet, although I was aware that he watched me throughout the meal. When we went into the drawing-room for coffee he seated himself beside me and said, 'Now, perhaps, I can have your company. Hamish is not going to monopolize you all evening.'

This didn't appear to be Hamish's intention; he had been my dinner companion, but now he joined Isabel. I saw them, across the room, deep in conversation, and the disappointment I felt was unreasonable.

I took the opportunity to ask Duncan about the valuation of Glenrannoch's antiques, and how long it was since the last had been made. He replied that he had already thought of that and put a revaluation in hand, values having risen so sharply, but when I asked if Ian was doing it, he shook his head emphatically, saying that Ian was not experienced enough. 'He's only been in the trade for two or three years.'

I was surprised, but Duncan shrugged. 'The man's a Jack-of-all-trades and master of none. He's been everything from a tea planter in South Africa to an insurance broker in Edinburgh, so hardly the man to do a valuation for probate. I employed a qualified valuer for that shortly before you came. There's so much stuff at Glenrannoch that it's almost like taking an inventory of a museum, but his report should be along any time now.'

I became aware that Ian, sitting nearby, had overheard.

His face coloured and anger showed in his eyes, but he said nothing until Duncan's attention was briefly distracted, then he remarked to me quietly, 'Duncan's qualified valuer will merely confirm what I already know – that there's nothing genuine here. Fakes, the lot of them.'

I stared in disbelief, thinking that Duncan was obviously right – Ian was not knowledgeable enough.

The man looked at me regretfully. 'You believe I don't know what I'm talking about, but I do. Your grandfather parted with the originals long ago, when the mills were going through a bad patch. Some of the portraits may be genuine, but most of them, like everything else here, are good reproductions. Ask Isabel. She knows.'

I didn't ask Isabel, and somehow I felt that Ian wasn't surprised. He knew that I was too shocked. Nor did I mention the matter to Duncan because we didn't have a chance to be alone together for the rest of the evening.

Ian Forsythe departed early, explaining that he had to be in Perth next morning and was leaving right away, and not long after that the party broke up.

As I unhooked the taffeta gown my thoughts fluctuated between Ian's news and what I had learned about Shuna from Hamish Cameron.

Perhaps it was because I wasn't concentrating on the endless rows of hooks and eyes that I let them become tangled and found it impossible to get out of the dress. Automatically, I rang for Flora, but to my surprise it was Jeannie who came scurrying to answer; Jeannie with her hair in rollers and a pathetically worn dressing-gown.

She apologized profusely for her appearance and I felt a tightness in my throat. When she had unhooked me I opened the wardrobe, took out a fleecy house-coat, and wrapped her in it.

'And you can put that thing in the dustbin,' I told her, tossing the worn dressing-gown aside.

She stammered incoherent thanks and I urged her gently to the door, but there she lingered, looking back at me, her eyes agog. She was obviously anxious to speak, but I wanted no further thanks and was about to say good night firmly when she burst out, 'Please, miss, there's something going on!'

'Something going on?' I echoed, amused. 'What is it? A village scandal?'

'I mean here, Miss Lavinia. At Glenrannoch.'

I had begun to brush my hair, but now my hand was arrested. Then I asked slowly, 'What do you mean?'

'Food, for one thing – it's disappearing, miss. After every meal, some of it goes. And – and the way Flora's behaving, like not being in the house to answer your bell, and blankets and pillows disappearing from the linen room.'

My hairbrush fell with a clatter.

'*You mean* – ?'

Jeannie nodded her head vigorously.

'Luke, Miss Lavinia. She knows where he is. She's looking after him, but I'm worried-like, because he's not anywhere in the house, and when she goes out she's away quite a while. Her room's next to mine. I hear her go, and I hear her come back.'

Jeannie had already half opened the door. I went across swiftly, and shut it.

'Listen,' I said urgently, 'you must tell no one about this. *No one*, understand?'

She agreed at once. 'That's why I came to you, Miss Lavinia – I thought you might help. There's no one else who would; somehow they'd get the truth out of her and take poor Luke away, but I'm fond of him, and Flora Fyfe's been good to me. 'Sides, she loves him, Miss Lavinia.'

'I know. I know.' My thoughts were racing. 'We must help her, Jeannie, and the best way we can do that is to keep this to ourselves.'

She gave a sigh of relief, and I guessed she had been forced to speak because the need to confide and the urge to protect had been at war within her. Now her knowledge was shared with someone she could trust, she felt better.

'Oh, miss, he didn't do it, did he? I've known Luke Fyfe ever since I came to Glenrannoch straight from school. He's like a child, gentle as a lamb, and he loved that puppy.'

'I'm quite sure Luke didn't do it, Jeannie. That's why we're going to keep silent, you and I. But I'm glad you told me. Now go to bed, and behave as if nothing had happened.'

She beamed proudly. 'That's the way I've been behaving, Miss Lavinia, but it'll be easier to keep it up now.'

'Good girl, but there's something you *must* do – come directly to me when you hear Flora go out tomorrow night, then go back to your room, and stay there.'

After Jeannie had gone, I sat down and thought long and hard. I could follow Flora if, between the time Jeannie came to me and the time I got downstairs, she was still within sight, or I could wait in her room until she returned. Wherever Luke was, I had to know, and Flora must be made to realize that I was her ally, not her enemy.

But two questions still remained unanswered. If Luke was innocent of strangling Jock – who was guilty?

And had the poison really been in my coffee?

CHAPTER TWELVE

My studio, if not entirely finished, was habitable. I could start work.

Next morning I set off for the mills with enthusiasm, cutting down to the ferry through Invercoe. This took me past Hamish's cottage and why I chose this route instead of the main glen road I did not know and later regretted, for as approached the house the front door opened and he emerge with Isabel.

My foot went down on the brake automatically, but it wa too late now. To reverse would attract attention and they seemed too absorbed in each other to notice if a car went by Better drive on, I thought, and wondered why I felt like a intruder just because a man and a woman came out of a house early in the morning and stood together, hands clasped A woman whose husband had driven off to Perth the nigh before . . .

My dashboard clock said nine.

I accelerated and shot past, my eyes on the road. Whether they saw me or not, I had no idea, nor did I glance in my driving mirror to find out. Spying was distasteful. Also, I didn't want to see their parting.

I drove on to the ferry feeling unreasonably depressed, and telling myself that nine o'clock in the morning was as good an hour as any for a friend to drop in on another.

And to stand on the doorstep in a lingering farewell?

I refused to heed the implication of that. I had always prided myself on never sitting in judgment on the love affairs of others. I knew already that there was a special quality in the friendship between those two; not only Aunt Mary had hinted at it, but Malcolm had openly indicated it in Isabel's presence the first time I visited Kyleven, when he referred to Hamish as 'he from whom she had no secrets . . .'

As a woman has no secrets from a lover?

Hell, I thought furiously as I drove off the ferry and headed towards Fort Willim. If a woman was good-looking, with a husband who was away a lot, a husband who was apparently something of a rolling stone and therefore very likely to be neglectful, it wasn't surprising if she turned to another man for comfort, even to a younger one. And many a man has loved a woman older than himself.

I let the Triumph G.T.6 have its head in de-controlled areas. Its leaping power had a tonic effect upon me, and with the additional need for concentration I was able to pull my mind away from that intimate little scene at Hamish's front door, but what puzzled me was my urgen need to do so. Looking the thing squarely in the face, I realized that I just didn't want to know about any relationship between them.

The sight of my studio was more than welcome. My long work desk was ready and waiting, the clear unblemished light shining down on it from above. All it needed was a drawing board, a good supply of cartridge paper, a stack of pencils, and I could set to work right away, undisturbed by the noise of the workmen fitting up shelves. Once lost in work, I was always deaf to the world.

Malcolm thrust his head round the door and said, 'I saw you drive in, and thought I might entice you to spend the afternoon with me. This weather is too good to use up indoors, but that look in your eye tells me I haven't a hope.'

I told him he was right, and that if I could lay my hands on drawing materials I would start right away. Supplies had been ordered, but not yet arrived.

'You could chase them up if you went to see Menzies and MacIntyre; they're the stationery dealers in Fort William. If the stuff hasn't come, I dare say they'll have something in stock for you to be going on with. I'll run you there.'

I thanked him, but declined, saying I would go down later, then I headed for the stock-room, intent on making a selection of fabrics first.

Malcolm came with me, determined not to be shaken off, trying to entice me with the prospect of lunch in the country, but, as usual, he underrated me. Designing clothes was as compulsive with me as painting was to an artist, or writing to a writer, and I had been away from it for too long. A sandwich and a cup of coffee at my desk appealed to me more, but when I said so he groaned.

'You're everything that kid cousin of mine says you are!'

'Moira? And what does she say I am?'

'Dedicated. She says you have that look about you. "She's got a dedicated passion for clothes", she said last night on our way home from your place. She added that you wear them well and that this was probably why Hamish Cameron couldn't take his eyes off you. She admitted she was as jealous as hell, so I told her to gear herself up properly if she wanted to lure him. She does, the poor kid, but she's clueless. Can't you make her realize that the rag trade isn't confined to rags? My dear Lavinia, you're blushing! What brought that on, I wonder? And I didn't know young women in this day and age could do it.'

Neither did I. It was a long time since I had blushed and was furious with myself for doing so now. It was sparked by Malcolm's remark that Hamish couldn't take his eyes off me last night and for some reason I very much wanted to believe it.

'Why does she want to lure him?' I asked at random, anxious only to turn the conversation away from myself.

'Because she's mad about the man. I'll have to get a bad reputation myself, then I'll have the pick of all the women I want.'

'What do you mean, a bad reputation?' I wanted to know, yet dreaded to hear, but too many people had hinted about Hamish Cameron's past and now my curiosity had to be satisfied.

Malcolm scoffed. 'Don't tell me you don't know. I can't imagine that self-righteous aunt of yours concealing the truth about the disreputable Hamish. He's got a record. A conviction. Only he was let off with a very heavy fine, which was lucky considering the offence. Of course, breeding race horses was out from then on and he was banned by the Jockey Club, which was why he quit Newmarket and landed up here as a vet.'

I stood stock still.

'You mean – ?'

'I mean that he used to breed race horses down at Newmarket. He was a vet as well, and the poor fool should have stuck to it.'

'Don't call him that! Don't talk about him like that!'

Malcolm raised his eyebrows. 'My, my, you're hot in his defence! Has he hooked you, too? First my aunt, then my kid cousin, and now you – I don't believe it. I thought you'd been around; living it up in London and all that jazz.'

'I was a hard-working dress designer in London, which I mean to be here, and that has nothing whatever to do with the way I feel about Hamish Cameron. He's been decent to me, and I don't care for people I like being maligned.

Now tell me what he was convicted for. If he *was* convicted.'

'Like it or not, my darling Lavinia, he was. Nobbling. Doping race horses, in other words.'

'*I don't believe it!*'

Malcolm looked at me with unexpected shrewdness and asked, 'Why not?'

'It's out of character.'

He shrugged. 'Facts are facts. He couldn't evade them.'

I became aware that we had come to a halt outside the stock-room. I pushed open the door and Malcolm followed me inside.

'What was he doing, living in Newmarket?' I asked at random.

'His people moved south when he was young.'

'And after – after this horrible business – he came here?'

'At my aunt's suggestion, I believe. A new start, and all that. Her parents and his had always kept in touch. His parents aren't alive any more, and the whole unpleasant business happened after they died, which was a good thing. But Camerons are plentiful hereabouts, and he stems from the Lochiel branch – *the* main branch. Are you sure I can't entice you out this afternoon?'

'Quite sure,' I said, and was hardly aware of his departure until I saw him through the window of the stock-room, driving out of the courtyard in his vivid gold Pontiac, golf clubs prominent in the back. I wasn't surprised when he turned out of the gates on to the road to Spean Bridge, and thought in passing that unless he changed radically this particular Matheson wasn't going to be an asset to the mills.

Then my thoughts took a quick turn back to Hamish Cameron. That I was shocked by the story about him couldn't be denied, but my swift defence of him had been instinctive and strong, prompted by the belief that a man who plainly loved animals would hardly be the type to dope race horses for his own benefit.

'*Facts are facts. He couldn't evade them.*'

Damn Malcolm Matheson! I thought furiously, hating him now for telling me the story. Hating myself for listening. But now I really did understand Duncan's veiled attitude to the man.

For the next hour I forced myself to concentrate on select-
ing fabrics for my first designs, then set out for Fort
William to visit Menzies and MacIntyre. The mills were
about a mile outside the town: I had need of fresh air
and decided to walk. I was strolling along the road, gazing
at the view across Loch Linnhe and watching a MacBrayne
steamer setting out for Skye, and thinking that I would have
missed the beauty of all this had I been driving, when a car
came racing up behind me. I leapt for the kerb, felt a blind-
ing pain as something hit me, and was only aware of a
flash of bright gold accompanied by the roar of a powerful
engine as I went pitching down into oblivion.

I wakened in a hospital bed. The face of a nurse swam
into focus, then retreated, replaced by that of a man in white,
with a stethoscope round his neck. I heard him ask how
I felt and murmured stupidly, 'Terrible,' then welcomed the
darkness which closed in again, obliterating the pain in my
head.

Next time I wakened more fully. Isabel was beside me. I
saw concern in her face, and thought how nice she was and
wished I could dislike her. There seemed to be some reason
why I should, but I couldn't think what it was. She put out
a hand and touched my forehead, and it was so gentle it was
like my mother's touch.

Someone other than Isabel asked if I could remember
anything, and I saw a policewoman with a notebook at the
ready. 'You were run down by a car,' she said. 'A hit-and-
run driver. Please tell me everything you can recall.'

Hit-and-run? *Malcolm?* I didn't believe it. But that flash
of gold and that powerful roar . . .

I shook my head helplessly, pretending to recall nothing,
and an officious voice said, 'She has had concussion. Not
severe, but she must rest.'

I saw relief in Isabel's eyes, and annoyance in the police-
woman's as they drew aside and let the Sister take over,
and before I fell asleep I was glad I had said nothing about
the Pontiac Firebird rushing up behind me.

Apart from concussion, there was no serious damage. Forty-
eight hours, and I would be able to go home, they told me
later. The pain in my head was less, but still there; not

enough to prevent me from thinking, however, and in the antiseptic silence of my room I thought as hard and as clearly as I was able, but out of it came only one coherent memory – the roar of a powerful engine, a bright flash of gold, an unseen face at the wheel of a car which deliberately bore down on me. It had been no accident, unless the car was out of control. The stretch of road had been deserted; not a soul in sight. So – no witnesses.

I wondered what had happened to the car. If it had been out of control, it would have crashed and the driver injured, or detained. There would have been no need for a police-woman at my bedside, waiting to question me about a hit-and-run driver, and when she paid me a second visit I re-peated that I couldn't remember a thing. I had seen nothing; heard nothing but the sudden roar of an engine. A powerful engine? I shook my head helplessly again, saying that surely any engine would sound powerful, rushing up suddenly out of nowhere.

The policewoman looked frustrated and went away, un-aware that I felt even more so because for the life of me I couldn't understand why Malcolm, of all people, should run me down.

Later, and disturbingly, I recalled other things; that Mal-colm had been in the main hall of the mills when the door leading into my studio passage had suddenly opened causing a wind to come hurtling through and sending my sky-light crashing; that the road in which the Firebird had hit me was that leading from Spean Bridge, where the golf club was situated, and that more than an hour had elapsed since he had driven out of the courtyard, heading for it, and before I left the mills to walk into Fort William. That had given him time to drive the ten miles to the golf club, turn round, and come back – or to park nearby and wait for me to emerge. And it had been he who advised me to visit Menzies and MacIntyre . . .

If I had been driving instead of walking, would he have risked a crash, causing damage to his precious car and, inevit-ably, detection, or would he have waited until some other opportune moment when I was on foot? Somewhere nearer home, perhaps on an isolated road near the glen?

I moved restlessly, feeling that all these bewildering

thoughts were simply sending me up a blind alley, and that my shocked state must be enlarging them into outsize questions which had no sense and no answers.

By the time Isabel came to see me next morning, I had managed to suppress them sufficiently to maintain my silence, and I was glad of this because Isabel had news. Malcolm's car had been stolen from the car park at the golf club yesterday, and had not yet been found.

Only her hands, agitated, nervous, betrayed her tension.

'Malcolm is in a state about it,' she assured me. 'Not so much about the theft of the car, but about what happened to you. The thief must have been making a fast getaway when he knocked you down.'

I asked slowly, 'What makes you so sure it was Malcolm's car that hit me?'

'I'm not!' She spoke quickly; too quickly. 'It just seems possible, that's all. Car-thieves surely try to get away fast, and it seems logical . . .' After the hurried answer, her voice trailed away uncertainly, and a silence fell between us. She finally broke it by asking, 'Are you certain you didn't catch a glimpse of the driver?'

I answered honestly that I had caught no glimpse, and the relief in her wide-set eyes convinced me that she was anxious to exonerate her nephew from any suspicion of reckless driving.

'If the car *was* Malcolm's, it's sure to be found,' I told her. 'It's unlikely that there's another Pontiac Firebird in the district, and it's very noticeable. I should have thought a car-thief would have gone for one less conspicuous.'

She agreed, but there was a restraint between us from that moment. I was glad when the nurse appeared with tea and so diverted the conversation. Isabel accepted a cup absently, but to me it was unexpectedly welcome.

'I can do with that,' I declared. 'I hope it's hot as love and sweet as hell.'

The nurse laughed and said I must be feeling better. I was. So much better that I was impatient to get out of here and back to Glenrannoch, because I had just remembered Luke, and that Jeannie might have been wanting to contact me last night.

To make conversation, I asked after Moira and Ian. Isabel

said that Moira was bored, as usual, and perhaps it was about time she got a job of some kind during vacations, and that Ian was still away in Perth.

'You remember,' she reminded me. 'He went later that night, the night we came to dinner. That was why he wasn't around to drive me into Fort William when my car went wrong next morning. I didn't discover it until Malcolm had already left. I managed to trundle it down to the local garage and then called on Hamish to see if he was going near the mills. Unfortunately, he had calls to make across Rannoch Moor.' She smiled suddenly. 'I saw you drive past his house and tried to hail you, but you didn't see me. By the time I walked down to the ferry, you had gone, of course. I was late getting to the mills that day, because I had to catch a bus from North Ballachulish on the other side.'

I wondered why she had to make such a lengthy explanation, and the only logical answer was that she knew I had seen her leaving Hamish's house after breakfast the next morning, and a cover-up story was necessary. I felt suddenly depressed again.

'And what of Luke?' I asked with an effort. 'Are they still searching the glen?'

She told me sadly that Mountain Rescue thought there was no likelihood of his being anywhere in the hills now, and the whole thing was entirely in the hands of the police, who were organizing searches farther afield.

'What puzzles me,' she finished, 'is how a man like Luke can evade detection, apart from hiding in some place like Ossian's Cave, and that doesn't really offer concealment because, as you know, it's no more than a cleft, and at a pitching angle at that. No one could stay comfortably in such a place. Anyway, it's been searched.' She added compassionately, 'This must have hit you hard, Lavinia – about Luke, I mean. And I was so sure you were right about him.'

'And now you're not?'

Her shoulders rose and fell, and suddenly she seemed tired; excessively tired. The kind of tiredness caused by worry and anxiety, which left no room for worry about anything or anyone else.

'If it's Malcolm you're anxious about,' I said gently, 'please don't be. If his car was stolen, he's in the clear.'

Her sharp reaction took me by surprise.

'*If* his car was stolen? Of course, it was stolen! Why shoul
I tell you so if it weren't true?'

I was so startled that I could only stare at her. This wa
an unexpected side of Isabel's normally serene and happ
nature. Tension seemed to crackle in the silent room, and no
even the sudden opening of the door broke it.

Duncan looked from one to the other of us, then demande
curtly, 'Are you upsetting Lavinia? I won't have her harasse
by questions, Isabel. Please leave her alone.'

I saw tears start in her eyes. 'I – I didn't mean – I'm sorry
Lavinia.'

I reached out and touched her sleeve, wanting to say tha
I had nothing to forgive, wanting to re-establish the likin
which had sprung between us at our first meeting, but suddenly that seemed long ago and now there was a rift betwee
us.

The next moment she was gone, and Duncan was placing
flowers beside me and saying that he hoped the hospital wa
right in discharging me so soon. 'I'll have a word with Siste
before I go. If you're not absolutely fit by tomorrow morning, you're to stay here.'

'I shall be perfectly fit. I feel better already, and Siste
says I can get up for lunch. All I have is a lingering headache, and that will be gone after another night's sleep.
Besides,' I finished, 'I want to get home.'

It was the first time I had referred to Glenrannoch as
home and, despite its shadows and its fears, and the things
which had happened there, I realized that this was how I
thought of the place now. A home which I wanted to bring
to life again, chasing away those shadows and fears.

Duncan said he would call for me in the morning, and
that he would tell Sister on his way out. I nodded absently,
my thoughts elsewhere, and was scarcely conscious of the
intent look he focused on me. I was thinking that I had to
talk to Flora, and soon.

'Did you hear what I said, Lavinia?'

'Oh – yes – and thanks, Duncan. You're very kind . . .'

'Kind? Is that how you think of me – only as kind?'

The awful thing was that it seemed to me now that this
was true. I couldn't think when the change-over had come

from strong awareness to fond acceptance.

'I like you enormously, Duncan. You know that.'

'Like?' It was a disappointed echo. 'I thought – hoped. You know how I feel about you.'

The tone of his voice made me feel guilty. I rubbed my forehead mechanically, and immediately he was solicitous again.

'You're in pain,' he said, but when I repeated that it was only the remnants of a headache he brushed that aside, eager to blame the concussion for the lack of response to him. But I knew that wasn't the cause, which stemmed from the stab of jealousy I had experienced when driving past Hamish's house yesterday morning, and the disappointment which had lingered with me all the way to the mills.

This was the reason why a division had come between Isabel and myself, and why I didn't want to know about any relationship between her and Hamish.

It hurt.

'I'm tiring you,' Duncan said, promptly making me feel even more guilty. 'I'll leave you to rest, then you'll be yourself again, and so will things between us.' He gave that flashing smile of his and finished, 'I always was an optimist!'

I was scarcely conscious of his kiss upon my cheek. I was glad when he went; glad to be alone. Thoughts were crowding in again, and prominent amongst them was the fact that where Luke was concerned – or, more particularly, where Flora was concerned – I needed an ally stronger than Jeannie, and I could only think of one possible person.

If I had prayed for him to arrive, my prayers could not have been answered more effectively, for soon after breakfast the next morning a nurse opened my door and announced that I had a visitor. 'Sister says you can see him if you like, Miss MacDonald, although it isn't official visiting time, but since you are leaving this morning . . .'

I was already up and dressed, waiting for Duncan to collect me. Instead, Hamish stood in the doorway, almost filling it. Sun streaming through the window lit his sandy hair and lightened his blue eyes, and suddenly I was remembering him as I had first seen him, looming solidly above me in fog. He seemed as dominant now, as then.

'I heard you were being discharged this morning. I cam
to see if you are fit to be.'

No greeting. No preliminaries. Directly to the point. Tha
was, and always would be, Hamish Cameron.

'I'm perfectly fit.'

'No headache? No hangover?'

'Ask the House Physician. He's been to see me.'

The nurse, departing, nodded affirmation.

'*And* signed her discharge papers. You'll be fine now, Mis
MacDonald.'

The door closed behind her.

'Right,' said Hamish. 'Ready, then? I presume you've n
overnight bag, since you were brought in as a casualty.'

I nodded, indicating the discarded hospital clothes. 'They
lent me those, and someone cleaned up my suit for me. .
gather it was a bit of a mess.' I was resorting to unnecessary
explanations as a stop-gap, a time filler, because his arriva
seemed to have thrown me off-balance. I said wildly, ']
can't come with you. Duncan is collecting me.'

'When?'

'Some time today. This morning, I expect.'

'Then I'll leave a message with Sister, telling him you've
gone.'

There was no protest I could make; he simply took charge
and I let him, feeling shakier than I expected as we walked
from the hospital to his ancient Bentley, then his strong
hold on my elbow steadied me and his voice said, 'Take it
easy. No need to hurry, Lavinia, my lovely.'

He shouldn't call me that; it was too disturbing, coming
from a man like him. From Malcolm, it would be no more
than a casual endearment, from Duncan a term of affection
which he would want me to take as something more, but
from Hamish Cameron, frequently taciturn and never
demonstrative, it went right home and set my blood pounding
so fiercely that I had to turn my face away, knowing it would
betray me.

Lavinia, my lovely . . .

But what of Isabel? The thought steadied my racing pulses
and brought me down to earth. What had happened to me,
to allow an innocent phrase to assume so much significance?

By the time he placed me in the passenger seat I was

calm again, but I knew that his sideways glance was summing me up. 'I hope you didn't insist on leaving the hospital,' he said. 'Another day safely in that bed mightn't have been a bad idea. At least I wouldn't be worrying about you.'

'No need to worry about *me*,' I said cheerfully. 'I've more lives than a cat.'

'So it seems.' The Bentley nosed its way through the hospital gates and headed towards home. 'And it seems you need them. Remember what I said, the day I told you about the real cause of Jock's death?'

I moved impatiently. 'That theory is exploded. The theory about the codicil, I mean. I was beginning to be convinced – really frightened, in fact – until this hit-and-run driver made for me yesterday, miles away from Glenrannoch. And that was largely my own fault. I was strolling along the road instead of keeping to the pavement. The car probably hit me accidentally, and the driver panicked and went on.'

'Stop kidding yourself!' His voice was explosive. 'Or are you trying to make excuses, covering up for someone at Glenrannoch?'

There he was absolutely wrong, and I said so. The car had belonged to no one at Glenrannoch. He caught at that. 'Then you *did* see it? Isabel said you didn't.'

I stalled. 'Only a flash of colour, and I might have been wrong. It happened so suddenly.'

He demanded to know what colour, and although I had managed to dodge this question with everyone else, I couldn't with Hamish Cameron.

'I think it was gold – this new burnished gold that's fashionable now. Lots of them about.'

'Not in these parts yet.' He drove for a while in silence, apparently intent upon the road, and I relaxed, thinking I was to be spared further questioning, but suddenly he said, 'You know Malcolm's new car was stolen from the golf club?'

'So Isabel told me.'

I felt, rather than saw, his sideways glance, and sensed a challenge in it, a touch of anger perhaps, as if declaring that Isabel wasn't a liar. I didn't think she was, but there was a strong maternal instinct in the woman which might make her protect her nephew. Alternatively, Malcolm might have abandoned the car after hitting me, and told his aunt

that it had been stolen, and she would naturally believe him.
My thoughts began to go round in circles again and I sighed
involuntarily. At once Hamish put out his hand and touched
mine.

'Forget it,' he said gently. 'We'll talk again when you've
got over this shock. But I want you to promise me – '

He broke off. We were approaching the ferry, slowing
down in a line of cars, and rounding the bend ahead of us
was Ian Forsythe's. Glancing at Hamish, I knew he had seen
it.

'So Ian has come home,' I said. 'I thought he had gone
to Perth for the rest of the week.'

'He comes and goes,' Hamish answered indifferently. 'That
happens in his line of work.'

'Which I gather he hasn't been in very long.'

'Who told you that?'

'Duncan. He said Ian's only been in the antiques business
for a couple of years or so, and is not sufficiently experienced
to value the collection at Glenrannoch.'

Hamish's voice seemed guarded as he answered, 'It's true
he is fairly new to the trade – '

' – but knowledgeable enough to state emphatically that the
antiques at Glenrannoch are all worthless. Fakes, in fact.'

The car slowed to a standstill, but only because the ferry
wasn't in and every car was forced to do the same. Nevertheless, I had the distinct feeling that Hamish put his foot
on the brake rather more sharply than necessary, but his
only comment was, 'He said that, did he?'

'Also that my grandfather parted with the originals years
ago. He told me to ask Isabel; that she knew.'

'And did you?'

'No. Duncan's put a valuation in hand for probate. That
will prove things one way or the other. What was it you
wanted me to promise?'

The ferry had berthed; cars were streaming off. When
the last had disembarked we began to move forward and I
saw Ian Forsythe's move on to the deck well ahead of us.

Hamish didn't answer until he had finished manoeuvring
the Bentley into position. I caught a glimpse of Eilean Munde
and the outline of its ruined chapel. Brenda was right – it

looked a pretty island; I must visit it some time.

Hamish said quietly and firmly, 'I want you to promise me that if you're uneasy in any way, frightened in any way, you'll telephone me. And use your bedroom extension. It will be more private, unless anyone listens in.'

'I haven't a bedroom extension.'

'Then what's happened to it?'

'I don't know what you mean. There hasn't been an extension in my bedroom since I arrived. Was there before?'

'Definitely.'

'How do you know?'

'Your grandfather often telephoned me from there when he became bed-ridden. I'd go and play chess at his bedside. He rang me from there the day he called me to witness the codicil. Flora will remember. She was the other witness.'

'Flora!'

'Why not? The woman can write; she's not illiterate. In fact, she's an intelligent woman.'

'She must be,' I said involutarily. 'She's hidden her son very effectively.'

The rattle of chains lowering the landing deck cut into the conversation. Cars revved. Further talk was impractical until we were driving up the curve towards the glen, past the piles of disused slate standing like memorials to the once prosperous industry of Ballachulish. Then Hamish said, 'What's all this about Flora hiding Luke?'

I told him all I knew, all I suspected. 'She's frightened. She knows they'll take him away.'

'Then all we have to do is assure her that it can't be done without her permission. Only she can sign the necessary papers and only you can order Luke to leave Glenrannoch. You're the owner.'

'It hasn't been finalized.'

Hamish said wryly, 'The wheels of God and the law grind slowly, but meanwhile no one else has any authority of possession, or the authority to order anyone out of the place.'

We didn't speak again until we reached Glenrannoch.

The day was warm; the heavy front door stood open on to the great hall, and as we mounted the steps voices came to us, echoing in its vast space – shrill, argumentative, but not those of Aunt Mary and Brenda. These tones were less modulated, the high voices of the two girls, Jeannie and Maggie.

'Ye'll say nothing, d'ye hear?' Jeannie's voice came to me clearly, its accent thickened, as always when she became excited or worked up. 'Ye'll keep a still tongue in that blabbing mouth o' yours, Maggie Munro!'

It was like walking into the middle of a play, with the two main characters centre stage and, standing up left, the silent figure of Flora, watching and listening. Jeannie had a broom and a duster in her hand, and at Maggie's feet was a scuttle of logs.

'That I won't, Jeannie MacIntosh!' She flung back. 'Too many things've gone from the larder, and milk from the dairy, and an oil stove, too, the one stored in the scullery. And when McCulloch from the village called today, what d'ye think he brought? Three gallons of oil, that's what! And oil hasn't been used in this house for many a year. What for, thinks I, what *for*? Well, I'd have to be right daft not to guess the answer – for the stove what's disappeared along with the food and blankets, and the rest. *She's* taking them, that old cow, Flora Fyfe – '

'Hold your tongue, girl!'

It was the first time I had ever heard Flora's voice rap out so venomously, and the girls spun round as if shot.

'You, Maggie – put those logs where they should be and get back to the kitchen.'

The girl heaved the logs sullenly towards one of the Gothic fireplaces, muttering something about doing a man's work, but Jeannie remained where she was, her colour high, her eyes on Flora's face.

I said, 'That's all right, Jeannie. You may go too,' and she spun round in relief, stammering, 'Oh, Miss Lavinia, thank God you're back!'

Flora came forward slowly and respectfully. 'I hope you're fully recovered, Miss Lavinia?' She spoke calmly enough, but beneath her apron I could see that her hands were tense.

I said, 'Come into the morning-room, Flora.'

When the door closed behind us I said quietly, 'Now tell me where you've hidden Luke. I want him to come home.'

Her rigid, emotionless face cracked. Her mouth moved

162

wordlessly. Behind me, Hamish said, 'She means it, Flora. Do you think Andrew MacDonald would have sent Luke away from this house? You told me once how kind he was to your son, even as a boy – and boys aren't always kind to those less fortunate. Well, this is Andrew MacDonald's daughter, and she's made the same way.'

She broke down then, and seeing a woman like Flora Fyfe break down is something I never want to see again; years of pent-up agony overflowing, a lifetime of suppressed suffering bursting its bonds.

Hamish urged her into a chair and I knelt beside her and took the work-roughened hands in my own, saying nothing until the strength which the years had given her forced back her self-control, then I said gently, 'He's safe, isn't he? You've looked after him, I know.'

She nodded wordlessly, the wrinkles on her face deepening.

'He is well?' I asked.

'Well enough.' Her voice choked. 'Safe. Or was.'

'And will be again. Take us to him.'

That was Hamish, and she turned and looked at him. So did I. There was so much kindness in his face that I could scarcely imagine it ever looking stern or forbidding.

I said to him, 'Tell her what you told me – that no one can force her to have her son committed, and that I won't allow him to leave this house. It's his *home*. He's safer and happier here than anywhere!'

I don't think she was aware of how tightly her hands held on to mine.

'You – mean this, Miss Lavinia?'

'She means it,' Hamish confirmed.

'But the others – your aunt, and Mrs MacDonald, and even Mr Campbell, though he's always been a fair-minded man. They'll insist on sending him away for good.'

'They can't, Flora. I won't allow Luke to be sent from Glenrannoch.'

It all seemed so simple now that I wondered why I hadn't worked it out for myself. The man would have to be a criminal for real pressure to be brought to bear, and it would have to be proved that he was responsible for Jock's death before he could even be prosecuted for that, and if the police

wanted to question him — which they would only be able
to do through his mother — I would simply remind them
that the dog was mine, that his death was accidental, and
that I wished the matter to be dropped.

It still took some time to convince Flora, and I think it
was finally Hamish's doing more than mine because she had
known him longer and he had always been protective towards
Luke, but finally she trusted us both and when I asked her
to take us to her son, to my astonishment she led us straight
to the chapel.

CHAPTER THIRTEEN

'But I searched here!' I cried. 'And so did everyone else.
I understand that the police even searched the family tomb
below!'

A flicker of self-satisfaction, a touch of triumph hovered
about her mouth.

'But not the Jacobites' hole behind it, Miss Lavinia. That's
been forgotten for many a year.'

I knew nothing about a Jacobites' hole, although I was not
surpised to learn that a chapel as old as this possessed one.

Flora took the key from its lock behind the porch and
we followed her inside. The first thing which struck me
was the dust about the place; in Luke's absence it had
accumulated. I noticed flowers on the altar and thought
wryly that although my aunt was diligent in this respect
her devotion apparently did not extend to using a duster
when needed. But the flowers were wilting, so evidently
she had not been here to replace them, which was fortunate
in the circumstances. One sound from Luke might have
betrayed his hiding place.

But there I was wrong, for when we reached it, it proved
to be impenetrable as far as noise was concerned, although
access to it was surprisingly easy. To the left of the altar
was the organ, with a door beside it leading into the vestry.
Right of the altar was a single row of choristers' stalls and

behind this were iron railings flanking a short flight of steps leading downwards.

At the top of the steps were a pair of wrought-iron gates; I had noticed them on my previous visit and admired their fine scroll work. Flora led us through them and down the steps to the family vault. Taking a key from a niche in the stone wall, she unlocked the door and stood aside for us to enter.

My hesitation was momentary. I had expected a dark, dank place; instead, it was light and the air was fresh. There was nothing particularly eerie or depressing about the vault. Four stone steps led down again, taking the floor level some feet farther beneath the earth outside, but it was not submerged like a grave. Stained glass windows were set high in the walls, and I saw that ventilators had been inset at some later time.

There were carved stone effigies on a centre tomb, and a ledge running round the walls in which were coffins of my ancestors. More recently, small alcoves had been set in the walls, with caskets containing the ashes of those who had been cremated. The old form of burial had evidently been abandoned by my family. The newest casket caught my eye, with an incription set beneath it in the stone wall and I saw that it was my grandfather's – the once proud, invincible James MacDonald who still wielded a certain power over my life.

I saw then that Flora was walking straight to the centre tomb and running her fingers along a carved frieze of thistles entwined with heather. I saw her work-roughened hand pause at a certain spot, the thumb upon the upraised base of a thistle, and for a moment she looked at us with another glint of triumph in her face.

'The police spent a lot of time searching the vestry upstairs, and the organ cavity, but not enough time here,' she said. 'I brought them to the vault myself and stood beside this tomb, with my back to this very spot while they looked around. Not that they could look far. After examining the walls they did try to lift the lid of this tomb because one of them said these old places often had cavities wide enough to hide Jacobites on the run, and they thought maybe this tomb marked the entrance to such a place. That was an anxious moment for me; if they had started to poke amongst the carving I would have had to stand aside, but thank the good Lord, they didn't. They were being very kind to me because I was going to a lot of trouble to help them, and they wanted to spare me. I had brought them down here myself and that made them less suspicious. I was a mother anxious for her son to be found, thinking of every place where they could look. Short of opening up the coffins, and they'd have to get the family's permission for that, there seemed to be nowhere else down here where they could search, and in less than five minutes they'd left the place.'

Her thumb pressed sharply. I heard a grinding noise behind me, and spun round. One of the large stone wall slabs was slowly turning on a central axis. I heard an indrawn breath of surprise from Hamish and a gasp which I knew was my own. We watched as the concealed entrance opened up before us, the slab coming to a vertical halt so that a gap was revealed at either side, large enough for a person to slip through.

It was chilly in the vault, but through the aperture leading to the Jacobites' hole came an unexpected warmth which was fresh, not damp, and a glow of light which bore testimony to the miraculous way in which the concealed entrance fitted, for not one glimmer of light had penetrated any surrounding crack.

The next moment I was inside with the others. The hiding place was no bigger than a single cell, and in it was the camp bed, rugs on the stone floor, a card-table bearing crockery and an oil lamp which, even in daylight, had to be lit because, unlike the vault, this place had no window. Even so, it was ventilated; beneath the low roof, above ground level outside, a primitive grating admitted air.

Luke sat on the edge of the bed, quietly carving a piece of wood.

He lifted his head, smiling, expecting to see his mother and holding up the wood carving for her to see, as a child holds up a toy, and I saw that it was an animal – the crude shape of a little dog. There were others on the table in front of him.

Flora said apologetically, 'You'll forgive me, Miss Lavinia,

166

for stealing that wood from the woodshed, but I had to keep him occupied during the times he had to be here alone. When it was safe and no one was around, I'd take him out into the fresh air, into that wood at the back of the chapel, and again for a walk every night before settling him.' She nodded towards the paraffin heater which stood in a corner. 'I borrowed that, too, ma'am, but I paid for the oil myself.'

'You shouldn't have done so – you'll be refunded,' I said with a catch in my voice. I was profoundly moved by this woman's protection of her son.

Luke made an inarticulate sound and scrambled clumsily to his feet, excited because Hamish and I had come to see him, and the next moment he laid aside the knife he was carving with – a sharp knife, good for whittling or cutting; a knife no one would entrust to a dangerous person – and held out the little dog to me.

'He wants you to have it, Miss Lavinia.'

I took it gratefully, and held out my hand to him.

'We've come to take you home, Luke,' I said, and took hold of his great hand. He came with me like a child.

As we left the Jacobites' hole, something made me look back. Flora was gathering up Luke's clothes and Hamish had picked up a pair of boots from a corner. Absently, I noticed that they were caked with dried mud.

Hamish asked if they were Luke's, but she shook her head.

'They were there when I hid him, Mr Cameron. Someone must've thrown them away long ago. They're pretty old, aren't they? You don't see that kind of studded boots around much these days.'

'A strange place to throw them,' Hamish said reflectively. His thoughts seemed to be moving along channels where I could not follow.

I didn't spare the old boots another glance. I was too intent upon taking Luke home.

The four of us were walking back to the house when Duncan's car appeared round the curve in the drive and slowed perceptibly at the sight of us. I could see him at the wheel, with Brenda beside him, staring in surprise. Then he whirled to a stop before the front steps.

Car doors slammed, and the sound brought Aunt Mary to

one of the french windows opening on to the terrace, then Duncan was striding to meet us with his mother tripping along behind him. Then Aunt Mary's sharp footsteps come clacking along the terrace, her capacious bag swinging against her hip and her bony fingers diving into it automatically as she exclaimed, 'My goodness me, my *goodness* me!' until her words were stifled by a sugared almond.

As Duncan halted in front of us I heard a sharp breath of apprehension from Flora, immediately followed by Brenda exclaiming, 'You've found Luke! Oh, I'm so glad! Now he can be taken care of properly, poor man.'

But Duncan was looking only at me and there was vexation in his voice as he demanded, 'What made you leave the hospital without waiting for me, Lavinia? You knew I was calling for you.'

'I called for her instead,' Hamish put in calmly, 'and if you'll all step aside instead of standing there staring, I can take her indoors. She's had forty-eight hours in hospital and quite a bit of excitement to follow, so don't harass her with questions. Anything you want to know, I'll answer for her.'

I was conscious of Duncan's clutch at self-control, and only then did I recall the reason for his dislike of Hamish. I had completely forgotten that the man had a record, and that to a lawyer this made him not only untrustworthy but a very undesirable type. Somehow the story had a quality of unreality about it which made it impossible for me to accept; I had told Malcolm that it was out of character, and I still thought so.

I felt unexpectedly lightheaded, and realized that this homecoming, on top of concussion, had been more than 'a bit of excitement'; it had been an emotional experience which now set up an almost violent reaction. I wanted to push my way past everybody, and found myself doing so, still holding Luke's big hand.

'He's come home, he's come *home*,' I said forcefully, 'and he's staying here, so you can call off the hounds, the lot of you!'

I felt Brenda's arm go round my shoulders. 'I'll take you upstairs, my dear. You are overwrought. As for Luke, Duncan will take charge of him.'

I shrugged her arm aside.

'No. His mother will. Hamish, will you call off the search? Tell them Luke is safe.'

I handed the poor fellow over to Flora, and went up the steps on to the terrace, clutching the little carved dog in a hand which shook. Then I turned and looked back at the small tableau of people who were now the central characters in my life. Hamish Cameron dominated them all, although he stood apart.

Flora was leading her son away towards the domestic quarters, and Duncan came striding up the terrace steps until he was at my side.

'My dear Lavinia, I'm as glad as you that Luke is found, but naturally he can't stay at Glenrannoch.'

'Why not?'

'Why not?' Aunt Mary shrilled. 'It isn't safe!'

'*Why not?*' I repeated stubbornly.

Brenda interposed reasonably. 'You know what he did to poor Jock.'

'But I don't. And neither does anyone. You've got to have proof to accuse a man of an act of violence, even to a dog.'

Suddenly I felt tired, and was glad when Hamish took hold of my arm. I hadn't noticed him draw near.

'Later,' he said gently. 'You can say all you want to later.'

'No,' I insisted. '*Now.* And I only want to say one thing. I don't believe Luke killed Jock, and I won't let him go away, so will everyone stop trying to get rid of him or I'll begin to think there's some reason behind it all. Is someone here trying to make a scapegoat of him?'

I was instantly ashamed. Aunt Mary looked outraged, Brenda dismayed, and Duncan concerned. He said in that understanding way of his, 'You *are* overwrought, Lavinia.. You don't know what you're saying.'

'I do, and I mean it, and I'm not going to apologize. But forget it, everyone, if it will make you feel happier.'

I turned on my heel, went indoors, and straight up to my room where I stripped and showered. I felt better after that, and decided that I really ought to apologize for being rude, and that I would take the first opportunity to do so. This came when I emerged from the bathroom and found Brenda waiting for me, sitting beside one of the tall windows.

'I knocked, but heard the shower running so I knew you couldn't hear me. I wanted to know if you were all right.'

'I'm fine. And I'm sorry I flew off the handle down there.'

She laughed. 'It does us all good at times, and no one took offence because we know that concussion can have after-effects.'

'Mine was mild and the only after-effect was a splitting head, now cleared. You can check with the hospital.'

'We did. I went along with Duncan, thinking you might be glad of a change of clothes.' She indicated a suitcase on my bed, containing make-up, underwear, and one of my tartan trouser-suits.

'That was good of you,' I said.

'We didn't know Hamish was calling for you.'

'Nor did I.' I began to cream my face, looking at Brenda through my dressing-table mirror as I did so. 'I'm glad of this chance to talk. I'm wondering why the telephone extension was removed from this room. I noticed the point on the skirting beside my bed. There appear to have been two. Was one for a house phone?'

I had deliberately examined the skirting when I came up, and now added, 'I'm glad the points weren't removed completely, because the instruments will be easy to reconnect, but why were they taken away?'

Brenda said it was her fault entirely. 'I should have had them installed again, but to tell the truth I completely forgot. The shock of James's death put the matter out of my mind. I had both telephones removed towards the end of his illness; I didn't want him disturbed.'

'But outside calls needn't have gone through to him, surely? Didn't the extension have one of those buttons to stop it ringing in here?'

'My dear, you didn't know your grandfather. The minute he heard the phone ringing downstairs he would lift the receiver to find out who was calling. He hated to feel cut off from the world.'

'Then he must have felt even more cut off when the phones were taken away.'

'By that time he was failing fast, too weak to either protest or care.'

I said slowly, 'Somehow I don't think you're telling me the whole truth.'

She gave a resigned sigh. 'I see I shall have to. You're a true MacDonald, Lavinia – direct and to the point about everything; impossible to fool, too. Well, there *was* another reason. When Mary was forbidden to visit her father, she was constantly ringing through to him from her room and upsetting him, so finally, on the doctor's advice, I had both instruments taken away so that he could be left in peace.'

I wiped the cream off my face with a tissue, still looking at her in the mirror.

'Why was Mary forbidden to visit her father?' When Brenda hesitated, I added impatiently, 'Don't hide anything from me. I'm one of the family. I have a right to know.'

'You have indeed, although I'd rather not refer to it. The truth is that almost from the day he began to be ill, certainly from the time it became apparent that he wasn't likely to recover, she was constantly reproaching him about his will and nagging him to change it in her favour. She insisted that she should rightfully inherit Glenrannoch.' Brenda gave a helpless shrug. 'Goodness knows, *I* didn't want the place, nor did I want to cut her out in any way. James provided well for me, and I was content. But Mary – well, you've been here long enough now to know what she is like. Full of resentments, real and imaginary. She believed I had influenced her father against her, and that when he died I would inherit Glenrannoch and be in a position to turn her out; I believe she even thought I might do so, because we've never got on together, but if the day ever came when she and I were left alone here (which heaven forbid!) the place could have been divided into two establishments with ease.'

'And she didn't like the idea?'

'One never knows what Mary likes, but I do know she would have been a great deal happier if *she* could have had the power to turn *me* out. I hate saying that, but it's true. She badgered poor James so much that I had to put a stop to it somehow. I appealed to Doctor MacFarlane and took his advice. But of course I should have had the extensions re-installed before you came.'

'No matter,' I answered easily. 'I'll have it put in hand

at once.' Brenda had reached the door before I added, 'What made my grandfather change his mind? What made him alter his will in my favour?'

Brenda looked surprised.

'But he didn't alter it until after your father was killed. He always intended that the inheritance should go down in a direct line to his son, even though Andrew had turned his back on it. He told me so when we married. Had I given him a son myself, that son would only have been second in the line of succession, Andrew being the elder. I understood and thought it right.'

'But the codicil – '

'Dividing Glenrannoch between Mary and myself, in the event of your turning you back on it also? That was an after-thought. Personally, I've always believed it was prompted by a desire to silence Mary's protests, and it did. She didn't make you particularly welcome when you came, I know, but to her you are at least "family"; I'm not. I have never once heard her complain about being cut out in *your* favour. Have you?'

That was true. I had not.

Of all the rooms at Glenrannoch, the one in which I felt most at home was the library. It had become a kind of refuge, a place where I could relax without fear of intrusion, for I had quickly discovered that neither Brenda nor Mary were great readers; Mary because her time was too much occupied with her hobbies and charitable activities, and Brenda – there my thoughts broke off. How *did* Brenda spend her time? Apart from arranging flowers and dealing with a few minor domestic matters, most of the responsibilities were left in Flora's capable hands and already the woman automatically discussed such things as catering and household matters with me, although I had had little experience in this line.

But I learned fast, and it was plain that Flora deemed it right that the new mistress should be consulted instead of the old. It was from Flora that I learned, and to whom I listened; Flora who initiated me into the established household routine and domestic management, and Brenda who stepped aside, allowing her to do so.

To me, it seemed that Brenda's sudden dinner party the other night, her planning of the menu, and her choice of guests without consultation with anyone, had perhaps been an impulsive clutch at former authority, a brief desire to retain earlier status; the queen of Glenrannoch stepping down from her throne but keeping one foot lingering there before finally abdicating. It had been an understandable gesture and as far as I was concerned my grandfather's widow was welcome to entertain at Glenrannoch whenever she wished. I decided to tell her so because it suddenly occurred to me that perhaps time was now hanging heavily on her hands.

Apart from weekly visits to the hairdresser in Kinloch-leven, occasional shopping trips, and pottering in the garden (as far as old Fergus, who had the proprietorial attitude of all gardeners, would allow anyone to encroach upon his territory without permission) I had no idea what Brenda actually did with her days. I knew she went to her Bridge Club in Fort William frequently, but I had never come home to find bridge parties in progress. Nor had I ever found her browsing amongst what she affectionately referred to as 'James's musty old books' – to which Mary always indignantly retorted that, musty or not, her father's library was an extensive and valuable one and she was glad to see his grand-daughter taking an interest in it.

Duncan had told me that it had been built up not only by James, but by his father and grandfather before him, and that James, in particular, had been an avid collector of books on Scottish history, particularly of Glencoe.

'He used to spend hours alone in there, steeping himself in it – and writing a lot, too. I used to wonder if he were planning a book himself, but he was a cagey old boy and wouldn't be questioned. This started about two years ago and we soon learned not to ask questions about what he was writing. My mother was glad he had an additional interest as he grew less and less able to take part in business affairs, so we used to leave him alone in there to his scribbling. The sad thing was that when he died we couldn't find any trace of a manuscript. He must have destroyed it in one of his moods.'

'What kind of moods?'

'Morose ones, when he couldn't bear anyone near him. At those times it was unwise to disturb him. The only thing that restored his good humour was chess, but unfortunately my mother wasn't a good player, and I had little spare time because I was becoming increasingly involved with my London tie-up. This gave Cameron the opportunity to get his foot inside the door, ingratiating himself with the old man.'

I protested that Hamish didn't strike me as being the type to ingratiate himself with anyone, but the remark earned only an indifferent shrug from Duncan, plus the comment that if Hamish had tried, it had availed him nothing because James MacDonald had not remembered him in his will.

I don't know why this conversation returned to my mind the afternoon after I came back from the hospital and wandered into the library, feeling in little mood for company. My grandfather's desk still held sheets of my drawing paper and a batch of discarded designs; I had taken the best ones to the mills to develop further. Tomorrow I would go back and continue with them, but today I felt lethargic and a session in the library seemed a better choice.

I was idly sketching when Duncan sought me out to tell me that his London office had called him urgently and he had to race off to catch a plane. He wanted me to promise to take things easy.

I said truthfully that I felt disinclined to do anything else, and that pleased him. The proprietorial air was back, but it sparked no pleasure in me as before. I had been glad of his protective interest when I first came to Glencoe, and now felt ashamed because I wanted, or needed, it no longer. On an impulse – of penitence? – I said swiftly, 'Come back soon, Duncan. Don't stay away too long.'

He came close to me then and I saw gratification in his eyes. 'I'll be back at the double,' he assured me, then kissed me lightly before leaving. I was glad he put no more into the gesture; perhaps he sensed that this was not the moment to be demonstrative.

I wished I could respond to him. I even told myself that perhaps the attraction which had sprung between us on arrival would come back, but in my heart I knew that I would never again feel more than affectionate trust of this man who, ideally, should be the one to fall in love with.

After he had gone, I sat staring at my drawing board, pencil dangling between my fingers, telling myself that Brenda had been right when saying that concussion could have after-effects. But in my case this was untrue and it was useless to seek excuses because a man known to be unscrupulous and dishonest had replaced in my mind a man who was wholly worthy.

Suddenly my interest in work flagged and, flinging my pencil aside, I wandered to the bookshelves. It seemed a long time since I had delved into the history of my ancestors, and now my fingers wandered across volumes on Culloden and Breadalbane, Cromartie and Inverawe, thence to the Annals of the First and Second Earls of Stair and the Memoirs of Sir Ewan Cameron of Lochiel . . .

'She fell in love, and ran away – with a Cameron of Lochiel.'

Shuna MacDonald, my lovely ancestress with whom I had such an affinity . . .

I jerked my attention back to the books and at last found what I sought. Immediately, I was carried into the past, when the Highland way of life was reaching its peak before beginning its tragic fall to extinction in the seventeenth century. I was lost in the turbulent days of William the Third, with the Clan Donald firmly entrenched in Glencoe, and the fatal morning of February 1st., 1692, rapidly approaching . . .

The day was bright, and along the shore road from Ballachulish a company of soldiers was marching towards the mouth of the glen. Someone was rushing to inform MacIain, and then came his sons, Ian Og and Alasdair Og, marching with a group of twenty men to meet the troops and find out their intentions – then relief because the Captain proved to be Robert Campbell of Glenlyon, uncle of Alasdair's wife.

Glenlyon was a vigorous man of sixty, whose weakness for cards and the bottle had incurred him so heavily in debt that he had seized the chance of a commission in the new Regiment of Argyll. Ian and Alasdair knew this, but greeted him politely. Glenlyon was cordial and apologetic as he told his Lieutenant to produce the billeting orders from his Commander; the MacIains were to house and feed the company because there was no room at the fort at Inverlochy.

Even more apologetically came the excuse that they had

175

come to collect arrears of cess and hearth money, a new tax imposed a couple of years ago, at which the MacIains had thumbed their noses. With his Ensign and Lieutenant, Glenlyon gave their paroles of honour that their intentions were not hostile, and the Gaelic code of hospitality compelled the clan to house and feed a company of hungry soldiers in a glen which could scarcely feed its own population at a time when winter food was running low. They took their guests on trust, welcomed them into their homes, shared their food and their beds and their roofs with them.

MacIain himself received Glenlyon and his company with dignity and friendship, but took the precaution of sending his teenage daughter to his summer shieling up in Gleann Muidhe to escape the soldiers' attentions – or perhaps because although he scoffed at the idea, he was then, if not later prepared to heed Alasdair Og's uncertainty.

I ceased to hear the solemn ticking of the library clock as the past took hold of me; I was there, joining in the evening ceilidhs in the houses, in the music, games, singing and story-telling; watching the forming of friendships and the swift growth of love affairs; sharing the unity of communal life based on mutual trust, so that within a few days Alasdair Og's uneasiness was being scoffed at and dismissed.

And yet I could feel his doubt persisting until his genial stubborn, forthright old father was demanding to know how he could possibly imagine they were under surveillance from the troops when he, the Chief, and his wife, had been left the privacy of their own house. He reproached his son for suggesting that this had been a wise move on Glenlyon's part, to avert suspicion.

And so followed nearly two weeks of genial companionship with the arctic winter conditions easing slightly on that memorable day of February 12th, and Glenlyon and his officer making their usual visit to take their morning draught with MacIain, and even accepting an invitation to dinner for the following night.

That same evening the two young MacIains went to play cards with Glenlyon in his billet at Inverrigan, Ian completely trusting, but Alasdair still uneasy and watching carefully when a runner arrived with a dispatch for Glenlyon whose hard-drinking face failed to hide the fact that he was taken aback by it. When asked by the young man what was wrong, his wife's uncle answered lightly that a soldier never knew what was to happen next, but he could play cards no more. There was trouble up at Glengarry. He would have to deal with it.

In the silence of the library I could hear the whisperings through the glen; I could feel the uneasiness and ever-increasing suspicion; I could see the brothers, on their way home from their card game, creep towards the window of one of the guard houses to overhear soldiers complaining that they would not mind fighting the men of Glencoe in battle, but this business could not be called honest soldiering. I watched as Alasdair promptly raced back and accused Glenlyon of duplicity; I heard the great man laugh and repeat his excuses about marching on Glengarry and demanding if he, his own nephew-in-law, really thought it possible that he could be preparing an attack on his niece, her husband, and their kin . . .

None of this satisfied Alasdair or his wife. They prepared for flight.

The hour fixed for the start of the attack was five o'clock, and as if to bring the whole thing vividly to life the long-case clock in the corner of the library boomed out five solemn strokes at that precise moment, taking me right into Alasdair's home as a servant rushed in, announcing that soldiers had been seen taking up positions with fixed bayonets, then I was watching their flight – Alasdair and his wife, his brother and others of the clan, collecting people as they went and making for the slopes of Meall Mor.

By ten o'clock the glen was asleep, except for the soldiers and guards at various posts. The night was dark; the weather had swung from moderate to freezing, with snow rapidly developing into a blizzard with a bitter gale from the north. I could feel the iciness of the night, the waiting silence, the grim foreboding between the bleak mountainous walls, and in the house of the Chief, I saw MacIain, who had dismissed Alasdair's last-minute warning and told him to go home, asleep in bed with his wife.

Then I heard the sudden knocking on the door of his house, followed by the friendly voice of Glenlyon's Lieutenant calling that he had come on urgent business; I saw a servant

admitting him with the Ensign, and watched them march
straight to the bedroom, where MacIain greeted them amiably and commanded the servant to serve drinks to his guests.
Then he began to dress, turning his back as he pulled on his
trews – and in horror I saw him shot by both, by one through
the back and by the other through the head.

He died instantly, falling beside the bed as his wife gave
a great cry and rushed to him; I saw her seized and her
rings torn off, her assailants using their teeth to wrench them
from her clenched hands; I saw her clothes stripped from her
until she rushed shrieking and naked into the blizzard – and
to her death.

I closed my eyes. I was shaking and sickened. All around
me was the horror of that night, with the young and the old
who could not reach the hidden passes being shot and left
for dead, their bodies thrown on to a rubbish dump and
abandoned. I could smell the acrid stench of smoke and
death in my nostrils, hear the weeping of the glen in my ears,
and see imprinted for ever in my mind, as they had been
imprinted for ever in history, the letters from Colonel Hill
to Hamilton, who was at Ballachulish with Duncanson, and
Duncanson's to Robert Campbell of Glenlyon, delivered
during that memorable game of cards:

'Sir, you are hereby ordered to fall upon the rebells the
MacDonalds of Glenco and put all to the sword under
seventy. You are to have special care that the old fox and
his sons do not escape your hands; you are to secure all
avenues, that no man escape. This you are to put in execution at five of the clock precisely; and by that time, or very
shortly after it, I will strive to be at you with a stronger
party. If I do not come to you by five, you are not to tarry for
me, but fall on. This is by the King's special commands, for
the good and safety of the Countrey, that these miscreants
be cut off root and branch. See that this be put in execution
without fear or favour, or you may expect to be dealt with
as one not true to King or Government, nor a man fit to
carry a commission in the King's service. Expecting you will
not fail in the fulfilling hereof, as you love yourself, I subscribe
this at Ballychyllis the 12 Feby. 1692.
ROBERT DUNCANSON.'

But beneath my horror ran a thread of triumph. The Massacre of Glencoe, remembered for ever after as 'slaughter under trust', had failed in its aim to cut off root and branch the rebel clan. The great majority had escaped despite blizzard and mountain hazards, for only the clansmen knew other avenues of escape which Glenlyon's men, in their ignorance, had left unguarded; secret routes used in affrays throughout the centuries by these wild and valiant tribesmen in their bastioned stronghold. The torrent of fusillades which echoed from Carnoch, Inverrigan, and Achnacon, and the flames of burning houses which lit the snow-laden sky, wiped out only a small section of an invincible and fighting people; people from whom had sprung men as proud and stubborn as James MacDonald, whose blood and character had been passed on to my father – and thence to me.

I thought with a sudden, choking pride: *I am a MacDonald, and proud to be.*

The sudden opening of the library door jerked me back to the present.

It was Malcolm, bearing flowers.

'I came to see how you were. Your aunt told me I'd probably find you here. She said you like this room as much as your grandfather did.' He glanced round expressively. 'I can't think why.'

I wanted to tell him that it was here that I had just discovered my true identity, and here where I had learned why my mother had fallen in love with my father. The Scots might be pugnacious, stubborn, and infuriating – but they were courageous, protective towards their women and, above all, men.

I pushed the volume I was holding back into its place and climbed down the library steps. Malcolm held out the flowers and said, 'For you, and thank God it didn't have to be a wreath!'

I burst out laughing. 'Whoever the hit-and-run driver was,' I said, 'his aim wasn't that good. I dodged just in time.' I saw to my surprise that it was six-thirty, and asked if he would like a drink.

'Not if it means joining your revered aunt.'

'Brenda will be there too.'

'She's out. A shopping trip to Oban, Mary said. Anyway, I came to talk to you, not them. I wanted to tell you that my car's been found, abandoned on a lonely road outside Fort William, with nothing but a drop in the petrol gauge to indicate that anyone had used it.'

'Nothing stolen?'

'Not even a costly new lighter my mother sent from America for my birthday. It was on the dashboard shelf.'

'A considerate thief,' I commented. 'One can only presume that he needed a car for urgent transport. A golfer late for a date perhaps?'

'Your guess is as good as mine. I merely want you to know that I wasn't driving it when you were knocked down.'

'You're the second person to assume that it was your car that did so. The first was your aunt. Why, I wonder?'

He said vaguely that it seemed the obvious conclusion; a thief in a hurry to get away and coming from the direction of the club. 'What else can one presume?'

'That he might have driven in the opposite direction, and that the car which hit me was an entirely different one.'

He was looking at me intently. Malcolm's eyes weren't always guileless. I said, 'If you're wondering if I saw anything, you must ask Isabel. I've answered all questions I'm prepared to answer on that score. By the way, how did you get home from the golf club without your car?'

He admitted rather sheepishly that he had pinched another. 'My Uncle Ian's, in fact. I saw it parked near the clubhouse and made use of it.'

'But your uncle was in Perth.'

'I know, but sometimes he leaves his car in Fort William and goes by train. He probably did so that evening because he dislikes night driving. Then he picks it up on the way back. When I saw it at the golf club I guessed Isabel had borrowed it in his absence; she goes for an occasional game when she has an afternoon off. I meant to go back and collect her, but she came home early. A friend had given her a lift.'

It all sounded very plausible. Too plausible. I didn't point out that it didn't tie up very convincingly because I had seen Ian Forsythe driving on to the ferry forty-eight hours later. I merely asked, as casually as possible, when his uncle had returned, and how he managed to get back to Kyleven without his car.

'But he didn't get back without it. Isabel and I used it to go to the mills next morning, and then a company car to get home, leaving Ian's in Fort William again for him to pick up on his return.'

'Which was when?'

'Earlier than expected. The day after, in fact.'

So it did all tie up, and any vague idea at the back of my mind that Ian Forsythe might not have gone away at all and that it was he who stole his nephew's car and attempted to run me down, faded into thin air. There was no plausibility about that either, for, like Malcolm, Ian Forsythe could have no motive for wanting me out of the way. Had that been the case, he could have disposed of me easily enough when he took me to Ossian's Cave; one slip on the mountainside could have sent me pitching down . . .

So it must have been the unknown car-thief, racing down to Fort William in the hope of escaping detection. It all seemed logical and acceptable now, even Isabel's anxiety to exonerate her nephew from any suspicion of reckless driving, although something about that still worried me. By the time she came to me with the story of the stolen car, she must have known that Malcolm had borrowed her husband's in its place and therefore could not have been driving the Pontiac.

If it was the Pontiac which hit me.

I seemed to be going round in circles, becoming prickly with suspicion and speculation. The wisest thing was to put the whole affair out of my mind and remember only what Hamish had said before we parted – that I was to telephone him if worried or frightened in any way. Duncan had said the same thing before dashing off to London. He had given me his office number and that of the hotel where he always stayed. I thought wryly that many a girl would enjoy having two men concerned about her. What *I* didn't enjoy was the necessity for it, and I could no longer delude myself that such necessity didn't exist. The more closely I became identified with Glenrannoch, the more obvious it seemed that someone was determined not to let me.

Malcolm didn't stay long, mainly because Aunt Mary joined us and refused to be shaken off, chattering away in

her feckless fashion while we drank sherry, the traditiona
pre-dinner drink at Glenrannoch. I resolved to order Campar
for my own consumption the next day, and a revolutionar
step that would be in her eyes . . .

I strolled across the garden with Malcolm. The evenin
was beautiful and in the distance I could see Eilean Munde
green against the sparkling waters of the loch, with the dir
outline of the ruined chapel. Now was an ideal time to rov
there. We had our own boat-house down by the loch and i
would by easy enough to cross the eight hundred yards o
water between the island and the shore of Invercoe. I wa
about to suggest to Malcolm that he might come with me
when a man and a woman came through the gap in th
beech hedge from Kyleven.

Ian Forsythe, and Brenda.

She waved, and they came towards us.

'I thought you'd gone on a shopping orgy to Oban,' Mal
colm chaffed. 'That was what Mary implied.'

Brenda laughed. 'Shopping, yes – an orgy, no. And wasn'
it lucky? Ian was going there and took me with him. I wa
glad, because I don't like driving.'

I thought how charming she looked. A change had com
over her since my arrival at Glenrannoch, the strain left upo
her face after her husband's death having completely dis
appeared. I had thought her lovely when we first met, bu
now she seemed to have acquired that second blooming whic
sometimes comes to women in their late forties, a mellow kin
of loveliness which often leads to a renewal of love in thei
life. She would marry again, I was sure. I hoped it would b
to someone local so that we would keep in touch.

I also thought what an ideal solution it would be as fa
as Glenrannoch was concerned. To have the two wome
remaining beneath its roof, to have to share my home wit
them permanently and act as a buffer between them, was
prospect I had thought about more than once and turne
away from instinctively, but to share it with Mary alon
would be simple. I would divide the house into two self
contained units and give one to her. She would then ow
it and feel that she had not been defrauded out of her right
ful share in the family home, and I would own my half an
live my life independently of her.

Ian Forsythe was asking how I felt after my mishap and repeated the assurances that I was perfectly well. He was handsome man, but I found myself reflecting that rolling tones usually got through life on their good looks. For sabel's sake, I hoped his present venture was providing tability at last.

And that reminded me of Duncan's remarks about him he other evening, and of Ian's verdict on Glenrannoch's ntiques. I should have asked Duncan if the re-valuation ad come; I was anxious to prove that Ian was wrong.

Malcolm waved a cheery hand and departed, and Ian aid something about getting down to the ferry to meet Isabel, vhose car was still laid up. I immediately said that she hould have borrowed mine; it had been returned from the ills and was standing idle in the garage, but Ian smiled harmingly and told me Hamish Cameron was picking her p at her office on his way back from a call at Glen Nevis.

'And I dare say he'd be only too pleased to bring her all ie way home, but I'll spare him the last lap to Kyleven.'

It was said amiably, but the implication was there – that e knew well enough about the closeness between his wife nd Cameron.

I didn't want to hear more and headed down towards the ch. Brenda called after me, asking where I was going, and looked back and said that I fancied a trip to Eilean Munde efore dinner. 'It's a lovely evening and I'll be back in plenty f time.'

'You'll need an oarsman,' Ian said, and somehow it pleased ie to be able to tell him that my father had taught me to w on the Thames down at Putney and that I would there-re be able to take the stretch between Invercoe and the land with ease.

'The Thames is tidal, same as the loch,' I said, 'and the irrents equally strong, but I'd like to know the best place land on the island.'

Ian recommended the south side, used by the local ferry-an when taking sightseers across. 'You'll see an opening etween the rocks, convenient for mooring.'

I thanked him and went on my way. What compelled ie to look back, I have no idea. All I saw was Ian strolling 1 towards the house with Brenda, and Aunt Mary, half veiled behind a curtain, watching them from her bedroor window. I was too far away to see the expression upon h. face, but even at this distance I could tell that she didn want to be seen, and that she stood rigid as a statue, spyin

I didn't like it and hurried away.

I did take the stretch between Invercoe and the island wit ease, and found the opening between the rocks which, as Ia said, made a convenient mooring place, but as I steppe ashore I was surprised by the depth of the water. No sha lows lapped here; the land seemed to go down in sheer drop, into a darkness so impenetrable that I could n see what lay beneath, whether rocks or shingle.

At close quarters the island was anything but eerie. It wa leafy and fertile, sprinkled with larch and elm, and to th east lay the smaller Isle of Discussion, where the MacDonald Stewarts and Camerons, who had once cropped the hay Eilean Munde in rotation, settled their disputes by deba and sometimes by blows, but there was no sign of cultivatio on Eilean Munde now, and no sign of habitation but that the ruined chapel.

I spent some time browsing amongst its ancient ston and found some of the graves of bygone Camerons as we as those of remote ancestors of my own. I also found th ancient Celtic stone about which Brenda had told me, an looking up through the open roof, judged that the chap had once been thatched.

I became unaware of time as I examined the crumblir limestone walls which were interspersed with slate in part Ancient buildings had always fascinated me and as a resu it was dusk before I finally made my way back to the sp where I had moored, and as I walked I found myself thin ing of characters of whom I had read in my grandfathe library, friends of the Clan Donald and many related them; men like Big Henderson of the Chanters, MacIair hereditary piper, and Big Archibald MacPhail, of Glen Orch who stipulated that when he died his body should be p across a piebald mare, '. . . and she will carry me to Gle coe, and the people of Glencoe shall bury me on Eile Munde . . . dare not lay me but beside the MacDonalds. P a sword in my fist and my face to the Camerons – I ha never turned my back on them!'

Nor had Shuna MacDonald, who fell in love with one. And nor would I, who had done the same.

I stood still abruptly, facing the truth for the first time. I loved Hamish Cameron, no matter what he was or what he had done, no matter if he were the lover of another woman, no matter if he felt nothing for me nor ever would. This was the man I wanted, and the fact that I might never have him made not the slightest difference to the way I felt. I could pretend no longer. Not even to myself.

Slowly, I went on, my feet mechanically finding the path back to the boat, yet reluctant to leave the island for it had laid a kind of enchantment upon me. If indeed it were haunted, it could only be the friendliest of ghosts, for only friends lay here together, men who had never crossed swords in emnity – and women who had loved them.

I rowed slowly back across the water. I could see the lights of Invercoe reflected in it and searched the gathering dusk for those from Hamish Cameron's house. There were none. I thought with a stab of disappointment that he was probably out on a case, and refused to heed the thrusting speculations as to whether he was with Isabel. That, at least, was unlikely because I knew that Ian was at home; I had seen him earlier with Brenda. I drew comfort from the fact, and wished I could have seen Hamish's tall figure waiting for me at the landing stage.

It would have been fitting and right to see him there, conjured up out of my emotions, brought to life by the force of my desire. So much seemed to have changed since I set foot on Eilean Munde – my world, my thoughts, myself – because I had come face to face with a truth I had been deliberately refusing to see, and now that I acknowledged it I could never be the same again.

I knew that this man had the power to stir my body and my mind to depths I could not yet comprehend, and although I knew he did not feel the same about me, and probably never would, a deep tranquility and gentleness lay upon me, so that the thought of another woman possessing him, sharing with him the passion I must hide and control, hurt me like a lash. There had been men in my life before, but none capable of stirring me so deeply or so permanently.

I let the boat drift ashore, guiding it desultorily towards Glenrannoch's landing stage. I didn't want to go indoors yet; I didn't want to face an evening with the family. I felt in no mood for two antagonistic women, not even for Duncan, had he been at home. There was a deep happiness and a deep sadness in me; a gladness because I loved Hamish Cameron, but a desolation because it must go unfulfilled. He liked me well enough; he felt concern for me, but there was no special quality about that concern. Not the quality I wanted him to feel, nor the depth and the warmth and the answering passion.

I shipped the oars and flung the tow rope towards a mooring post, but before the loop encompassed it the rope was caught and held, pulling me towards the wooden steps, then his hand – the hand I wanted so much to see – was reaching down to help me ashore and I knew then that desire could be strong enough to work miracles. He was here, waiting for me. And not by chance. I knew instinctively that he had come for that purpose.

He looped the rope, knotted it, doing the whole thing automatically because his attention was focused on me alone.

He said quietly, 'You look lovely with the wind in your hair . . .' and his face came down to mine and his hands ran through my hair, holding my head still as he kissed me, gently at first and then searchingly, wildly, desire leaping to desire. I murmured incoherently as he pressed his cheek against mine, then covered it with soft, biting kisses that were demanding yet protective. There was no one in the world but our two selves; no happiness so deeply shared . . .

It was shattered by a woman's voice, by a dog's loud barking, and out of the dusk the Forsythes' Great Dane came leaping in furious welcome. We broke apart as Isabel's tall figure emerged from shadow, and I knew without being told that she had seen us before we saw her, although her smile and her greeting were casual and self-possessed.

We all went up to Glenrannoch. I was unable to look at Hamish. When we reached the house I achieved a measure of composure, sufficient to urge them both to stay for dinner. Isabel declined, but she did come in for a drink. Hamish accepted my invitation, and announced unabashed that he had telephoned me earlier, only to learn from Brenda that I had gone across to the island.

'That's why I was there to meet you,' he finished. 'You seemed a long time coming back.'

My delight because he admitted this in front of Isabel was the ridiculous delight of a woman in love.

It wasn't until after Hamish had left that I wondered why he had telephoned. He forgot to tell me.

Throughout the evening, with Brenda and Mary present, his manner was the same as usual. When he looked at me there was nothing different about his glance, nothing to indicate that he even remembered that wild, sweet moment by the loch. But I remembered it and always would. I might tell myself later that my desire must have been so obvious that his response was inevitable; that any man would react in such a way to undisguised invitation in a girl's eyes. The realization that it must have been there didn't shame me. I had had no time to cover it – and was glad.

Two things happened the next day. First, although it was Saturday, I went to the mills and spent a long and stimulating morning on my first Mactweedwear designs. I worked as one inspired, returning home to find that the telephone engineers had not only re-installed the outside line in my room, but the house phone as well. If the midnight walker returned I had only to lift a receiver to contact Duncan or anyone else in the house.

And that was the second thing which happened. The midnight walker did return, but Duncan was still in London and instead of ringing through to Brenda or Mary I lay there listening to the approaching footsteps because beneath my leaping apprehension something arrested me, a sudden awareness that tonight there was something different about that step. It was as firm, as loud, as deliberate as before; it still had a metallic ring about it, but not the identical ring. It was this difference which tempered my apprehension with curiosity. It was as if the midnight walker was wearing different footwear, and no ghost would do that . . .

I leapt out of bed, flung the windows wide, and stepped out on to the balcony at the precise moment that the figure halted below, and looked up. I saw the enveloping plaid swinging from the shoulder and half wrapped around his body, and the head covered with a Balmoral bonnet. But I

saw no face. Not because it was in shadow, but because ther
was no face to see.

Then the figure turned and marched away, the metalli
ring echoing on the stone flags of the terrace. It was definitel
a different echo. A blunter sound, as if the studs on his shoe
were not the same as before.

I called sharply, 'Stop! You there, *stop!*' but the figur
disappeared down the terrace steps and across the garde
until trees and darkness covered him.

The extraordinary thing was that this time I felt no fear
I was too angry. I listened to the booming strokes of mid
night echoing from the great hall, and all I could think wa:
that the practical joker timed his exits and entrances well
But he should check his props. He should make sure that h
wore the same metal-studded footwear each time.

Or *she* should. It could, after all, be a woman. A kilt, ar
enveloping plaid, a bonnet as of old, all could hide a
female figure and a female head of hair. And had the figure
worn a kilt or trews? From the height of my balcony it had
been difficult to see; all I had noticed was the concealing
shawl-like plaid, and the covered face.

For of course it was covered. A scarf, a dark handkerchief, or the present-day gangster's disguise of a nylon stock-
ing could smother a person's features entirely.

And no ghost did that.

But it was the footwear which worried me; that difference in the sound. Why had the change been necessary?
And wasn't there something else at the back of my mind,
some scrap of knowledge which I found myself unable to
dredge up, but which I knew to be important? Something
I had read somewhere . . .

I pulled on a robe and raced barefoot down to the library,
and as I went I had a feeling that time was running with me,
carrying me towards a climax, and that I was determined
to force that climax because I had had enough of being
persecuted.

It was some time before I found the book I wanted, but
when I did, I curled up in a deep arm-chair, my bare feet
tucked under me, and read avidly about the personal history
of Alasdair MacDonald, believed to be the Twelfth MacIain
of Glencoe, although earlier records had been scanty between

John of the Heather and his own birth, but one thing was certain – like his forebears, he had been a man of gigantic mould, mighty in strength; flaunting the fierce red hair of his family, and growing to a height of six feet seven inches . . .

Six feet seven inches – even looking down from my balcony I had seen that the midnight walker did not approach that height. Did a ghost shrink? The idea made me laugh, sparking my anger, urging me to read on . . .

As a young man MacIain had been sent to Paris, a custom in those days with the sons of Highland chiefs. Here he acquired a veneer of sophistication which could never subdue the wild savagery of his race, but which gilded his personality and perfected his French, much spoken in the Highlands but without Parisian polish. He came back, as he was expected to, burnished with an elegance worthy of his rank, so that when he received his father's sword and the white rod of leadership, and the traditional Bard recited at length about his family's honour and courage, he looked every inch the leader of the clan, distinguished by his bearing and by his dress.

Not for him the traditional brogues of deer-hide; not for him the kilt of the common people; he wore tartan trews, skin-tight and shaped to the leg, and a plaid pinned on the shoulder with a fine silver brooch shaped like the head of a wild beast, with jewels in its eyes and nostrils, and on his feet he wore shoes buckled with silver . . .

I snapped the book shut, and the sound echoed triumphantly in the silent room. *Metal-studded boots?* They had never been worn even by the roughest Highlander. Brogues of deer-hide for the common man, tough and hard-wearing and tied in cross-bands round the ankles; silent on the rough earth so that no enemy could hear them coming. And for their splendid Chief, with his Piper, Bard, and Sword-Bearer, his gillies and his bodyguard of the strongest tacksmen in the glen, elegant buckled shoes. Anything less would have been an indignity.

I opened the book and read on. Although a chief inherited his rank and honours, he had to prove that he merited them by demonstrating his valour and his ability to lead; this he did in war, and in cattle-raiding and plundering, so proving to his *clann*, or children, that he could not only lead but care for them. This Red Alasdair had mightily accomplished, but for all his savage leadership he lived in a highly civilized manner compared with his people, his house at Carnoch being two storeys high, with a roof covered with blue slate from Ballachulish, and having private chambers as well as a council room, an immense table for feasting, splendid carved chests, panelled walls, closets to hold the wife's fine laces, foreign drinking glasses, and, most precious of all, a cup of French silver from which he always drank, brought back from Paris in his youth and looted by his murderers on that infamous night.

Now I was quiet, sitting very still and thinking hard. 'Take no heed,' Hamish had said at our very first meeting, 'when people claim to know the actual site of MacIain's tragic home.' I had felt then that he was trying to warn me in some way, and now I knew this was so, for very shortly afterwards Aunt Mary had told me the story of the midnight walker, the ghost of the Twelfth MacIain, haunting Glenrannoch because it had been built a century later on the site of his own house.

But Glenrannoch was close to Clachaig, and Carnoch was now the village of Glencoe, and neither site could possibly be confused with the other. Some other house had stood here, no doubt; the ancient chapel proved that, for it was older than Glenrannoch itself, but rich as MacIain the Twelfth had been compared with his people, he had owned no private chapel. That had been built by a later MacDonald long after his death, and if the historian who wrote this book was correct, MacIain's home had been nowhere near this spot. Nor were any of the other places claimed to be traditional sites.

By morning I felt I knew all there was to know about the immortal MacIain, that Carnoch was undoubtedly the site of his home, and therefore no legend could be associated with him at Glenrannoch.

I also realized why the midnight walker had worn different footwear this time. He had been forced to because the iron-studded boots, caked with dried mud and hidden in the Jacobites' hole, had been removed the day we brought Luke out of there. Hamish had picked them up, and presumably

Hamish had taken them away.

I was certain now that the midnight walker must be a member of this household, with access to the chapel and a knowledge of the hiding place; someone who had kept that secret spring well oiled and in perfect order, for the concealed entrance had opened at a touch; someone, moreover, who never delved into my grandfather's library or troubled to check on MacIain's attire, otherwise they would never have made the fatal mistake of wearing the wrong shoes.

Except, of course, to make their footsteps heard. That had been the most necessary thing of all.

It was imperative to talk to Hamish, but as I dialled his number from my own room I saw the fingers of my bedside clock pointing to four-fifteen. I couldn't disturb him at this hour; I had been up since midnight, but like everyone else he would still be asleep. I flopped on to the bed and promptly did the same.

When I awakened I heard the sound of whistling outside. It was the newspaper boy delivering the Sunday papers. It was nine o'clock.

Half an hour later, eating a solitary breakfast, I heard the familiar sound of Duncan's Jaguar zoom up the drive. He must have caught an early morning plane and picked up his car at the airport. I had never seen him look so tired, and wondered if the urgent case which had called him to London had not gone well.

I poured some coffee, strong and black, and as he accepted it the telephone rang. 'If it's anyone for me,' he said wearily, 'I'm not back yet. I must catch up on some sleep.'

To my surprise it was Angus Matheson, asking if Duncan had returned. His voice, loud and imperative, echoed down the line and across the room, and after a moment's hesitation Duncan said, 'I'd better take it, I suppose.'

I handed the receiver over, wondering why the Managing Director of the mills should be telephoning on a Sunday morning, then I picked up the newspapers which, from the look of them, either Mary or Brenda, or both, had been reading and discarded, and took them up to my room, paying no attention to Duncan's monosyllabic conversation, except for an awareness that he sounded anxious to terminate it, which was understandable considering the office was closed

In my room I sat upon a window seat, waiting for the ping which would indicate that the outside line was clear but Matheson's call seemed to be going on for a long time I scanned the papers, but it was in no mood for reading, impatient now to telephone Hamish.

As I waited, my mind was already rejecting the possibility of the midnight walker being a member of the household because the list was unconvincing. How could it be Brenda, dainty as a piece of Dresden china, or gaunt Aunt Mary, whose quick, mincing steps could never be disguised? And obviously it couldn't be Duncan, not only because he had been away in London last night, but on the occasion of the walker's last visit he had been in his study, and promptly gone racing outside in search of him.

Nor was it likely to be Flora, heavily built though she was, when the security of herself and her son depended upon the goodwill of the owner of Glenrannoch. Nor could it possibly be the beaming, bouncing Jeannie, plump as a little hen and too good-natured to indulge in cruel practical jokes.

That left only Luke, and sour Maggie Munro; the latter, I knew, had gone home to visit her family at Orchy for the week-end, which meant that she had left the house on Friday evening and would return tomorrow morning.

And nothing in the world would convince me that it was Luke. Apart from his obvious devotion to me, he had neither the intelligence to hatch such a plan, nor to carry it out so methodically.

The telephone pinged sharply; the line was clear. I leapt up, and the newspapers scattered at my feet. One page had a piece torn from it, and as I gathered up the sheets I wondered why, because it wasn't from the women's page but prominent amongst the general news. I could understand Aunt Mary tearing out a recipe or Brenda a new fashion design, but why a news item?

I tossed the paper aside and dialled Hamish's number, listening impatiently as it rang out. Then came another sound – the faint click of someone lifting another extension. Mary? Duncan? Brenda?

I said into the invisible ear, 'Sorry, I'm making a call,' and the other extension was immediately replaced.

Well, I thought reasonably, they didn't have to apolo-
ize for cutting in – and squashed the suspicion that they
idn't want me to recognize their voice.

There was no reply from Hamish's number.

few minutes later Aunt Mary came through on the house
hone and asked if I was going to church. I said no, not this
orning, and immediately drove off to Hamish's house,
oping that by the time I got there he would be in.

He was not, but Mrs McPherson, who came later on Sun-
ays, had just arrived and suggested I should wait; Mr
ameron had left a note saying he had been called out on a
se, but shouldn't be long.

She went back to the kitchen, leaving me in the book-
ned room which seemed dearly familiar although it also
emed a long time since Hamish had brought me here on
at foggy morning and told me the story of poor Luke
yfe. I experienced now, as I experienced then, a feeling
relaxation. His bedroom slippers had been kicked off by
e hearth, the Sunday papers scattered . . .

Except one, folded carefully and placed on his desk, dis-
laying a news item circled in red.

Curiously, I picked it up, and when I had finished read-
g my heart seemed very still. Then I glanced at the name
the paper and the page number, scribbled a note asking
amish to telephone me urgently, then raced back to Glen-
nnoch, praying that the newspapers had not been cleared
om my room.

My luck was in; they were on the window seat where I
d left them, and the newspaper and the page number were
entical.

I went downstairs, and as I descended I heard church
ells begin to peel, and the sound of Aunt Mary's Busy-
ini stuttering on its way. That meant that neither Brenda
r Duncan had gone, or either the Jaguar or the Singer
ould have been used.

I guessed who had torn that item from the Sunday paper,
d why, and was filled with anger curiously tinged with pity,
cause the action must have been a defensive one, a pro-
ctive one, but it had also been rather stupid because it
uld only be a delaying tactic. By now the news would be in

every surrounding home; to tear it out had been a vai[n]
attempt to conceal it from the occupants of this house. Mysel[f]
in particular?

I heard their voices in the study, Duncan's and his mother'[s]
and when I opened the door and went in they stopped dead
looking at me. Something in my face must have told the[m]
what I knew, for neither spoke.

I said, '*You* tore it out, didn't you, Brenda – the new[s]
about Duncan's London firm and Hamish Cameron's inno[-]
cence?'

Duncan answered quickly, 'I came back to tell you an[d]
to explain to the directors – '

' – but Angus Matheson got in first. He'd read it, hadn'[t]
he, and that was why he phoned?' My voice shook wit[h]
indignation. 'I hope the board asks for your resignation.'

'Lavinia! I swear to you that I knew nothing. It all hap[-]
pened before I joined Humbold and Strickland.'

'Now called Humbold, Strickland and Campbell, an[d]
crossed off the Law List following investigations into thei[r]
involvement with a group called Modern Enterprises, [a]
crooked set-up operating dubious schemes from the soun[d]
of things. The Law Society heard the case on Friday, henc[e]
your urgent departure; you didn't tell anyone you wer[e]
going until the last minute, pretending it was an urgen[t]
call, although you must have known the investigation wa[s]
scheduled for that date.' I tried to control my anger, an[d]
failed. 'I've heard of shady lawyers, but never met on[e]
before!'

Brenda's blunt, squat little hand shot out and stung m[y]
cheek. I was glad she did it. The shock steadied me. I[f]
the whole nasty business had taken place before Dunca[n]
joined the firm, I had no right to accuse him of being par[t]
of it.

'I'm sorry,' I said, and meant it. 'I suppose you wanted t[o]
spare us.'

'Particularly my mother. I hoped to get back this morn[-]
ing before the Sunday papers arrived; I knew they woul[d]
have picked up the story from the London evening papers
which we don't see here. Unhappily, I was too late. Afte[r]
the case was heard, I had a lot to deal with – Strickland i[n]
particular. We were in the office all night, and all day yes[-]

erday, thrashing things out and trying to wind up the mess he'd landed the firm into.'

No wonder he looked fatigued, I thought, and felt compassion stirring beneath my still-smouldering anger. I felt it for his mother too, who had torn the item out in the vain hope of shielding her son; a protective instinct and a natural, maternal one, but inevitably a waste of time.

I asked Duncan, 'Did you honestly know nothing? Hadn't you the slightest suspicion that false evidence had been presented on behalf of Modern Enterprises in cases of nobbling, of doping race horses?'

'How could I? I worked only on Industrial Law, the branch handled by Humbold. I was once articled to him, and after I qualified I came home to handle the legal department at the mills; Industrial Law again. That's the branch I've specialized in. A couple of years ago I had the chance to buy Humbold's interest in his firm when he retired; by that time Strickland had worked his way up to a partnership. He was the sharp one, and of course very much younger than Humbold. He brought Modern Enterprises in as one of his clients. I'm sure old Humbold didn't know what was going on. I took over the straightforward industrial cases which he handled, and knew nothing about Strickland's. It is he who is guilty, but that doesn't do me much good, since my name is now linked with the firm. Yes, Angus Matheson is calling a meeting of the directors on Monday, and I'll answer to them as frankly as I am answering you. I knew nothing.'

'Except that Hamish had been wrongly accused and found guilty. Framed, in other words.'

'I know that now. I didn't before. How could I? The only good thing to come out of this is the proof of his innocence, and that of others, and, believe me, I'm glad about that.'

'So is Lavinia. In fact, it is the only thing she does care about.' I hadn't imagined that Brenda's voice could be so acid, but it was the voice of a mother defending her son and therefore excusable. I felt sorry for her; sorry for them both. She went on to demand sharply, 'It's true, isn't it? You don't care about Duncan, despite all his kindness to you. It is Hamish Cameron you're in love with. Do you think I can't tell?'

I didn't bother to deny it. It was useless to try. I saw the hurt in Duncan's eyes and turned away from it.

'If you marry him,' Brenda said, 'you'll lose Glenrannoch.'

Duncan pointed out fairly that this wasn't so. 'Her grandfather didn't stipulate that she had to marry a Matheson, merely that she should retain the name MacDonald. Marriages between Mathesons and MacDonalds have been traditional, that's all. Lavina is free to marry whoever she wishes providing she fulfils the rest of James's stipulations.'

I was tempted to say that Hamish had not asked me to marry him and was unlikely to. Instead, I answered, 'Someone is trying to make me lose Glenrannoch now, either by trying to be rid of me or by frightening me away. The midnight walker returned last night, but he made one big mistake, and that mistake told me that he – or she – is someone in this house.'

I think Brenda gasped, but I was only aware of Duncan's reaction, which was characteristic. He forgot himself and thought only of me, urging me to tell him everything. I did so willingly enough; about the iron-studded boots hidden in the Jacobites' hole and how they had been discovered there when we brought Luke home. 'And only someone in this house could know about that secret hiding place.'

Brenda gave a shrill laugh. 'Rubbish! What about old Craig, the gardener from Kyleven? He's the only person who goes there now, apart from Luke who cleans the place. The boots probably belonged to one or other of them.'

'They weren't Luke's. Flora said so.'

'She'd be bound to.' Brenda shrugged, but her stubby fingers were moving agitatedly. This news about her son's firm had shaken her.

'Then they must have been an old pair Craig threw away,' she said indifferently. 'But what does it matter? It isn't important.'

'But it is. Whoever owned them had to replace them with another pair when they masqueraded as the midnight walker last night, because Hamish removed the others. I noticed the difference in sound immediately. I've never heard of a ghost who changed his boots.'

'I've told you all along that it was some practical joker,' Duncan said.

'And an ignorant one,' I added. 'He should have checked on legendary Highland footwear. That was his big mistake. They were never studded with iron.

Duncan ran a tired hand through his hair. 'I wish to heaven I'd been here last night, but at least I'll be here to catch the bastard if he gives a repeat performance tonight. I'll wait up for him and meet him face to face.'

I could tell Brenda was exasperated and that she couldn't forgive me for harassing her son further, but all she said was, 'For goodness sake don't mention it to Mary when she comes home from church, or she won't let the matter rest all day.' She glanced at her watch. 'Matins must be half-way through by now, so we've at least another half-hour before she comes twittering home. That gives me time to cut flowers for the lunch table.'

When the door closed behind her, Duncan smiled a little sadly.

'I ought to hate Hamish Cameron, but I don't. I guessed he was in love with you the night you wore Shuna Mac-Donald's gown, but even so, I went on hoping.' His voice shook a little, but he covered it with a cough, and when I impulsively held out my hand, he took it and kissed it gently. 'I'm glad for his sake, and yours, that he's cleared. I shall tell him so.'

I decided to wait for Hamish's call in the library, and had scarcely entered the room before he rang. I snatched up the extension to forestall anyone from answering elsewhere in the house, and said swiftly that I must see him. At once.

He suggested lunch at the Kingshouse Hotel, at the top of the glen. 'We could meet somewhere on the way – say at the foot of Aonach Dubh? I'll bring my car, and be waiting before you get there.'

The conversation was too brief for anyone to have had time to listen in, unless they had picked up another extension simultaneously. It seemed to me that the ping which followed my replacing the receiver had a double echo, but decided it was due to my imagination, because as we talked

I had heard Duncan walking across the great hall towards the stairs on his way to his room, and a moment later, as I left the library, I glanced towards the window and saw Brenda walking briskly across the garden, secateurs in her hand.

As I approached the bridge across the Coe, people were walking home from church and cars driving back up the glen. There were a few picnickers and parked vehicles, but no sign as yet of Hamish's ancient Bentley. It didn't matter. I knew he would come. Meanwhile, the sun was warm; the atmosphere that of a lazy summer Sunday. My footsteps settled to a leisurely stroll, and by the time I reached the foot of Aonach Dubh all returning church-goers were out of sight.

I glanced at my watch. I was late. The walk had taken longer than anticipated and my final desultory steps had added to it.

There was still no sign of Hamish. It was odd that he should be late after telling me that he would be waiting. The tone of his voice had suggested an impatience to see me.

It seemed as if the minutes ticked by with agonizing slowness. Farther down the glen I could see picnickers beginning to drowse in the sun after their midday meal. My disappointment increased, then became acute, for suddenly I was convinced he wasn't coming. The eagerness in his voice must have been imaginary on my part.

Common sense dictated that I should go home, yet still I lingered, hoping against hope to see his car suddenly appear. To kill time and to occupy my mind I crossed the road and began to wander at the foot of Aonach Dubh, idly searching for lumps of volcanic lava which still lingered from the time of the great upheaval of the Caledonian Chain. And it was then that I heard someone call my name.

It sounded like Aunt Mary.

I stood very still, alert and listening. Her voice came echoing down the slope, calling for help. I guessed at once what had happened. She had taken one of her Sunday walks after church, searching for coloured pebbles to use in her craft jewellery; these hill walks were a habit of hers, and one to which no one paid much heed. She was an agile woman and sometimes wandered far. Her late return never upset Sunday lunch because at Glenrannoch a cold buffet was always left on the sideboard, an institution inaugurated by my grandfather so that the servants could attend church also.

Today my aunt must have climbed farther than usual and become stranded in some inaccessible spot. If I could locate where she had parked her car, it would give me some indication of the point at which she had started her hill walk, but I could see no sign of Busy-Mini. That puzzled me. Surely she wouldn't have left it outside the church but would have driven here to save time?

Her cry came again – 'Lavinia – help me!' – but although I scanned the heights very carefully, studying every projecting ledge within range and every visible nook and cranny, I could not see her as she, apparently, could see me.

There was only one thing to do. Go in search of her.

I set out at once, thankful that I had donned stout walking shoes, the Kingshouse being the kind of place where climbers and hill walkers felt at home whatever they wore, and as I progressed I heard my aunt's voice coming nearer, the note of terror in it verging on panic. Yet still I could see no sign of her.

I passed the ledge where I had found Jock and scrambled on up the slope. The track was rough, worn by generations of hill walkers. It became steeper the higher I climbed, at one point curving sharply left to avoid an outcrop of rock which jutted forcefully from the hillside, forming a precipitous drop beneath.

Pausing briefly to gain my breath, I glanced over my shoulder and was surprised to see how far I had come. Much higher than previously. The floor of the glen, sliced by its winding road, seemed very far away, and from this point I could see most of the pass as it curved up from Loch Leven towards Achtriochton. I could see the waters of tiny Loch Achtriochton sparkling in the sun, the river and the glen curving away from it towards Rannoch Moor, but hidden from view by the mountainous projection of Gearr Aonach, the centre slope of The Three Sisters.

I glanced back swiftly towards the western entrance to the pass, praying even now for a sight of Hamish's battered

Bentley driving up from Invercoe, but there was none. I was on my own, isolated on this rocky slope, with my aunt's voice crying even louder for help. Louder — or nearer? I looked carefully around, but still could see no sign of her, whereupon bewilderment deepened for if she had fallen into some hole, or foolishly ventured into a hidden cleft to chisel pebbles out of the rock face with the small tool she always took for this purpose, how could she possibly see me? How did she know I was here?

I felt an unreasonable apprehension, a momentary flicker which I thrust down impatiently. I was becoming tense with suspicion these days, imagining threats where none existed. My foolish aunt had probably fallen and sprained her ankle and was lying sprawled amongst the scree above, peering anxiously through a screen of coarse mountain grass. It was the obvious explanation.

I cupped my mouth in my hands and shouted to her that I was coming, urging her to keep calling so that I could follow the direction of her voice, then I pressed on, exasperated and yet concerned. Stones slithered beneath my feet and pelted down the hillside behind me, so that I momentarily stumbled, halted, and paused again for breath.

It was then that I first detected the sound coming up the slope behind me, like a double echo of my footsteps, but heavier. My whole body went rigid, then relaxed when the sound ceased. Imagination was playing tricks with me; there was no one on this slope by myself and my aunt, whose voice continued to call piteously and, I realized thankfully, much nearer. It would not be long now before I found her.

For the first time I began to wonder how I was going to get her down. It wouldn't be easy, especially if, as I suspected from the note of panic in her voice, she was hysterical. I would have to calm her somehow, even if it meant shaking some sense into her, and if she was injured, I would have to make her as comfortable as possible and leave her while I went back and contacted the nearest Mountain Rescue Post.

I called again that I was coming, and heard her sharp and inarticulate cry in answer — then silence.

And in that silence I heard again the uncanny double echo of footsteps thrown back at me by the pitching hillside. The crags high above, spreading to the distant peak of Stob Coire, evidently played tricks with sound, enlarging and distorting it. I called my aunt's name again, and it was thrown back at me, hollow and unrecognizable, but instantly comforting because it assured me that the illusion of being followed was indeed nothing but an illusion.

This time there came no answer to my call, and I felt a sharp stab of fear. Had she fainted? Was she severely injured? I wished now that I had heeded Hamish's advice about going for help before risking my neck on these unpredictable slopes, but, as usual, I had acted in my impulsive way, and there was nothing to do now but press on.

I came upon her suddenly, arrested by her scream for help close by. I turned sharply, and found myself at the entrance to an unseen cleft in the hill face. For a moment, dazzled by the sun, my eyes could not accustom themselves to the darkness of the cleft, then gradually a shape focused and I saw that it was my aunt huddled within the slit.

But she wasn't alone. There was another shape, that of a man who pinioned her with one arm, his face and figure a shadow. But it was familiar to me.

Hamish. Dear God in heaven, Hamish had tricked me into coming here!

CHAPTER FOURTEEN

Suddenly Mary screamed, 'Get away, Lavinia! Get away—*fast!*' and in the brief second that I hesitated a glint of gun cut through the sliced rock and high-lighted a gun levelled at me.

The bullet whistled above my head as I flung myself to the ground and rolled sideways, and then I heard deep panting breath as he sprang. Simultaneously I hurled myself away again and his body shot past and went catapulting down the mountainside. In that same flashing second I was seized

by powerful arms and lifted up, and I saw the hurtling bo
pitch over the rock projection below, to sprawl finally at t
foot of Aonach Dubh like a broken puppet.

It was Ian Forsythe, and I knew at once that he w
dead.

Hamish's voice said, 'I'll take care of her, Luke. You mu
help Miss MacDonald down.'

I can't remember how long it took to reach home aft
we made the descent and Hamish had contacted the neare
Mountain Rescue Post to take care of Ian's body. Throug
shock and confusion I was conscious only of joy becau
Hamish was with me and because my horrifying belief th
he was the man within the cleft had been wrong.

He would let me ask no questions until we were back
Glenrannoch, and to tell the truth I had no inclination
talk. Nor had Aunt Mary, now stunned into uncharacterist
silence.

Hamish had left his car concealed beyond the elbow
of the pass. I wondered why, but knew he would explai
later. Everything would be explained later.

But I had to wait until Aunt Mary lay with her feet u
on a couch and Duncan was giving her brandy. My ow
shock didn't equal hers, perhaps because I was younger an
more resilient, or because Hamish sat beside me, grippir
my hand as if he would never let go. Nor did I want him to
His nearness was all I needed, but Aunt Mary looked lik
a woman whose spirit had been broken. Her thin arm
clutched her clumsy *petit-point* bag as if it were the onl
safe anchorage in a reeling world, and now I remembered th
she had been clutching it in the same way as she crouche
within the cleft.

'Easy does it,' Duncan said kindly. 'Sip, don't gulp. The
we'll pack you off to bed. No need to talk.'

Hamish said abruptly, 'There's every need. She'll tal'
Campbell, and we'll all listen.'

Duncan protested that Aunt Mary had had a harrowir
experience and should be allowed to rest.

'She can rest when she's told us everything.' There wa
a relentless note in Hamish's voice. 'And that means the lo
Mary. Why Forsythe took you to that spot and why yo

went with him so willingly.' At my aunt's protesting murmur he continued more gently. 'I watched you go. I saw you arrive in Forsythe's car, which he parked alongside some picnickers farther down the glen. Amongst a group of tourists' cars it was unlikely to be noticed by Lavinia when she came along, besides which she entered the pass farther up. For the same reason I'd left my own car out of sight; I didn't want it to be seen by whoever followed her. I anticipated that someone would; what I didn't anticipate was that someone would come ahead and lie in wait for her, but of course it took Forsythe less time to drive to the church and pick you up, and then head for the pass, than it took Lavinia to walk there.'

I cut in swiftly, 'So that was why you suggested I should meet you on the way!'

He nodded. 'You'll have to forgive me for using you as bait, but I had to force things to a head. I knew any phone call you made would be tapped, or any incoming call for you likewise.'

Brenda protested indignantly that she had never heard such an abominable accusation and that neither she nor her son would dream of listening to other people's conversations.

'Nevertheless, one of you did. It couldn't have been Mary, because she was at church. Was Forsythe waiting for you when you came out?' he asked her.

Mary nodded mutely, but when Duncan, calmly ignoring both Hamish and his mother, held the glass to her lips again she brushed it aside and the brandy spilled on to her faded bag. At any other time her bony fingers would have wiped it away in vexation, but now she didn't even notice.

'He'd come to meet me specially, he said. Isabel had gone with Moira and Malcolm to lunch with friends at Oban and he made an excuse not to go with them, so that he could see me. I – believed him, of course. He suggested a walk like old times. We used to take hill walks together after church when we were young. I used to slip away from Father and meet him, and it was on one of these walks that he proposed to me . . .'

Her voice broke, and a quiver of surprise ran through me. So it was Ian Forsythe, not Alistair Matheson, whom she had loved and expected to marry. I looked at her once-pretty, faded face and felt the first deep rush of pity I had really felt for her since coming to Glenrannoch.

Brenda said sharply, 'That's enough, Mary. Stop getting maudlin about the past. Duncan is right – you must rest.'

Mary rallied at that. Her stepmother had only to speak to set her bristling with opposition.

'Duncan is wrong. You can't believe that, because in your eyes he can never be – just as he couldn't in my father's. To the day he died my father believed he could trust Duncan, and nothing I said would convince him otherwise. I was a nagging, embittered spinster, and who would listen to a nagging, embittered spinster? My only consolation was that he had long ceased to trust you.'

Duncan put in soothingly, 'Mary, my dear, you don't know what you're saying.'

She sat upright, hugging her clumsy bag to her flat breasts, her eyes sparkling.

'I know what I am *going* to say,' she snapped back, 'and I should have said it when Lavinia first arrived. It was dishonest of me not to, but I've been dishonest for a long time, not merely since the will was read, but before that – when I found what my father had been writing in the library. I stole it. He was bed-ridden by that time and the diary was in the library desk where he used to sit day after day. We all wondered what he was doing, didn't we? Do you remember, Brenda, how you joked that he was writing his memoirs? And you, Duncan – you said it was probably his own version of the history of Glencoe and if it kept him occupied, let him get on with it. Oh, you were both so indulgent because it suited you well; it kept him out of your way; you could both do as you liked – Brenda carrying on with Ian and you, Duncan, turning a blind eye on everything but your own ambitions.'

Brenda blazed, 'How dare you! This time you've gone too far!'

'Not far enough,' Hamish cut in. 'In what way have you been dishonest, Mary, and what should you have told Lavinia when she came?'

'About the codicil. The right codicil. The one Duncan

didn't produce when the will was read. The one you and Flora witnessed and no one else knew about but me – and Duncan, of course, which was why he kept it back. And I let him because, like Brenda, I benefited more that way.'

Duncan said impatiently, 'The woman's rambling. Everyone knows I produced the codicil when the will was read.'

'The first one, yes. The one leaving Glenrannoch to myself and your mother if my niece rejected it. And I was glad, until I began to wonder just why. I thought you must have done it for your mother's sake, because you knew my father had finally cut her out completely. Myself too, as far as Glenrannoch was concerned. I was to have no more than a comfortable income for life, because he was tired of my nagging – ' She choked indignantly, patted her bulky bag, and went on. 'That's what he calls it, here in his diary. *Nagging!* "My daughter gives me no peace," he wrote, "for ever nagging me to leave Glenrannoch to her, and my wife gives me no peace for the same reason, and neither is fit to be mistress here." I've read it so often I know it by heart. Especially the part about you, Brenda. He'd found out about you and Ian, and that was why he turned you out of his room. "She never loved me. How could she, so much older than herself? I was an ageing fool, but I treated her well. She might at least have waited until I died before giving herself to another man. Poor Isabel – I wonder if she knows." But *I* didn't feel sorry for Isabel. I never have. She took Ian from me when my brother jilted her.'

Suddenly she shrank back, for in one swift movement Brenda was at her side. Mary clutched her bulky bag tighter.

'Oh no, you don't, Brenda! You'll never get it. The diary has been mine since the day I found it, and I've carried it with me wherever I went because no one would ever suspect that I carried in this bag anything but what you call my "clutter". The simplest places make the best hiding places. There are other volumes, all locked in my room, but this is the most important, and having it with me meant that I could read it as often as I liked. That's how I knew that my father decided to replace the earlier codicil with another, also the day on which Hamish and Flora witnessed it, and the clause

he altered about Lavinia having to keep the name Mac
Donald if she married. There was an argument about that
but Hamish persuaded him – '

Duncan cut in sceptically, 'How do you know all this?'

'I've told you, From the diary.'

'He was bed-ridden then. He couldn't get up.'

'But he did. The day after the second codicil was signed
he felt better. Have you forgotten, or were you feeling so
elated that you didn't pay much attention to things at
Glenrannoch that day? My father rallied, the way he
always did when he'd made a decision, or settled something that was worrying him. I saw him come downstairs and
go into the library. We met at the foot of the stairs and he
said. "Where is my wife? Is she out?" and I nodded, because
she was. I'd seen her drive off to her Bridge Club at Fort
William – or so she said. Except that you don't belong to any
Bridge Club, do you, Brenda? I know, because I checked
long ago. It's been your excuse when you've gone to meet Ian.

Hamish said patiently, 'You were saying how your father
came downstairs . . .'

'That's right. He was wearing that shabby old dressing
gown of his, the one he would never part with. I tried to
get him to go back to bed, but he ordered me to keep quiet
and went into the library and slammed the door. I heard
the rattle of keys as he unlocked his desk. I lingered for
a while, wondering if I ought to call Doctor MacFarlane,
then decided not to in case it threw my father into a rage,
but after a while I took him a cup of tea. He nearly threw
it at me and told me to get out, and couldn't I see he was
busy? That was the day I saw the diary for the first time
and realized what he did in the library. That day he made
the last entry of all, about the new codicil and why he had
countermanded the first one.'

' "At least I can trust her son," he wrote. "He has pride
in Glenrannoch and should make a good master here, if
Andrew's daughter turns her back on the place or refuses
to come." He wrote a lot more about his reluctance to let
Glenrannoch pass out of the family, but of course he knew
I would never marry and have children now and it was
important to leave it in the hands of someone who would
care for it and take pride in it, and he believed Duncan

would. He was right there, I suppose – you've always been ambitious, haven't you, Duncan? Socially as well as professionally.'

Suddenly my aunt's bony hand dived into her capacious bag and brought out a thick, hard-bound notebook. She held it out to me. 'Look for yourself, Lavinia. Turn to the last entry of all. I should have shown you this long ago.'

My grandfather's handwriting, vigorous in the early pages, grew more sprawling, more spidery as the pages turned, but the final one was written by a hand which had suddenly regained its strength, a last rallying effort recording the truth for all time . . .

'Today I took the final step in ensuring the future of Glenrannoch if Andrew's girl refuses it, or should die. In that event I've named Duncan Campbell as sole inheritor, though I never thought the day would come when I would contemplate a Campbell living here, but that ancient feud was over long ago.' Then came the part Aunt Mary had quoted, and the final words: 'I sent for Hamish Cameron to act as witness, Duncan declining, being a beneficiary, but of course I wanted him there as lawyer, and I acquainted Cameron with the contents of the new codicil because he is a trusted friend. Then the thing had to be re-drafted because I'd left in the stipulation about my grand-daughter retaining the name of MacDonald in the event of marriage, linking it with her husband's but taking precedence over it, and Cameron declared that no true Scot would tolerate that. We had words, as usual, and damn me, Cameron won. He pointed out that to hyphenate a name with another had always been a sign of weakening the name in Scots tradition, and that a pig-headed old Scot like myself should know that without being told.

'And then the argument broke out, with my stepson telling Cameron that what I wanted to stipulate in my will was no concern of his, and that hot-headed descendent of Lochiel saying I could bequeath Glenrannoch wherever I wished, but I had no right to dictate to some unknown girl what name she should take after marriage, or to her husband either. He demanded to know what I wanted my grand-daughter to marry – a man, or a lap-dog? Then he said something which went right home, though I took good care not to show it. He said he was sure my son's wife had been proud to bear *his* name, as a wife should.

'That was why I had the clause struck out, and signed the deletion to make it legal, and then I sent for Flora Fyfe to be second witness because she was here and on the spot. All I told that good soul was that she was witnessing my will. And after that, Cameron and I played chess and, by God, I beat him soundly.'

The writing grew suddenly tired, but there was one more entry.

'Soon I shall leave that shadowy, unhappy room of mine. I recall that when I brought my first bride to Glenrannoch she didn't take to it. She said it was haunted by the unhappiness of someone who had gone before, and declared it was Shuna MacDonald, whose husband had been a bully and a tyrant. Jessie was never an imaginative woman, so maybe she was right. Family history records that Shuna's husband was not a man the MacDonalds were particularly proud of; tyrannical we may be, fond of getting our own way, but bullies to our womenfolk, never. But with Jessie the room gradually lost its atmosphere for we were happy together. Now I shall be glad to leave it, for the unhappiness has returned. Pray God, it doesn't linger behind after I am gone . . .'

The writing grew weaker, but I could still read it. 'I also pray God that Andrew's girl will come, although I've no doubt she can be as stubborn as her father . . . *my son* . . . *my son* . . .

Tears blinded me, and somehow I knew that they had blinded James MacDonald as he wrote those final words.

I felt as if I had been meeting my grandfather for the first time, listening to his voice, looking into his heart; so much so that Aunt Mary's next words seemed to call me back from a distance.

'Knowing what I did,' she was saying, 'I expected the second codicil to be produced when the will was read. I was astonished when it wasn't, and puzzled too, but oh, so thankful! At least I was to have half of what should rightfully be mine, half of Glenrannoch. So it suited me to keep quiet, even if the other half still went to Brenda. She would tire of it, I thought, or perhaps sell it to me; maybe

nd herself another husband and go away. Nothing would
onvince me that she would remain here, not even for Ian, and
was sure that a girl who had lived in London all her life
ould never settle here. Lavinia would be up and away
n no time, I thought, so all I had to do was wait. But recently
've begun to wonder why Duncan really kept back the second
odicil and let Lavinia go on believing that his mother and I
ould inherit after her. I began to be uneasy the day she
ld me she had heard the midnight walker, because Brenda
ad told me that my father heard him before he died. Now
suspect she made it up.'

She turned to her stepmother. 'Why did you say that?
'o make sure the story was passed on to Lavinia to frighten
er away? I prattled, I know; you've always told me so.'
he waved her thin hand. 'But it doesn't matter – I'm facing
acts now. If Duncan had revealed that he would be sole
nheritor in her place, she would have had cause to be
uspicious of him when things began to happen to her,
nd it was better by far that others should be suspected.
Myself – and even his mother. But you were in league with
our precious son, weren't you, Brenda? What did he
romise for your silence?'

I could never have imagined that my neurotic aunt could
peak so calmly.

Then I noticed that Hamish was on his feet, blocking
ne door, and Duncan was trying to push past him, saying
e wasn't going to stay here listening to such a pack of non-
ense, and in my mind everything was suddenly clicking
nto place – the important things, like Hamish telling me
nat someone was trying to get rid of me, and why.

'Don't you see?' he had demanded. 'Because of the
odicil.'

But he had not been present when the will was read, so
e had no knowledge that the second codicil had been
ept back. He had assumed all along that I knew of its con-
ents; he had been telling me that Duncan was my enemy;
elling me to open my eyes; telling me that the man wanted
ne out of the way, and wondering why I couldn't under-
tand.

And when I decided to remain, refusing to be frightened
way although efforts to make me had started as soon as I

arrived, there was only one thing left for Duncan to d
Marry me – or have me killed. His position as family lawy
had given him full control of the reins, but at all costs he ha
to be above suspicion.

To do him justice, I felt that in marriage he would hav
spared me, especially if, in time, I made everything over t
him.

But there were still some things unexplained.

'Where did Ian come in? How was he involved?'
asked.

Hamish answered before Duncan had a chance to.

'He was in it up to his neck, not merely because o
Brenda, although his wife knew of their relationship an
turned a blind eye because, poor soul, she actually loved hin
but because he was up to his eyes in debt. His busines
was a failure and the financiers, a group called Moder
Enterprises, were turning the screws, threatening him wit
ruin unless he paid up. All Isabel's capital had gone, tryin
to save the boat. So Ian became their tool through one o
their directors here on the spot – Duncan Campbell.'

'You told me you had nothing to do with Modern Enter
prises, that you knew nothing about them!' I flung the word
at Duncan.

'If he said that, he was lying. He financed it, with Strick
land. He was co-partner right from the beginning, and no
a sleeping partner, either, although he managed to concea
the association pretty well working up here, apparentl
exclusively, for the mills, until Humbold retired and he wa
able to buy the old man's interest in his legal firm. Th
last thing Duncan wanted known was his link with Strick
land because although the man was apparently a respectabl
lawyer, I've found out since that his personal affairs wouldn
stand close scrutiny, although poor old Humbold was unawar
of that. It's taken me three years to investigate Moder
Enterprises thoroughly. It wasn't coincidence which brough
me to Glencoe when I had to leave Newmarket – I came t
keep an eye on Campbell, to do a bit of private-eye worl
You've been uneasy about my presence here ever since
arrived, and with good reason, Campbell.'

Aunt Mary demanded shrilly, 'What *are* you talkin
about, Hamish? Who and what are Modern Enterprises?

'A group I've been watching ever since I became one of their victims. A group operating all sorts of crooked schemes. Amongst their "enterprises" they sponsored a number of promising race horses from various stables, and their proposition to sponsor two from my own seemed a fair and sound one. Part of my obligation was to allow the horses to be inspected during training, and always before a race. Strickland usually came alone – he had a fair knowledge of horse-flesh and of racing, and although I didn't like him as a man, we respected each other's opinions as far as horses were concerned. He always deferred to mine because of my veterinary qualifications, and never interfered with my training programme. Everything seemed fair and square and above board. His co-director, listed merely as R. S. D. Campbell, never put in an appearance – he merely handled the accountancy side, Strickland told me. But before that last, fatal race, the one which victimized me, Strickland brought him unexpectedly and without my knowledge.

'It was lunch-time and one stable-boy was keeping an eye on both horses in their stalls. Strickland and his partner went straight there, and dismissed the boy on an errand, saying they would keep an eye on the horses – I met the lad coming across the outer courtyard beyond the stables. I had a weekend guest – Isabel's uncle, an old family friend and a retired director of the mills. I was taking him to see the horses. Naturally, I asked the stable-lad what the hell he was doing, leaving them unguarded, and he told me they were all right because Strickland and his partner were with them. We hurried over and were just in time to catch a glimpse of Campbell driving off – in the same Jaguar he's running now. Isabel's uncle recognized him at once, and if you'd glanced in our direction, Duncan, you'd have seen him – old Robert Matheson himself, who's known you since your mother married James MacDonald. Afterwards, it seemed pretty significant to me that you didn't even stay to watch the race.'

'Because I happened to be in the stables with Strickland didn't mean that I had anything to do with the actual doping,' Duncan scoffed.

'But he admitted it at the inquiry. He wasn't going to let his partner go scot-free! I heard from my lawyers late on

211

Friday all the details which haven't yet reached the Press. But they will. You and Strickland made one big mistake when you victimized me – I'm not the sort of man to lie down under that sort of thing. I fight back, no matter how long it takes. So I came to Glencoe and went to work. I found out that you and Strickland had been articled to Humbold at the same time; that you founded Modern Enterprises between you; that when Isabel's husband got into financial difficulties you had a good hold over him, and made the most of it. Bit by bit I filed every piece of evidence with my lawyers. You don't think it was by chance that the Law Society became wise to the activities of Humbold, Strickland and Campbell, do you?'

I could hear the loud ticking of a marble clock on the mantelpiece. I could hear Aunt Mary's breathing and Brenda's skirt rustling as her stumpy little hands clenched and unclenched in her lap. Only Duncan seemed to be absolutely silent, but I could see his mouth twitching in an effort at self-control.

Aunt Mary said in distress, 'I've wronged you, Hamish. I've believed that story about you always, but I'll never believe the worst of you again.'

But Hamish wasn't listening. His anger was spilling over.

'How did you go to work on Ian Forsythe?' he demanded of Duncan. 'By using your charming mother's influence over him, as well as your financial hold, to persuade him to do whatever you wished, even to masquerading as the midnight walker in an attempt to frighten Lavinia away? *And* making him tell her that the collection of antiques at Glenrannoch were fakes?'

Duncan shrugged and, half turning to me, said, 'Did Ian say that? I told you the man was ignorant, didn't I?'

Hamish declared. 'But he wasn't. He really did know something about antiques, thanks mainly to his wife, but as a businessman he was a failure. And there's one obvious way in which you doubled your pressure on him – you promised him a share of the collection if Glenrannoch became yours. With that alone he would have got on his feet again. Making Lavinia believe they were worth nothing was simply a red herring to indicate that there was nothing between the pair of you – likewise your detrimental criticism of him. All part of the act. But you made one mistake. You made him tell Lavinia that her grandfather got rid of the originals at a time when the mills were going through a bad patch, and that Isabel knew all about it. He told her to check with her, knowing full well that she wouldn't go to anyone to ask if her grandfather had pulled a fast one behind everyone's back, which is what substituting a genuine collection of antiques with fakes amounts to. But *I* checked. Isabel had no knowledge of such a thing, so I guessed you wanted Lavinia to believe the collection at Glenrannoch was worthless simply as part of your scheme to convince her that you and Forsythe were not in league in any way.'

Suddenly Hamish turned his anger on to Brenda. 'Was it you who sent him to meet poor Mary after Church today, telling him where Lavinia was setting out for and to use her aunt as a tool finally to get rid of the girl? I issued an open invitation over the phone, and it worked.'

Suddenly I recalled Brenda hurrying across the garden after I had spoken to Hamish, secateurs in her hand, apparently intent on cutting flowers for the lunch table, but heading towards the gap in the hedge, although the direction she was taking made no impression on me at the time.

Suddenly Brenda leapt from her chair and ran towards the door, but I was there before her. Her slight figure pulled up sharply and her strong, stumpy little hands clenched in anger.

'Before you go,' I said, 'I want to know who killed Jock.'

The woman burst into hysterical laughter. 'That wretched puppy! It was expendable.'

'Be quiet, Mother!'

But this time Brenda paid no heed to her son. She was fighting only for herself.

'It was his idea – Duncan's. My boy has always been so clever.' The venomous glance she threw at him indicated that she had changed her mind now. 'What importance was a wretched little animal, anyway – and a stray, at that?'

'Or an unfortunate man, subnormal from birth?' I flung back.

'Precisely. That shambling creature has always been an irritation to me, but your pig-headed grandfather would never let him be sent away. And, after all, he came in useful.'

'As a suspect? An animal-killer? A dangerous mentality about the place, so that if anything worse happened he could be blamed?' I heard my voice crack, but still I went on. 'I was right – he was to be used as a scapegoat. Did you poison the coffee meant for me?'

Aunt Mary gave one of her quavering shrieks and cried, 'Coffee? The coffee Brenda poured out that day and I served to you? I remember now – she said, "That cup is Lavinia's – make sure she gets the right one." But Jock spilled it, and licked it up . . .'

'I suspect it wasn't the first attempt to poison Lavinia,' Hamish added. 'There was the tisane Mary made for her one night. Don't look so startled – I've kept an eye on everything as far as possible, through Flora. The woman trusts me, and little has happened in this house which she hasn't known about. Andrew MacDonald meant a lot to Flora; consequently his daughter does, too. She told me how Mary came to the kitchen to make the tisane; it had to infuse a while, Mary said, and left it there for a few minutes because you, Brenda, called her to speak to the vicar's wife on the phone. Flora went out to the dairy to get the nightly glass of milk she gives to Luke, and when she returned you were at the kitchen table, stirring the tisane. You said something about cooling it a little; that Mary had made it too hot and it would scald Lavinia's throat. Then Mary came back and said that the vicar's wife wasn't on the phone after all, that nobody was. You shrugged, and said good night, and left Mary to pick up the tisane and take it to Lavinia. And in the morning, when Flora took round the tea, she could see Lavinia had been ill, but there were no dregs left of the tisane. Lastly, there were the climbing boots, hidden in the Jacobites' hole behind the vault.'

'We knew nothing about those. They didn't belong to us,' Brenda scoffed.

'Of course they didn't. They belonged to Ian Forsythe. Isabel identified them for me. She hadn't seen them for ages, she said, and asked where I found them, so I let her think old Craig had acquired them somehow and left them in the chapel, but told her nothing about the midnight walker or that the boots had been hidden in the Jacobites' hole – a convenient place from which to pick them up when wanted, and to hide them when not. The rest of the gear – trews, plaid, Balmoral bonnet – Ian already had, so there was no need to hide those, but a clumsy old pair of iron-studded boots would have been noticed at Kyleven. Isabel would have been sure to ask why he kept them; she might even have thrown them out, and they were the most essential part of the charade. And since Craig had access to the chapel Ian knew where the key was kept and so had access too.' Hamish turned to me and finished, 'This is why I telephoned you, the evening you went across to Eilean Munde – I wanted to see you privately to tell you about the boots and what I suspected they were used for, but I had no opportunity. We weren't alone all evening . . .'

Except for one brief, delirious moment when everything else was forgotten . . .

All the same, I wished he *had* told me, because it might have made me recall something which I remembered now – that it was Duncan who first made me believe that Highlanders had worn iron-studded footwear. 'Many claim that spectres of warriors roam the hills, clad in boots capped with rawhide and studded with iron . . .' He had said that as he brought me to Glenrannoch, planting the idea firmly in my mind, so that when I heard the midnight walker I would be ready to believe the story about MacIain's ghost.

But I had no opportunity to remind him of this because he was saying to Hamish, with a sneer in his voice, 'It's a fine, plausible story, but prove it. Prove that my mother realized she had poisoned that damned puppy, so strangled it and threw its body in the herbaceous border near the spot where that idiot was working. And no matter what she says, it was *not* my idea.'

'Even though you strolled over to Kyleven, ostensibly to have a professional chat with Ian Forsythe? Between the pair of you, you're filling in the details pretty well. The police should find it easy to get at the truth, and,' Hamish added quickly, as Duncan edged nearer to the window, 'trying to run away won't avail you anything because I've already primed them about my suspicions and I can definitely prove your hold over Forsythe. Isabel put me in the picture in that respect. I've been her friend and confidant for a long time.'

'No more than that?' sneered Brenda.

'No more than that,' he answered quietly. 'She discovered Ian had borrowed heavily from Modern Enterprises, and that they were bringing pressure to bear, and of course I had found out Duncan's part in that organization. But we haven't yet heard everything from Mary. What additional persuasion did Forsythe use to get you up the hillside, apart from wanting the pleasure of your company?'

'He said he'd found some attractive stones in a cleft up Aonach Dubh,' my aunt admitted, 'and that he would help me to collect some. I – I was very touched, and of course I believed him, but when he pulled me into the cleft I was frightened. It was so narrow, and dark, and he hadn't even a torch to show me the stones, and all of a sudden he was – different. Cruel and savage, as I'd never known him. He told me that my niece would soon be passing by the foot of the slope and that I was to shout to her for help. He pushed me to the ground and I nearly lost my precious bag. When I grabbed it, he struck at me and told me to let the damned thing go. He was trying to pinion my hands behind my back, but I clung to the bag with both arms because the diary was in it, so he held me fast from behind with one arm across my shoulders and the other pressing something into my waist. I couldn't believe it was a gun, but he vowed that if I so much as moved he would let me have it, and if I didn't get Lavinia up here, he'd also let me have it. So what could I do, but obey? Forgive me, Lavinia – I led you into a trap, but if I'd known that he intended to kill you and that my stepmother or Duncan had sent him – '

It was then that Brenda lost control of herself and burst out, 'He was a fool to use that gun! He wasn't meant to fire it, only to use it to force Mary to do what he said.'

Duncan rounded on his mother savagely. 'Do you want to give *everything* away?'

Her face went white. For a split second she was silent, then she spat contemptuously, 'You've done so yourself!'

I heard Hamish speaking into the telephone. He was calling the police.

Brenda made a dash for the door, but her son caught her

arm. 'Don't be a fool. How far d'you think we'd get? It's all up now. Running away will only make things look blacker for both of us.'

We were alone — Mary, Hamish, and myself. Into the quiet room my aunt said, 'I'm glad Ian is dead. At least he has been spared shame and dishonour.'

But had he? I wondered. Brenda, who cracked so easily, would break under police examination, only too ready to exonerate herself and blame others — especially a man who was conveniently dead. Even her maternal instinct wasn't so strong that she would protect the son who had landed her in such a mess.

And what of Isabel? How much had she suspected? I remembered her agitation when she came to see me in the hospital at Fort William, and I wondered now whom she had been more anxious to protect — her husband, or her nephew. I strongly suspected that it was Ian, for since she had been at the golf club that afternoon she must have seen his car there and known he had not gone to Perth.

Had she suspected that he was the car-thief and for some reason had remained in the vicinity, apparently returning — as Hamish and I had seen him — a couple of days later? She could have feared that it was he who ran me down, presumably by accident. Or had her fear been prompted by the suspicion that it was no accident? How greatly had she been aware of the kind of pressure being brought upon her husband?

I doubted if I would ever know, because Isabel was a woman of intense pride and loyalty.

As if reading my thoughts, Hamish said, 'Isabel found out that Ian had not gone to Perth that night because she telephoned him there after breakfast the next morning. He always stayed at his manager's flat above the shop, and the man told her that not only was Ian not there, but was not expected. The answer was the same from the Edinburgh branch. Both men were anxious to see him, and accused him of staying away because things were in a bad state. She was alarmed then, and came to see me right away.'

And I had been jealous, hurt, hating to see her leaving Hamish's cottage so early in the morning . . .

The memory shamed me.

Perhaps Mary was ashamed too, for she said quietly, 'I shall tell Isabel that Ian took a false step up there on Aonach Dubh, and that I saw it happen. She must be made to believe that his death was accidental, which,' she finished with a catch in her voice, 'it was, wasn't it?'

CHAPTER FIFTEEN

Sometimes I wonder how I could ever have thought Glenrannoch sinister, the place is so different now, its sombre grandeur lightened just as I once visualized, and its rambling space condensed into the self-contained wings which I also visualized, with Mary living in hers and my husband and I in ours.

It took some persuasion to make Hamish live in his wife's home, but he yielded in the end because he realized that to take me away from Glenrannoch was something which should not be done – although, rather than lose him, I was ready enough to go.

'But don't forget you'll be a Cameron,' he insisted. 'Keep MacDonald for your professional name if you want to, but Cameron will be your legal one and by that you'll be known.' And I, like Shuna MacDonald before me, could never say no to a Cameron of Lochiel, which is why I am Mrs Hamish Cameron in private life and Lavinia MacDonald only at the mills, and since their prosperity was my grandfather's greatest interest, and since Lavinia MacDonald designs have put Mactweedwear on the market in a big way, I've added more lustre to the name of MacDonald and somehow I think the old man would be well satisfied with that.

Other things are good too. My husband's name is respected throughout Argyllshire, Perthshire, and beyond, and the twins, James and Andrew, now seven, haunt the stables where the pure-bred stud Hamish raises is one of our greatest prides. And then there's Shuna, four, and, according to her father, myself in miniature – with a passion already for dressing up.

Hamish's house beside the loch has become an animal clinic and surgery, and Isabel is my close friend as well as neighbour. Mary has kept her word in keeping silent about Ian. No one but she, myself, and Hamish really know what happened up there on the slopes of Aonach Dubh — except poor Luke, who can never reveal it. And I sometimes wonder whether the whole incident wasn't, to him, a bewildering accident from which he mercifully saved me.

Perhaps Isabel doesn't smile so much as in the old days, but that is because she no longer has to pretend that all is well with a marriage which was all wrong.

Duncan's duplicity hit the headlines, and in his absence the directors of MacDonald-Matheson unanimously voted him off the board — and out of the business. An official statement was put out to the Press, hiding nothing.

Now Angus Matheson is Chairman of the mills in my grandfather's stead — the first Matheson ever to hold the position. Times change, and tradition must go with them.

And so Glenrannoch became mine, and as long as she lives, Mary will own her half of it. If, after she has gone, we or any future generation want to restore the place to its former size, the division can be taken down.

One incident will remain forever in my memory.

After Brenda and her son had been taken away from Glenrannoch I went up to her bedroom and found the portrait of James MacDonald slashed across and across. He had left her nothing; she was penniless, out on her ear, with an unpredictable future and only age spreading ahead of her. I stood in front of the portrait and could feel the hatred and bitterness in her as she attacked it, and I wondered how many other lies she had told me — about her first marriage, and her worthless husband, and her valiant desire to bring up her son alone. How much of it was true, no one would ever know, because no one could ever get to know a woman like Brenda — except any man who married her.

Hamish sent the portrait to be restored, and it now hangs in its rightful place amongst my ancestors on the great staircase — the side of the staircase which is in our wing, the other, with its quota of family portraits, being in Mary's. Also in Mary's part of the house is the bedroom where I spent so many uneasy nights. It is hers now, and the uneasiness must have gone because she is happy there. Also gone is what she called 'Brenda's vulgar bathroom', replaced with a far less flashy décor.

There is a communicating door linking the two houses, but Mary, with surprising tact, never intrudes. It is the children who use the door for the most part, running in to see her whenever they want to, and always sure of a welcome. The children have had a rejuvenating influence on my aunt.

It is the children who have also helped Luke. Perhaps they most of all because they are aware only of his great gentleness, with themselves and with their pets.

The other change is in Moira, now well established in my department at the mills, and fulfilling a potential which I always sensed in her. She started from the ground up as I did, and no longer looks as if her clothes have been cut out with a knife and fork.

But the greatest change is in Malcolm Matheson, for with the growth of my design department a new job was created for him, and one eminently suitable. Collections of Lavinia MacDonald's Mactweedwear designs are not only shown in Edinburgh, Glasgow, and London, but on the Continent as well, and Malcolm is the organizer, the PR man, the unflagging publicity chief, with flair and American showmanship plus dynamic energy. So it isn't surprising that my designs are now crossing the Atlantic and that Malcolm's sights are ever expanding.

Sometimes I feel that I want to resist his irrepressible drive because cities no longer appeal to me, and I long ago parted with the London flat which, unbelievably it now seems, I thought I might need as a bolt-hole. I am linked with the present although time has healed its wounds and brought peace.

Not that my marriage is a placid one. I married a hot-tempered and hot-blooded husband, with the passion and the tenderness and the warmth which goes with such a man. This I expected, coming as he did in direct line from Ewan Cameron of Lochiel, who was the archetype of a Highland chief, as was Red Alasdair, Twelfth MacIain of Glencoe; arrogant, emotional, stiff with pride and extravagantly brave, so how could a marriage between two people with such blood as ours ever be a milk and water affair?

Once, I asked my husband why he never tried to open my grandfather's eyes to the duplicity of his stepson, but Hamish merely shook his head, looking at me in that very human way of his and saying, 'Disillusion an old man, hurt one who had already hurt himself when he broke with his own son – do you think I could do that, Lavinia, my lovely?'

No. He could not do that. And I love him the more because of it.

Catherine Gaskin

'Catherine Gaskin is one of the few big talents now engaged in writing historical romance.' *Daily Express*

'A born story-teller.' *Sunday Mirror*

A Falcon for a Queen

All Else is Folly

Blake's Reach

Corporation Wife

Daughter of the House

Edge of Glass

The File on Devlin

Fiona

I Know My Love

Sara Dane

The Tilsit Inheritance

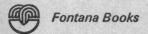 *Fontana Books*

D. E. Stevenson

'D. E. Stevenson has made peculiarly her own this province of feminine fiction—the kindly, ironical observation of ordinary life which retains a wonderful zest and freshness in its presentation.' *Glasgow Herald*

The Musgraves

Crooked Adam

The Four Graces

Gerald and Elizabeth

Kate Hardy

Katherine's Marriage

Spring Magic

The Tall Stranger

The Two Mrs Abbotts

Vittoria Cottage

'Mistress of the light novel.' *The Times*

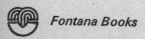

Fontana Books

Fontana Books

Fontana is best known as one of the leading paperback publishers of popular fiction and non-fiction. It also includes an outstanding, and expanding, section of books on history, natural history, religion and social sciences.

Most of the fiction authors need no introduction. They include Agatha Christie, Hammond Innes, Alistair MacLean, Catherine Gaskin, Victoria Holt and Lucy Walker. Desmond Bagley and Maureen Peters are among the relative newcomers.

The non-fiction list features a superb collection of animal books by such favourites as Gerald Durrell and Joy Adamson.

All Fontana books are available at your bookshop or newsagent; or can be ordered direct. Just fill in the form below and list the titles you want.

FONTANA BOOKS, Cash Sales Department, G.P.O. Box 29, Douglas, Isle of Man, British Isles. Please send purchase price, plus 8p per book. Customers outside the U.K. send purchase price, plus 10p per book. Cheque, postal or money order. No currency.

NAME (Block letters)

_____

ADDRESS

_____

_____

_____

While every effort is made to keep prices low, it is sometimes necessary to increase prices on short notice. Fontana Books reserve the right to show new retail prices on covers which may differ from those previously advertised in the text or elsewhere.